Tangled Strings

Christopher Clark

.

ISBN 978-0-9939713-2-7

Cover Design and Formatting:
Caligraphics
www.caligraphics.net

Cover image from www.pngtree.com

Chapter 1

"Out! Just out Bob," the man shouted, pointing toward the sky with his index finger.

"Is there a mark?" the man on the other side of the net asked, walking toward the sideline where his inside-out forehand had landed.

"Well Bob, there are a couple of them," the man answered, returning with some reluctance to the scene of the call and circling two marks in the green clay with his racket. "I'm not sure which one it is, but I saw it out. Great shot, just missed. Back to deuce."

"You know Larry, that felt in when I hit it and I see a mark right on the line there." He was leaning on the net, resisting the urge to walk around to the other side. "That's happened a few times today. If you don't see it land, you can't just call it out you know."

"What are you saying?" the mark-circler asked in a tone of feigned outrage. "It was out. I saw it out, period." With that, he dragged his right foot down the line and through the clay, erasing any and all marks in the area. "Come on, let's play."

The other man swiveled and began walking back to the baseline, looking around to see if players on neighboring courts were paying any attention to the dispute. He had taken about five angry steps when he stopped, pulled a ball from his left pocket and turned back to look across the net. He bounced it once, then wound up and smacked it as hard as he could directly at his opponent, who was standing on the baseline with his arms crossed in a way that suggested he didn't like having his calls questioned.

The ball – a Penn 4 – short hopped him, which made it difficult to avoid. The cross-armed mark-circler tried to protect himself with his racket, but managed only to deflect the ball right into his groin. He dropped to the court and began writhing in pain -- a 60/40 mixture of legitimate discomfort and practised theatricality.

If nearby players hadn't noticed what was happening on court 7 by then, they certainly did at that point. It wasn't every day that one player dropped an opponent like a poacher taking down an African antelope.

"My ball was in," the poacher screamed. "And so were 10 others before it. We're done here." On his way to the court-side bench to retrieve his bag, he picked up another ball and fired it toward the injured antelope who was still lying on the court, his sweaty shirt absorbing clay with every flinch. The second shot missed its target and rattled off the back fence. "*That* was out. *That's* what an out shot looks like," the poacher screamed again.

Six courts away, Gil Pence heard every word of the angry exchange and saw, through the fence that separated the club's hard courts and clay courts, that one player had gone down hard, screaming in pain. *Couldn't happen to a nicer guy* he thought but dared not say. The head tennis pro had to play everything right down the middle, just as he was doing now, feeding balls for a monotonous hour to a member who could hit 10,000 balls every day until the Rapture and never improve.

"Hang on a second Carl," he said to his aged pupil. "I think I should see what's going on over there."

"OK, but you're not going to charge me for the time, are you?"

"Ah, we've only got 10 minutes left, but no, don't worry about it," Gil said feeding the final ball just out of the old man's reach. "Would you mind picking up the balls while I see what's going on? Thanks."

The poacher nearly knocked Gil over as the two men crossed paths between courts 1 and 7. "Bob, what happened? Are you OK?"

"I'm fine but you should check on that fucker Larry. He's putting on quite a show out there writhing around on the ground. And one more thing, I'm not playing him ever again. Find someone else, OK."

"Sure, ya, but what happened?" Gil pressed.

"Look Gil, I'm sorry. I'm not mad at you, but you know how he is. He calls everything out. No one wants to play with the guy. I gotta go."

With that, the poacher headed to the clubhouse, where half a dozen people were sipping drinks and already speculating about whatever had happened out on court 7, although none of them had seen anything or talked to either combatant.

"Fucking Larry," the poacher said as he passed them, on his way to the change room. "Why is he still playing here? What do you have to do to get kicked out?"

Out on court 7, the antelope had pulled himself to his feet and was dusting the clay from his clothes when Gil walked across to check on him.

"What's going on Larry? You OK?"

"I am not OK, thanks very much Gil. And I want to file a report about what just happened here. For whatever reason, Bob there fired a ball at me. Got me right here," he added, pointing below his waist to make the point. "That's dangerous and uncalled for. I don't know why he's still a member of this club. No one wants to play with him."

"Let's not get ahead of ourselves, OK Larry? Tell me what happened. He mentioned a few calls he didn't like."

"One call, that's it. He didn't say anything for a set and a half, and then boom, he just freaks out. I saw that ball out,

OK? Jesus, I can't believe I have to explain this to you. He's the one who attacked me."

"OK Larry, look, just give him a minute to get out of the change room and on his way. Then we'll go up together, maybe get a lemonade."

"A lemonade isn't going to help, Gil. You should be talking to him, giving him a warning, writing it up, not questioning me. I did nothing wrong. Nothing."

The conversation continued for 10 minutes, during which the antelope offered nothing new. Gil settled him down, delivered the promised lemonade and headed for his office. He wanted to slam the door shut and scream at the walls, but instead he left the door wide open and calmly brought his computer to life.

He scrolled down through two weeks of emails to the message he wanted. It was from his old college coach. It wasn't unusual to hear from him, but normally the note was nothing but small talk and updates about his former teammates. This message was different.

"Gilbert, I hope this finds you well in the thriving metropolis of Memphis. I was at the Challenger event in Chile this week and started thinking of you. There wasn't anyone in the tournament better than you. Honestly, no one. I know you miss the competition. I know you think about giving it one last shot before you're an old man. Now's the time. Seriously, now's the time. Give me a call. I'd love to help you get back in and see what we could do. Rackets up, Coach Ramsey."

Gil read the email over and over as memories of his four years at Michigan washed over him. It hadn't all been great, but on balance it was probably the best four years of his life. He'd gone in expecting to turn pro at some point, but a stubborn case of turf toe had sidelined his plans in the months following his graduation. That was three years ago.

At 26, he was not old by any real world measure. But in the tennis world, his window was nearly shut. Coach was right: It was now or never.

Chapter 2

The neighbors gathered in groups up and down the street, chatting and catching up. The scene could well have been mistaken for a block party, except for the burning house on the south side of the street that served as the focal point of the conversations.

Nine firefighters from two stations were dousing the structure, ensuring anything that hadn't burned up would be destroyed by the water. The good news filtering through the crowd was that no one had been home when the fire started. Not even a hamster or a goldfish. The absence of casualties freed up the crowd to gossip and speculate about everything from the cause of the fire to the whereabouts of the homeowners to the health of their marriage.

Everyone knew who owned the home; very few actually knew them, however. Sergei Ivanov was the kind of tennis player you only saw in the early rounds of minor tournaments. You might catch him on Tennis Channel if he were playing someone more famous. That made him a celebrity among his neighbors, but a definite nobody in professional tennis.

A few die-hard fans in Mobile knew him because he had been a star on the University of South Alabama tennis team before turning pro five years ago. He and Svetlana had moved into the house two years earlier, coming back to the city after a less than fruitful experience living in Florida.

Fresh out of college, he did what everyone did and moved to a tennis hotspot. They chose Florida over California because it was more affordable. But after three years kicking around the Challenger circuit, qualifying sporadically for ATP World

Tour events and seeing his ranking slide in and out of the top 200, Sergei was frustrated and on the verge of quitting. That was when Svetlana sat him down and pitched a new strategy. They would go home – not to St. Petersburg, their birthplace – but to Mobile, where he had enjoyed his greatest tennis success, where he could reunite with his coach, and where they could live more easily on their dwindling income and savings.

They chose the Hannon Park area and had to work hard to spend $300,000. For that, they got a six-year-old Tudor style with fruit trees and a pool in the backyard. It would be a great place to raise kids when they decided to have some. In the meantime, it was home base for the Ivanov 2.0 project. He began working regularly with his Jaguars coach. Tom Wilkins had recruited the scrawny 17-year-old from Russia almost a decade earlier and had always felt responsible for unleashing the full Southern experience on the kid.

"Sure, come on back and we'll see what we can do," he said when Sergei floated the idea of returning to Mobile, essentially to give his career one last shot. "I'll be on the road some with the team, of course, but I'd love to help. You can pay me when you start winning something."

Money. It always came back to money – with tournament directors, agents and sponsors to be sure -- but even more so with a group of friends who'd invested in him shortly after he turned pro. The friends were mostly young professionals who'd been students when he took the Jaguars to two successive NCAA finals. Excited by their proximity to a potential tennis star, they'd formed a syndicate to bet on his success. With investments of anywhere from $10,000 to $200,000, they were backing a long shot, hoping to bask in the glory of a Wimbledon or U.S. Open victory one day. It was like betting on the K.C. Royals every spring to win the World Series that year. It almost certainly wouldn't happen, so you got terrific odds. Then, when it did happen, you looked like a genius and cashed a very healthy check.

The thing was, the Royals and every other Major League Baseball team had a better chance of winning the World Series than Sergei and his fellow mid-range professionals had of winning any high level tournament, never mind one of the four Grand Slams. But even the most remote chance was enough for the 20 or so people who had joined the syndicate five years earlier. The funds paid for most of Sergei's considerable expenses as he clawed his way up the world rankings.

With little to show for his efforts, however, Sergei had not attracted any new investors for more than two years. The moods of his original investors ranged from indifference to anger to outrage, informed largely by the amount of cash they had sunk into the long shot and how well their more traditional investments were doing.

No one on the street that morning, watching the Ivanov home crumble to the ground, was an investor. And no one that morning had seen the man two hours earlier who had snuck into the Ivanov backyard and sat down, leaning on a large peach tree. There he used an elastic to wrap a bed sheet with paper and cotton batten. Next he tucked a book of matches under the elastic, but not before using one of the matches to light a low-tar Marlboro. As the cigarette burned, he jimmied a basement window, stuck the burning cigarette into the matchbook and dropped the entire bundle through the open window. The hardest part of the exercise was lighting the cigarette while wearing gloves.

By the time he walked around the block and retrieved his rented Kia Forte, there were plumes of smoke drifting up from the Ivanov basement, into their grand foyer and up the winding staircase to the oversized master bedroom, complete with hotel-style ensuite and dedicated walk-in shoe closet.

An hour later, it was all gone.

Chapter 3

The meeting was scheduled to begin at 9:30 but only the bagels, coffee and token pieces of fruit arrived on time.

Baffled by how to resolve the simmering dispute, Gil had consulted with the general manager of the club, forgetting for a moment he had an MBA and got off on meetings like they were online porn. His plan was to bring the warring factions together in hopes of brokering some kind of Middle East peace plan. Gil was skeptical.

His skepticism was not abated when neither the poacher nor the antelope showed up at the appointed hour. Looking out the conference room window, he could see Bob Bendheim sitting in his car, 25 steps from the door to the clubhouse. He was sipping coffee and staring straight ahead, showing no sign of leaving the vehicle or entering the building.

There wasn't a hint of Larry Spangler in either the parking lot or the building. He hadn't even responded to the invitation/summons to attend.

"He's probably on his way," said the general manager, Tony Di Pietro, who was seated at the head of the table, resplendent in a blue striped shirt and checked tie under a blazer he left buttoned as he sat down. "Let's go over the agenda while we wait."

"Agenda? What are you talking about? We just have to get these two knuckleheads to kiss and make up, don't we?"

"The more formal we make this, the more weight it will carry. There may come a day when we have to boot one of these guys. We have to do everything by the book."

"We're not trying to fire a public school teacher Tony. Can't you, or the board I guess, just tell Spangler to buzz off?"

Di Pietro was about to explain the finer points of the club's constitution when the door swung open and Bob Bendheim marched into the room, letting everyone know how he felt about the circumstances before uttering a word.

"Well?" he grunted, tapping his foot unironically.

"Good morning Bob, thanks for coming." Di Pietro stood to shake hands. "Have a seat. Can we get you some coffee?"

"I have coffee, thanks. Where the hell is that Spangler idiot?"

"Then have a bagel. He'll be along soon. Gives us a chance to catch up. How're Karen and the grandkids?"

Everyone in the room knew the moment Bendheim reached for the bagel, he was hooked, like a smallmouth bass going for a spinnerbait.

"Top up his coffee, would ya Gil?" Di Pietro said as the disarmed poacher took a seat. "So, Bob, how many grandkids do you have now? I can never keep track."

There were two surefire topics among most members of the club, given the demographics involved: extended family and health. Everyone had kids; most had grandkids. And many had begun to experience the kind of health challenges connected with the AARP portion of their lives. If he had to guess, Gil figured hip replacements were slightly ahead of knee replacements, but neither could touch incidents of cancer – severe and less severe – among the members.

Bendheim was well into the story of his grandson being named MVP on his high school volleyball team when the door opened again, this time revealing the widely loathed Larry Spangler. He entered somewhat more timidly than had Bendheim, sans coffee, not sure what to expect.

"Larry, hello, thanks for coming," said Di Pietro, again standing and shaking hands, ushering the newcomer to a seat far away from the proud grandpa, who ended his grandson story abruptly and glared across the table.

"Ah, OK, ya," Spangler muttered. "Am I late? I thought your email said 10:00."

"Oh, it probably did. My mistake," Di Pietro said, shooting Gil an almost imperceptible wink. "Anyway, no matter. Sit down and, Gil, can we get Larry a coffee?"

Again, Gil poured coffee and watched as the overdressed general manager assumed complete control of the room and meeting without either combatant realizing what was happening.

For 30 minutes, he listened and cajoled, joked and nodded, letting both men air their beefs with each other and with the club and world in general. In less than an hour, he somehow persuaded them to stand up and shake hands, albeit with some reluctance. Then he closed with all the elegance of Roger Federer in his prime, picking a rocket return off the baseline and sending it back with more pace and direction to win the point.

"Now that we've cleared this matter up, I would like you – actually, it's not really me or Gil at all. The board would like you to just acknowledge that we've had this talk, just to keep things official and professional."

With that, he produced two sheets of paper and asked each man to sign one. They did so with barely a fuss, agreeing with the flurry of their pen that if there were a similar dispute any time in the following calendar year, the board would be entitled to revoke their membership. Each man assumed the provision was aimed at the other, while Gil just watched in amazement. *He could have asked them to sign over their time-shares in Florida, and they would have done that too.*

Having signed, the two men left quickly without speaking to each other. Gil poured himself a coffee and raised his mug to toast Di Pietro. "I'm not sure how the hell you did that, but it was amazing to watch," he said. "What's in those bagels?"

"The secret's in the cream cheese," Di Pietro said, biting off a large chunk of a bagel he hadn't touched during the meeting and chewing vigorously. He washed it down with the rest of the coffee, removed his blazer and threw it over the back of an empty chair. "What else is going on Gil? Something is bugging you, has been for a few weeks, but I can't quite tell what it is."

"What are you, a goddam mind-reader? How much time have you got?"

"As much as it takes," he laughed, reaching for another bagel, bypassing a bunch of bananas on the way.

Chapter 4

As his house was burning to the ground, Sergei was 1,500 miles away on a practice court, trying to add more kick to his second serve. So he was one of the last people in his circle of friends to learn about the fire. Among a flood of sympathetic texts he saw after his practice, one stood out. The message included a video of the destruction, edited to show the moment the roof collapsed, sending sparks, flames and timbers across his yard and driveway. Unlike the other texts that offered sympathy and inquired about his health, it included only four words: "We'll be in touch."

Sitting in the change room, Sergei thought he was going to throw up. They had done it. In the moment, he couldn't untangle his feelings, but somehow the loss of his home was secondary to the awful realization that the men who had been threatening him would, in fact, carry out those threats. *They weren't bluffing.*

Running toward his car, he punched his phone and tried to reach Svetlana. She had planned to stay at the hotel that morning and possibly meet some friends for lunch. They were in Puebla City, Mexico, where he was playing in the Abierto De Puebla tournament. They'd chosen it because the very next week, Sergei could play in the Jalisco Open in Guadalajara. It was 400 miles away, which meant they could drive and save money. On paper anyway.

This was the third year they had entered the two tournaments, and they knew what to expect. The first year they wondered if they'd somehow entered the Baja 1000 off-road race, as they navigated their way west from Puebla, around the ridiculous traffic and congestion of Mexico City and on to Guadalajara.

There was an entire circuit of Mexican tournaments in March. San Luis followed Guadalajara; Leon followed San Luis. Some years there were only two or three. It varied every year, depending on sponsors and local support. In the years there were four, it was madness to enter them all, unless you exited early each time. If that happened, you beat a path to the next tournament and hoped to win enough matches to make the trip worthwhile. It was very much like doubling down after a lousy hand in Vegas. Except in Vegas, all but the most serious gambling addicts know they can't really influence the outcome of their bets, no matter how many times they blow on the dice or tap the cards rhythmically for luck.

On the Challenger circuit, nearly all players believed they had the talent to break through to the World Tour if they practised more, worked harder or – in a handful of cases – took the right cocktail of banned substances. It was that hope that convinced Sergei and dozens of other middling professionals to spend much of the month of March in Mexico, staying in crummy hotels, raiding the laughable player buffets, and bowing and scraping before sponsors who demanded better results for the pittance of cash they sent the players' way every year.

Those who weren't in Mexico could be found in China or Europe, slogging from tournament to tournament, and doing everything they could to earn the points that would move them up the rankings, potentially into the big time. Of course, players playing big time tennis were doing everything they could to stay there, lest they be sent back to Mexico in March.

Svetlana had received texts from most of the same people

– with one notable exception – and was racing from the hotel to the tournament. She'd skipped her lunch date and instead gone for a long walk in a circuit that kept the hotel in her view and reasonably close. Sergei had the car, so she had to wait for a cab to arrive in what could charitably be called an up-and-coming part of town, where the Holiday Inn was the newest structure around, designed to be a catalyst for further development.

As she was climbing into the back seat, she got Sergei's call.

"Turn back please, back to the hotel," she blurted, motioning wildly behind her.

Confused, the driver slowed down but didn't change direction.

"Back, back," she screamed. "Go back. Hotel!"

Sergei arrived only minutes after her confused cabbie returned her to the hotel. Sobbing, they embraced in the lobby, oblivious to the attention they attracted.

"Come up to the room," he said quietly. "I have to show you something. I'm so sorry."

It took him almost 10 minutes to explain the series of events that led to someone torching their house that morning. For months he had hidden the threats from her, determined not to worry her and to solve the problem himself. As he explained, she doubled over in pain, sliding off the bed and onto the floor, sobbing so violently she had trouble breathing.

She pushed him away when he tried to hold her, first with her arms then with her legs, kicking wildly at forces she didn't understand and a feeling of despair she had never experienced.

Sergei had never felt so helpless. He too collapsed on the floor and began convulsing.

Chapter 5

It took investigators less than half a day to discover someone had set fire to the Ivanov home. Once they found the telltale evidence in the basement, they stepped up security around the property and worked with police to comb the yard for evidence. There was none to be found, just as there was nothing to learn from neighbors interviewed in the days that followed.

"OK, professional job, sure, but why make it so obvious?" asked fire chief

Geronimo Joseph to the pair of investigators sitting in his office two days later. "The bed sheet? Come on. And when are we gonna talk to the home owners, the Ivanskis or whatever their name is? Where the hell are they again?

"Mexico, sir. He's a tennis player."

"I play a little tennis on the weekends, but if my house burned down I'd damn sure head back to find out what the hell was going on," Joseph shot back. "Have we even heard from these people?"

"Jose talked to the wife, ah, Svelte Llama, or something like that. He said she was crying the whole time on the phone. Didn't seem to know what they were going to do. That was yesterday I think."

"Alright, OK, let's try again today. Jerry, see what you can do. There's no time difference is there? Just find out, OK?

"Also, I've got this message from a neighbor. Says he has to talk to me. Seems he might just solve the case. Didn't we canvass all the neighbors that day? Wait a second. Isn't this place five minutes from the Dew Drop Inn? And isn't it damn near lunch time? Whatcha say we get us some burgers and onion rings, then drop in on this neighbor fella while we're, ya know, in the area? Who's with me?"

With that, the trio left the office, climbed into the chief's bright red Ford F-150 and headed for Hannon Park. They could almost taste the onion rings as they swung out onto Government Street.

Traffic was light, and many drivers made room for the truck, as though the chief had turned on the lights and siren. As a result, lunch was earlier than usual, landing them at the Ivanov house by 12:45. They parked on the street in front of the house. The driveway was still covered in debris.

Consulting his iPhone, the chief located the nearby home of Nester Pidwerbecki, three down and across the street. Like many nearby homes, it sat well back from the boulevard, framed by oak trees front and back and a wrought iron fence along the sidewalk. The boards and batten had been cared for meticulously, and the lawn had a certain Augusta National feel to it. Black letters spelled the name Pidwerbecki on the pristine white mailbox, its red flag raised to indicate the mail had arrived that morning.

Moving slowly after their impressive lunch, the fire-fighting trio strolled down the sidewalk, through the fence opening and to the front door. They didn't bother with the mail.

"Mr. Pid-wer-specty?" Joseph asked awkwardly when a man answered his aggressive knock.

"It's Pidwerbecki, and yes. You got my message, good."

"I did. Do you have something to add to what you told our investigators the other day? I'm fairly sure someone spoke to you that day, right?"

With that, the man opened the screen door all the way and motioned for the group to come in. The sidekicks waited for a signal from Joseph before making a move. He signaled his decision by walking through the door and heading for the nearest couch in the large sitting room off the foyer.

"Got anything to drink Mr. Pick-turn-specki?"

"It's Pidwerbecki sir, and I can offer sweet tea if you're interested. Three glasses?"

It took the officious man several minutes to pour the tea, arrange the glasses on a tray, fan a row of cookies on a plate and carry the whole arrangement from the distant kitchen. Placing it on the giant ottoman in the center of the room, he sat on the edge of an arm chair, one leg folded over the other, but leaning forward as though the weight of what he had to say was tugging at him.

"I think someone set fire to that house, and I know who it was," he declared with an obvious sense of relief. He had the expression of someone who had just revealed the identity of the Boston Strangler.

Joseph coughed up a chunk of cookie and leaned forward to meet his host. "I'm sorry, what? You know who did it? Why didn't you mention this the other day?"

"You know, with all the excitement I didn't realize what I had seen. But now that I've slept on it and thought about it. Well, that makes a difference, you know?"

"I suppose yes. So tell us, what did you see?"

With that, the man stood up and started pacing. He shot a glance out the front window and adjusted the blinds to further obscure the view from the street. "Look, I didn't actually see anyone light the fire, if that's what you mean, but I know who did it."

"Alright, tell us."

"Well, first you have to understand I pay attention to what goes on in this neighborhood, on this street. I mean, I watch and remember. I see what others don't see."

"Do you have a job, sir?" Joseph asked, leaning back, crossing his arms and wishing he hadn't rushed through his lunch to meet Nester Pister-speckity, or whatever his goddam name was.

"I'm semi-retired. I still teach a little, here and there, helping out when needed."

"What in God's name did you see? Spit it out."

"It's better if I show you."

He produced an iPad as if by magic and sat down beside Joseph on the giant ottoman, nudging the tray of cookies aside. "I posted it this morning, but I wanted to show you in person and explain why it's important."

The Pidwerbecki Facebook account was largely a collection of photographs documenting the man's insatiable thirst for lawn care perfection – green grass and shrubbery porn for liked-minded enthusiasts whose idea of a fun morning was double-cutting the front lawn in a crisscross pattern and then delineating its boundaries by cutting a razor-sharp edge along the length of the sidewalk and driveway, all the while casting an eye for a pesky weed or dandelion that needed to be uprooted by hand with the precision of a vascular surgeon.

"Here, here it is."

The video he clicked looked like it might have been shot from the moon or a neighboring state. By staring and concentrating, Joseph and his cohorts were able to recognize the street and then the Ivanov home.

"OK, watch on the left," the man said, excitedly, indicating with a thumb which side was the left side. "Here it comes."

Right on cue, a UPS truck rolled down the street, slowed slightly near the Ivanov home, then continued along the street and over the horizon. As the truck disappeared from view, the cinematographer had jerked the camera back toward the street, and sure enough, it was possible to see wisps of smoke starting to rise from somewhere behind the Ivanov abode.

It wasn't exactly We-Have-a-Pope smoke, but it was there.

Then the video ended.

"That's when I called 9-1-1," Pidwerbecki said, his chest pumped out, his cheeks starting to flush. "If you freeze it, here I'll show you, if you freeze it you can see the licence plate of the truck. You should be able to find out who was driving, right?"

Joseph couldn't decide whether to laugh first and then punch the stupid man in the face or to punch first and laugh second. His sidekicks were equally dumbfounded but uncertain if they had simply missed something important. So they remained quiet and waited for their boss' reaction.

"With all due respect Mr. Pid-ster-dicky, what the hell are you talking about? I see a UPS truck driving down the street. Am I missing something. Is there a grassy knoll somewhere here?"

"There's no need to be rude," Pidwerbecki said, standing up and removing the tray of cookies. "I would have thought it obvious that the truck slows down right in front of the house as the smoke starts to appear. Either the driver is looking to make sure the fire is going or he ignores it. Both are suspicious actions, don't you think?"

"Well, no actually. I don't."

"Look," Pidwerbecki said, slightly frustrated. "If you're driving along in a neighborhood you probably know quite well, and you see smoke coming from a house, wouldn't you report it. Wouldn't you stop? I mean, not you. You're the fire chief. Of course you would. I mean anyone else. So if he didn't stop, well, that's suspicious."

"We don't know he saw it. We don't know what he thought if he did. Maybe he saw it and thought someone was burning leaves. Or roasting weenies. Even if he did see it, so what? Are you saying the UPS guy started the fire, then drove around until the smoke appeared, just to make sure the house would be destroyed?"

"I'm saying it's a possibility, and I have the video evidence right here." With that he grabbed Joseph's ice tea from the table and placed it on the cookie tray, out of reach of everyone there. "That's what I'm saying. I'm just trying to help. Why are you so hostile and close-minded?"

"Look, Mr. Pis-ter-shecky. We have a lot of work to do on this case. We can't even talk to the homeowners and there are no real clues. It seems like a professional arsonist, which raises a ton of questions. None of which, believe me, have anything to do with a UPS truck that happened to drive by that morning. Honestly, do you know what's more suspicious? It's a neighbor who happened to get a video just as the house started to burn down. That's pretty good timing, wouldn't you say? That's a hell of a lot more suspicious than a goddam UPS driver."

Joseph stood up about halfway through his rant, and was on his way to the front door as he delivered the last line. The sidekicks were following so closely that they bumped into him when he spun suddenly before reaching the door.

"Please don't call us with any other theories, OK? But thanks for the cookies. And the tea."

Chapter 6

Svetlana Ivanov sobbed on and off for most of the night before regaining something close to her composure. Sergei remained by her side the whole time, aching to make it all better but unable to do anything other than supply Kleenex and water as required.

When dawn broke, they were asleep on the floor where they'd collapsed very early in the morning. Two hours of sleep helped a little. She woke first, stepped over her husband and had a long, hot shower. She resisted the urge to curl up on the shower floor and let the water beat over her, hiding whatever tears she might have left to shed. Instead, she forced herself to look ahead, to make a plan, to figure out what the couple would do to make things right. She had always been the thinker of the duo. *If he'd come to me when this started, we would still have our house. Still have our life.*

Sergei heard the water running and for a spark of a moment considered joining her in the shower. It was something they did regularly at home, but especially in hotels. Before the thought had formed fully in his mind, however, he remembered everything. Every twisted, rotten thing – and who was to blame. *Me.*

Instead, he changed his clothes, straightened up the room a little and sat in the uncomfortable desk chair, waiting for her to emerge. His memory was sketchy; he thought he had told her everything over several hours of screaming and crying the night before.

He wasn't sure what she was going to do when she

emerged from the bathroom. He set the odds of divorce at roughly even. She had put up with a lot, sacrificed for years, in support of his long-shot tennis dream. It would hardly be surprising if she decided this was too much -- that a husband who didn't tell her he was being blackmailed and consequently put her life at risk was not worth keeping. She wasn't the athlete. They wouldn't come after her. It made a lot of sense for her to bolt that very day.

She would get half their dwindling but still significant nest egg. The house and all their belongings were insured. She could start over without taking much of a financial hit at all. No kids. And, as Sergei's friends often reminded him, he was punching well above his weight class with her. She was gorgeous and smart and would easily be able to find someone new, if and when she wanted.

To his relief, she chose the other option, at least for the moment. She committed – again – to his career and their marriage. After exhausting the hot water supply for much of the hotel, she stormed out of the bathroom with a towel wrapped securely around her torso and another wrapped around her head. Instead of dressing, she shooed Sergei from the desk chair and set up shop with standard-issue hotel stationery and pen. If she could write it down, organize her thoughts, she always felt better. It was the way they had made all their major decisions together. The sight of her taking charge gave Sergei hope for the first time since he watched his house burn to the ground on his 4-inch iPhone screen the day before.

"Tell me again when they first contacted you, how it began."

He repeated much of what he'd said the night before, apologizing for everything. This time around, rather than sobbing and punching him in frustration, she took careful notes. After an hour of questions and answers, she had constructed a timeline of sorts, tied to tournaments and their travel schedule.

It was the kind of thing Sergei had never considered doing. He had fielded their approaches and fended them off, without ever trying to step back and analyze what the hell was going on. It wasn't as though her makeshift timeline had cracked the case or anything, but seeing it all laid out somehow made him feel better. Not better exactly, but less culpable.

"These guys are fucking serious and organized," she said as she examined her handiwork, a pencil stuck in her mouth. "I'm not saying it was OK not to tell me," she said, taking his hand and softening her gaze. "I'm not saying that at all. But Jesus, I'm amazed you were able to function for the last 18 months worrying about all this."

Athletes dealing with scandal or tragedy often said their only peace was on the playing field or court, where they could do the thing they knew best and forget for a moment the tumult all around them. Sergei never said that, never thought it. As far as he was concerned, that was utter bullshit, a cliché along the lines of giving 110 per cent or playing with your back against the wall.

But over the last year or so, he'd experienced that very thing. It was the only time he didn't feel pressure. The messages were sporadic, often months apart. They asked him to lose a specific game in a set or lose his serve at a designated score. Sometimes he answered back to refuse. Sometimes he didn't bother answering. Either way, he resisted the increasing pressure from faceless bettors who profited by betting in real time on point-to-point results, capitalizing on the inside knowledge they created.

"Alright, we have a pattern here for sure," Svetlana said, finally. "Let's get some lunch and figure out what to do next. "Does Vlad know about this?"

"No. Absolutely not."

She was strangely relieved her husband had hidden the facts from his brother as well, even if they barely spoke. Telling him while keeping her in the dark would have felt like more of a betrayal.

"It's probably time to tell someone," she said, flatly. "Someone who can help us figure out whether to talk to the cops, or the ATP."

She had just finished writing ATP on her sheet, when she stopped and looked at Sergei again, suddenly less certain.

"Hold on a second. They burned our house down, so of course that means you didn't help them. But it started two seasons ago. Oh my God, Sergei, did you help them already? What really happened?"

For the second time in 24 hours, Sergei came clean. It wasn't quite as painful the second time around because he wasn't trying to explain why someone had torched their house. But it was still wrenching.

"OK, there's some money. In an account. But I haven't touched any of it. None."

"What? You took their money?"

"I didn't take it. They just put it in an account and told me it was there. I've never touched it. I don't even know how much is there."

"I don't understand," she screamed. "You have their money? What else did you do? What the hell is going on Sergei? What?"

"I don't have any money. They just kept telling me it was there, I guess to try to suck me in? Last month, I told them it had to stop. I told them I'd never help them, no matter how much money they put in that account. But I couldn't exactly call the cops. I don't even know who they are. I know a couple of guys playing in Spain who threw a few points, that's it. And they're done, off the tour forever. I was terrified of being linked to something, because of the money. I was just trying to ignore them. Ignore everything."

"How? How do you talk to them?"

"It's all texts. I don't know who they are or where they are. Nothing. The numbers change all the time. They would tell me what to do in a tournament, and then they sent a confirmation number for money going into some account, but I promise you, I never, ever looked at it. I've never touched it. I just wanted to get out and forget all about it."

With that he tossed a plastic cup half full of Pepsi toward the balcony, intending to have it plummet to the ground in a grand gesture of frustration. When it hit the screen leading to the balcony, the effect was somewhat less grand, more pathetic than anything.

Svetlana giggled, despite herself. He uttered a long series of Russian expletives but couldn't help laughing himself. They fell onto the bed where their collective exhaustion, helplessness and fear somehow brought them closer. He tugged at the towel still wrapped tightly around her body. She responded by removing the towel from her head and pulling down the covers. Smarter than the cup-throwing incident suggested, he followed her lead, shedding his clothes and climbing into bed next to her. For an hour, they enjoyed a version of the peace of mind Sergei enjoyed on court, focusing on each other and forgetting briefly about their burned out home and how it suddenly symbolized their life in general.

Chapter 7

Gil pulled into his parking spot at the club Saturday at 6:30, in lots of time to get ready for his first lesson of the morning, at 7:00. He walked the long way around to his office, doing a perimeter scan of all 16 outdoor courts. When he got to the very back court, he did a double take.

There were at least 100 balls on the court, most on the side opposite the ball machine, which was in position on the north side of the court, ready to fire balls all day long. Except the ball machine had a curfew. It didn't stay out overnight. There was a spot in the nearby storage shed for it. Same for the balls, which were now wet with dew.

What the hell?

The kid working the sign-in desk was supposed to put the machine and balls away before going home at night. The lit courts meant members could play until 10:00 p.m., and often did.

Gil headed for his office to check the schedule and see who had worked the night before. He turned his key to open the main clubhouse door and felt no resistance. The door wasn't locked. Suddenly queasy, he opened the door slowly and looked around.

The pro shop looked OK, as did his office which he had locked at 7:00, when he left the night before. Going up a flight of stairs, he entered the bar and social room, where players gathered after matches to drink and watch the courts below from an expansive balcony.

The sliding doors to the balcony were wide open – which

was just as well because had someone tried to close them they might have broken one of the empty beer bottles lying near the door. There were bottles behind the bar too, along with empty bags of chips and other snacks. With 15 minutes before the first players arrived for weekend play, he was standing in the middle of a frat house.

From the ground floor, he heard the kids working that morning begin arriving. He came down to meet them, knowing they wouldn't have worked the night shift if they were scheduled that morning.

"Who was here last night, Janet, do you know?"

"Ah, no, sorry Gil. Why?"

"Go upstairs and look around, but be careful and don't touch anything. It's a mess up there. Then, you and Aisha go out to court 16 and get the ball machine ready. It was left out overnight. The balls are probably ruined. I don't think they'll work in the machine, that's for sure."

The ball machine was an enormous pain in the ass for nearly everyone at the club, even when it was put away properly at night. If the tennis balls got the least bit wet and swelled up by 1/16th of an inch, the machine would jam. But like a photocopier that quits if one piece of paper goes in slightly askew but doesn't shut down until another 25 pieces of paper are jammed in six hard-to-reach locations, the ball machine could swallow up 10 soggy balls before quitting. It took someone with a broomstick and superhuman strength to ram the balls out of the launch tube, as though loading a Civil War musket over and over.

Few people used the machine. It was the die-hards who couldn't get a game on a given day and faced the alarming prospect of going 24 hours without hitting their flawed groundstrokes off the back fence or into the net. When the thing broke down, which it did about once a month, Gil delayed calling the repairman for a few days, to give himself and most of the members a break from the infernal thing.

Janet and Aisha managed to get it working again, using a hopper full of dry balls after collecting the wet balls and spreading them out to dry in the rising sun. Gil, meanwhile, called Tony Di Pietro at home. As club manager, he often dropped by on weekends, but never at 7:00.

"What Gil? Is everything OK?"

"Ya, sorry to call. Well, no, I guess not everything is OK. But, I mean, no one is hurt or anything. Not yet."

Before Gil finished explaining what he found, Di Pietro was dressed and on his way. One of the summer students, Randy Jorgensen, had worked the night before. Gil called him and got his parents.

"Randy stayed at a friend's last night after his shift Gil. Sorry, he's not here," the woman Gil knew only as Mrs. Jorgensen said. "You know, since I've got you on the phone -- Randy would kill me for doing this -- but I just want to say how much he loves working for you and everyone there at the club. It's really great."

"Well, that's good to hear. When you talk to him, please have him call. I texted but haven't heard back." Gil said. "Sorry to have bothered you so early on a Saturday."

"Oh, no problem. I just got home from my hike. It's beautiful along the river this morning Gil. Randy doesn't always have his phone on. He's kind of a people person, you know, and isn't always on his phone like a lot of the kids."

"Uh huh, OK. Thanks."

Oh Mrs. Jorgensen, you have no idea.

Di Pietro arrived within 15 minutes, about the same time as Gil's 7:00 lesson, Howard Forrester, who seemed only mildly interested in the commotion all around him and headed out to Court 1 to start his usual session.

"Hey, Howie, morning," Gil started. "I've got a few

things to look after here, as you can see. Would you mind hitting with Anne? Good to get a fresh look at that serve of yours anyway." Anne Hollings was the assistant pro. Gil had hired her the previous year and considered it one of his best moves at the club. Women loved hitting with her, as did some of the men. Like Gil, she had been a collegiate stand-out whose game was still top notch. A few members from the Mesozoic Era refused to take lessons from her and barely acknowledged her presence. Old Howard Forrester fell into that camp.

"Er, I can wait a few minutes Gil. Go ahead and finish up. I'll be out here."

"The thing is, it could take most of your hour, and Anne is here, ready to go. Whatcha think?"

"I think I could come back later. I noticed on the court sheet, you have an hour free at noon today. I could rearrange my schedule and come back then."

"Ya, that's generally my lunch hour. I've got eight hours of lessons today," Gil replied, letting the statement hang there for the old man to consider.

"It's the same number of hours either way. I'll come back at noon. In the meantime, since I'm here, maybe I'll go use the ball machine."

Of course you will.

"Great idea. I'll tell Anne you're doing that and have one of the girls get you set up."

Gil was so annoyed that he briefly forgot why Di Pietro was there.

"I've had a look around Gil. Not good, of course, but no serious damage. Anything taken from the pro shop?"

"Don't think so. Haven't actually gone through it all, but it just looks like someone had a party upstairs."

"Jorgensen was scheduled," Di Pietro said, looking at the clipboard he had grabbed from behind the counter.

"Ya, can't reach him this morning. Called his house, but he's not there. His mom says it's lovely along the river this morning, if you're wondering."

Di Pietro didn't smile or acknowledge the comment. "Alright, keep trying to reach him. I've called maintenance, and they can have this cleaned up by noon. I'm going to close the second floor to members until then. You've got the ball machine squared away, right? That's everything, as far as we know?"

"Ya."

With that, they heard the pop of the ball machine from across the grounds on court 16, as it began firing balls at Howard Forrester. He launched the first one over the fence and looked around to see if anyone had noticed. He then got into something he thought of as the ready position for the next ball, which he hit a few feet lower against the top of the fence. He was in mid-season form.

Chapter 8

Flipping through her messages from the previous day, Liz Catalano was not surprised to see a call from Sergei Ivanov. She had planned to call him that afternoon.

Catalano had been legal counsel at the Association of Tennis Professionals for eight years. She enjoyed the job about 50 times more than her previous job as managing partner at Heinrich, Scheff, Carling and Dobbin, a medium-size labor law firm in Manhattan. No one there could understand why she would leave such a prestigious position at all, never mind to join the ATP, which they understood had something to do with tennis.

"Those idiots have no idea how shitty the job is," she told her husband in bed, the night before she gave her notice at the firm. "No amount of money is worth the hassles."

Said hassles included arbitrating disputes about office size and location between and among the 15 partners, chasing said partners and 70 or so wannabe partners every month for their billable hour reports, representing the firm at an endless parade of social events and fundraisers, and – most tiring – handling the increasingly messy decline of the firm's founder, Octavius Heinrich, whose 85-year-old mind and body were in a race to the end.

There was no way Heinrich would ever retire. He had nothing to which he could retire – no spouse, no kids, no friends and no particular interests beyond the daily machinations of the firm, which he understood less and less with each passing month.

When she joined the firm, her bucket list did not include being a corporate nanny to the eldest member of the firm, no matter how highly regarded he was or how many kind gestures he had made to various other rich white men over the years. There was no 'senior babysitting' skill box to check on her LinkedIn profile.

She made the decision to leave without knowing where she would end up, but followed her husband's advice and focused her search on her one true love. Catalano didn't start playing tennis until she was 30, well past her athletic peak. She had danced competitively as a teen and always been able to throw a baseball better than her brothers, but she didn't even pick up a racket in her youth.

She went with a girlfriend to a public court one day mostly to be polite. She was more excited by the plan afterward to find an outdoor patio and drink lattes. The friend loaned her a racket and gave her a few rudimentary tips. Within a few weeks, she was feeling more comfortable hitting the ball back and forth.

After a month of Saturdays, they signed up for lessons at a club they saw driving home one day. At age 47, she often smiled when thinking how that chance outing, with someone she no longer even talked to, had completely changed her life.

Not only did she become a tennis addict, playing at least three times a week and arranging vacations around playing and watching the game, but she had then reset her career by joining the ATP, initially as a member of the legal team and then as chief counsel. That required a move to the ATP Americas headquarters in Ponte Vedra Beach, Florida. Her husband's enthusiasm for chasing dreams had vanished with that news. He had no desire to leave New York and essentially made her choose. The ultimatum put their marriage into depressing relief, and she bolted for Florida. With no kids to complicate matters, she had made the transition with surprising ease. Her professional and social lives were now intertwined with the sport in a way she could never have predicted. She loved it and often said so to anyone who would listen.

She'd never met Ivanov in person, but she was pretty sure they had spoken once or twice by phone. It wasn't unusual for players outside the top 100 to rely on advice from her office more so than their more successful counterparts. The very best players had agents and advisors who identified and solved their legal issues. Players like Ivanov navigated that world alone. Even if Ivanov had an agent, he would have to split his time among many middling players to make a living, giving each only a few hours per month and handling only the most basic tasks.

She fielded a handful of calls and texts per week from players looking for advice about sponsorship deals, international tax rules, labor regulations and even divorce laws. Sometimes she could help with some general advice. Other times she encouraged them to seek the advice of an attorney who worked directly for them and could delve into the issue more thoroughly. Her friends occasionally called this passing the buck; she called it issue management.

As she prepared to return Ivanov's call, she was certain it was the first time she would be speaking to a player about his house burning down, an attack local authorities were now publicly labeling arson. When she saw the news the day before, she had put in a call to her counterpart at the quixotically named Tennis Integrity Unit. Formed in 2008, its mandate was not to crack down on bad lines calls and rampant foot faults in club-level tennis, but rather to investigate match fixing. A cynic might have argued its mandate was to make enough noise to assure the public match fixing was being rooted out: to remove any suspicion about matches they were paying to watch – the way airport security makes people remove their shoes to demonstrate how safe that day's flights will be.

Since match fixing had hit the headlines in a big way a few years earlier, the TIU had doubled its staff and budget and accused a meager seven players and officials of actions they couldn't actually prove in court but for which they issued bans ranging from six months to two years. Catalano knew a couple of the people working there and believed their motives were pure. She also knew high-level, organized match fixing was nearly impossible to detect and stop. They caught the ham-handed amateurs from time to time, but they had never arrested, or even identified, any of the international gambling crooks whom everyone believed ran the most significant match fixing schemes.

As she expected, the TIU was unaware of the Ivanov fire. They played a perpetual game of catch up, investigating players' actions after tournaments, when results look fishy and the crooks betting on the fishy results were long gone – both physically and online, covering their virtual tracks expertly.

"Morning Sergei, Liz Catalano returning your call from yesterday. How are you doing? I heard about your house."

"Thank you Mrs. Catalano. Yes, it's been…"

"Call me Liz, please. Go on."

"Yes, OK, thanks. It's been a terrible few days, for sure. We're in Mexico. Lost in the quarters. Supposed to head to Guadalajara next, but we don't really know what to do."

"Is Svetlana there with you?"

"Ya, she's here. She's right here, actually, sitting with me."

"Maybe she could go back and see what's going on at home. I'm sure you have to talk with insurance people and maybe the fire department. Did I see right in the news? Was it arson? Do they know that already?"

"We talked to someone from the fire department, but it was early and we're not really sure what's going on. It almost seemed like he was blaming us or suspicious of us. I don't know, but we got a weird vibe from him. But ya, we need to be there soon. It's just that Guadalajara is a big tournament. I have points to defend from last year when I got to the semis."

"Can I speak with Svetlana? If she's right there."

There was a muffled discussion in Russian for about 15 seconds and then the bright, overly upbeat voice of Svetlana Ivanov came on the line.

"Liz, how are things in Florida? We need some help down here."

With Sergei out of the loop, the two women quickly developed a game plan for the next week and beyond. The Ivanovs would drive to Guadalajara as planned, but from there Svetlana would fly, via Mexico City, back to Mobile.

Sergei would follow her the moment he was bounced from the tournament, which could be 24 hours if he lost his first match or a week if he got to the final.

"Svetlana, there's one more thing I really should mention, and I know it's not something you've thought of or want to hear…but I talked to the Integrity Unit – you know them, right?"

"Yes, well we know it exists. We've never talked to them or met anyone. I mean, it's just something you read about."

"Of course, ya. Anyway, they're gonna want to talk with you at some point. Don't panic or be insulted. It's just a routine thing. When the fire people say arson, they have to at least open a file, talk to you, produce some kind of report. It's really just routine, you know?"

"If you say so. Doesn't seem routine to me, but OK, whatever. How will that work?"

"You'll hear from someone soon. Next week maybe. That's

really all I know. I'm not allowed to be involved or know exactly what they're doing."

"Liz, I want you to understand: We have no idea why this happened. We didn't do anything or talk to anyone or do anything wrong."

"I know, I know. It's not you. It's them. They have these policies now. It's routine, that's all."

"Routine my ass," Svetlana cursed when she hung up. "There's nothing routine about the tennis cops asking questions about this. Nothing. How much do you trust her?"

"Liz? Well, she's helped before, but that was just some minor stuff when we were looking for an agent and trying to drum up some sponsorship money, remember? Nothing like this."

"This is exactly why we need an agent."

"So expensive."

"I know, I know. What if we signed up with someone now? Could he help us?"

"I'm not sure. It's not like there's agent-athlete confidentiality. If we mentioned this going in, no one would be interested."

"Ya, you're right. But we need some help from someone and it sure as hell isn't going to be the ridiculous Tennis Integrity Unit."

Chapter 9

Ten years earlier, Nikolai Popescu didn't know it was possible to spend €3,000 on a suit, never mind €800 on a pair of shoes and another €600 for a shirt and tie. But then, he'd been working what he now considered a loser job in his uncle's bakery in Bucharest.

He was lucky to make the equivalent of €5,000 in the summer when he worked full time after school was out. The most the job ever paid him in one calendar year baking and delivering bread was the equivalent of €22,000. He could spend that now on a weekend in Paris with his girlfriend if he was in the right mood.

His mastery of numbers had been apparent early on, when he could add columns of two-digit figures in his head at the age of 5. It was a party trick for the most part, something his parents delighted in showing off to friends and neighbors.

Nik recalled the first time his father took him to a horse race. He was 8. The night before, his father sat him down to explain the finer points of the racing form. Within 20 minutes, Nik had grasped the basics of pari-mutuel betting and the odds assigned each horse. He didn't immediately understand exactas and trifectas, but once his dad explained it was like picking all the winners on the Olympic podium, he got it.

They left at 9:00 the next morning and spent an hour or so touring the race track, visiting the paddocks and concession stands and wandering around the viewing stand. Nik noticed everyone had the racing form his dad had shown him. That was disappointing: He figured his dad had something special there. If everyone had the same numbers and stuff, how would they pick the winning horses?

"We have a system," his dad said, chuckling at the question.

Nik stood as close as he could to the betting window as his dad placed their bets on the first race. The system let them down the first time, and again the second time. Nik noticed other peoples' systems were letting them down too. As soon as the race ended, they all threw their losing tickets into the air, creating a confetti storm of lost bets.

They bet on four more races that afternoon, and won some money on two of them. Nik didn't ask his dad how they ended up overall. He had figured out they lost money. But his dad didn't seem disappointed or worried, or even surprised. That last part stuck in Nik's mind. People were upset when they lost, but they weren't surprised. And losing never seemed to stop them from betting the next time. If anything, it made them bet more, and sooner. He didn't understand that.

They started going to the track together once a month or so, more often in the summer. Nik was never allowed to bet his allowance money, but once in a while his dad would bet on one of his suggestions. He had to have a reason for the pick, and he always did. He read the racing form, front to back, and found more info by going online. His dad never did that, but there was so much there. It made the racing form look kind of wimpy. Plus, Nik soon noticed you could place bets there too. People placed bets without actually going to the races. That seemed weird to him. He loved going to the races with his dad. He loved plotting their strategy on the drive there and reviewing it on the way home. He loved how so many people seemed to know his dad and always said hi. They usually rubbed his head or smiled at him too.

Nik was 13 when his dad had a stroke and died. No one was more surprised than his dad, who had turned 58 two weeks earlier. It happened while Nik was at school. The principal drove him to the hospital 10 minutes away. His mom and sisters were already there, and soon all his uncles and aunts showed up. His dad never regained consciousness. It was a Tuesday. Nik felt the loss most painfully that Saturday, when they didn't go to the track. Instead, they had a funeral.

"We should have it at the track, mom. That's what dad would want."

"Don't be so silly Nikolai. That's not a respectable place."

That was news to Nik, who considered it every bit the hallowed ground as the church where the service took place or the graveyard where a bunch of overdressed people buried him later that day. They weren't nearly as friendly as his dad's friends at the track. He thought of that when a few of the track friends came over to him at the back of the church and rubbed his head or smiled at him. But these smiles were different – pained and sympathetic, a goodbye rather than a hello.

Starting the following month, Nik spent his Saturdays not at the track but at his uncle's bakery. The family needed the money, his mom said. It was unfair in every way Nik could think of. He missed his dad so much his stomach hurt. He read old racing forms in bed at night, remembering the bets they made and the winners they celebrated. He thought about it at the bakery, doing stupid jobs for very little money.

If we need money so much, how come Uncle Fritz pays me almost nothing?

One day, Nik adjusted the price of a delivery he was making on his bike. It was easy to do. The prices were hand-written, as they had been for decades when his uncle's father had opened the business. Nik bumped it up 10 per cent and kept the difference. He hardly slept all week, fearing he would be busted when he showed up the next Saturday. But nothing happened. And nothing happened when he bumped it up 20 per cent. And nothing happened when he started doing it on sales over the counter when his uncle was out smoking or busy in the back.

In no time, Nik was making more by skimming than in legit pay. He had no problem with it, except for the fear of getting caught. But that fear diminished with each week, and he kept devising better ways of boosting his take.

He offered to help with the ordering of supplies. He'd listened to his uncle complain about doing that for years, so he figured out how the system worked and offered to pitch in. He mastered it immediately, and within three months, Uncle Fritz had handed over virtually all the ordering to him. He ran it straight up for six months, aware there was an audit at the year-end. His first January order had one additional account, into which he directed five per cent of the money he paid out to suppliers. It was common for some prices to go up at the beginning of the year, so there was a natural cover for the increase if Fritz had looked into it. But, of course, he didn't. Nik knew he wouldn't.

He started doing the same thing for the large corporate orders the bakery filled every week. Their bagels and pampushkies were sold to a medium-size grocery chain with locations across Romania and neighboring Bulgaria. Nik skimmed eight per cent from those orders. The whole system was hand-written and based on trust and decades of inertia. No one in business with the bakery had any reason to believe there was anything wrong.

The most challenging part was taking care of the actual cash he was skimming. He dutifully gave his official wages – a paltry sum compared to what he was really making – to his mom every week. After two years, his uncle gave him a tiny raise. Nik pretended to be grateful and handed over the increase too. But every week, he had a bag of bills and coins to make disappear. It was simple enough to hide them in his backpack each day, but he couldn't exactly open a bank account in town and show up every week with his cash deposits. Fourteen-year-olds just didn't do that.

A decade later he would face a similar problem, but with vastly larger sums. Laundering illegal money was often the biggest challenge of any criminal activity, and he began grappling with the problem at age 14. His initial solution was to buy a waterproof duffle bag and stash it in a hollow tree on the edge of the woods near his home. He became quite good at ensuring no one saw him stop there once a week or so. It worked well but was a temporary solution. It also raised a question he hadn't considered when he started stealing from his uncle: Why was he doing it?

Leaving the cash in the tree did nothing to help his family, who certainly could have used more than he and his mother were earning officially at their jobs. He wasn't benefitting at all from the scheme. At first he had done it to even things up with his uncle, who clearly was taking advantage of his father's death to get some cheap labor. It wasn't until years later that he realized the act of balancing all those numbers and calculating the risks he was taking had more or less replaced much of what he loved about the track. He could never replicate the joy he felt with his father, but the rest was surprisingly similar.

When he turned 16, he could open a bank account without attracting much attention. Always cautious, he opened accounts at six banks, all operating independently from each other. Once a week he went to one of his banks and made a modest deposit – money earned doing odd jobs, if any of the tellers expressed an interest. He went at varied times, combining the errand with a baking delivery, so he dealt with different people at different banks nearly every week.

On his 17th birthday, after the modest party his mother organized with three of his friends, he locked his bedroom door and reviewed his year-end results. He had amassed the equivalent of €50,000.

For all the success he enjoyed in subsequent years, he took the most pride in that sum. He had figured out an entire system to triple what his tight-fisted uncle paid him. And he did it without anyone ever suspecting a thing. He knew his father would be proud of him.

His math acuity earned him a scholarship at the Transilvania University of Brasov, almost three hours north of Bucharest. It was his ticket out of the bakery and the unspoken but growing expectation that he stick around to take over the business when cheapskate Fritz retired.

He studied hard at school, but not in any official courses. He went for a few weeks, mostly to look for cute girls, but then settled in to follow the plan he'd made when he accepted the scholarship. Because he was required to maintain an 80 per cent average to keep the scholarship money flowing, he knew his first year would be his only year. Like a can't-miss basketball prospect forced to play in college before being drafted into the NBA, he looked at the year as an investment in his future. He was a one-and-done student.

His plan was to find a way to parlay his tree money – moved now to three banks in Brasov – into a business of some kind. Not a business in the sense he would open a shop, hire employees and pay taxes. That was for squares like Uncle Fritz. He had something less formal and more profitable in mind.

It took him most of the year to develop the connections he needed, but by the time a guidance counselor was informing him the scholarship tap was going to run dry because of his spotty attendance and low grades, he had found a London flat to rent and was getting ready to move.

"It's an opportunity I can't refuse," he told his mother. "I can always go back and finish, but these things don't come around very often."

She accepted reluctantly, without really understanding what her math genius son would be doing in London. But he was happy and independent, and that was enough for her. Well, that and the money he sent her every month to supplement her income.

He joined the Garfunkel sports oddsmaker as a junior associate, but the title meant almost nothing. Garfunkel was relatively new to the growing gambling industry in Britain. Known historically as bookies, modern oddsmakers like Ladbrokes, Betfair and 888sport operated legitimately, taking bets on everything from Premier League football matches to Royal Family baby names to American election results. Millions of gamblers worldwide wagered on their sites every day, rivaling Las Vegas sports books as the epicenter of global sports gambling.

Garfunkel did all that and made a respectable return for its handful of publicly reported investors. But the partners who owned the majority of the business had not teamed up just to collect betting fees like the other 20 oddsmakers in the country. They were going to make millions following their own rules.

They had hired Nik to work that side of the operation, given him 5 per cent of the business in exchange for a €200,000 investment and had quickly been rewarded when he turned out to be a natural.

That's how Nik could afford a closet full of €3,000 suits, at age 23, two years after moving to London.

Chapter 10

When Randy Jorgensen was finally able to recharge his phone, the text messages from Gil and his mother started pouring in. It took a few seconds for him to realize they were both texting about the same thing and that his decision the night before to trust someone he barely knew might have backfired.

He'd slept over at his pal George's, as he often did on weekends, where his phone had died sometime overnight. With it still plugged into the kitchen wall at George's house, he called his mother first. It was 9:30.

"What happened at the tennis club last night?" she asked immediately. "They called here before 7:00 this morning and said something about vandalism. What happened Randy?"

"Ah, nothing mom. Well, OK, I don't actually know. I was there 'til 8:00 or so, but then some of the members' kids showed up. I know a few of them from school, but not really. Anyway, they said they'd close up. George was there with his car, and he didn't want to wait 'til 10:00. Why, what happened?"

"Your boss, what's his name?"

"Gil?"

"Ya, he's the one who called so early this morning. He said there was a lot of damage, bottles all over the place. Something about a ball machine. I don't know what he was talking about. He sounded upset."

"Geez, I'm sorry."

"Don't tell me. Get over there and tell him. You need that

job this summer. You need to make it right. Do whatever he asks."

"I don't know. It sounds bad."

"It is bad. That's why you have to fix it. Do you have a ride over there?"

It was only then Randy noticed George and his parents were sitting at the kitchen table listening to his half of the conversation. His father nodded to indicate he would drive Randy wherever he needed to go.

"Yes, I do. I'm just not sure what I should say."

"Be honest. You screwed up Randy. You really did."

"OK. Bye."

He hung up and dropped his head into his hands.

"Not good?" was all George said.

"Ah, no."

"I'll come with you, tell him I had to leave early and kind of forced you to come with me."

"Thanks. Don't think that's gonna work. Mr. Martino, if you can drive me I really appreciate it. The sooner the better I think."

"Sure enough kid. Remember, things always seem worse in the moment. Someday, you'll laugh about this."

George nearly spit up his coffee, listening to his dad try to be cool by contradicting everything he'd ever told him about responsibility. But he decided not to point that out right then.

The car ride was silent, aside from the Sirius classic rock channel George's dad dialed up instinctively.

"Good luck," was all he said when he pulled up the clubhouse and let Randy out.

"Thanks sir. And thanks for the ride."

When he walked into the clubhouse, he felt like he was living the dream about showing up somewhere without pants. Every eye in the building fell on him. It was awkward, but as he looked around he didn't see anything out of the ordinary.

No broken windows, no graffiti on the walls, nothing out of place at all actually.

Maybe this won't be so bad.

"Jorgensen. Get the hell up here."

He didn't recognize the voice or the person yelling down at him from the second floor. He hadn't met Tony Di Pietro during his first month of sporadic shifts. He disliked him already.

"Yes sir."

When he got to the top of the stairs, he saw half a dozen maintenance people working in every corner of the area. *Ugh.*

"Come in here please," the man in the suit said, pointing toward Gil's office.

He'd never really been summoned to the principal's office, not for behavior issues anyway, but he figured this was what it must feel like. Gil was sitting behind his desk, with a look on his face that suggested Randy had raped and killed his mother.

Geez, lighten up everyone.

He took a seat.

"Mr. Jorgensen," the man in the suit began, standing over him menacingly. "We're going to ask you once about what happened here last night. We expect you to tell us the entire truth, without any bullshit. Do you understand?"

He didn't wait for an answer.

"When we finish here today, you will be fired. Your level of honesty will determine whether we call the police about this vandalism. Is that clear?"

Randy's lip quivered and Gil felt just a pang of sympathy for him.

"Do you understand young man?"

"Yes, but, I mean. Ya."

Stammering and sobbing, Randy told his sad tale of

trusting the wrong people and leaving his job early to hang out with his friend. He didn't know all the names of the kids he'd left in charge, but he freely gave up the names he knew. There was no code, no honor among thieves. He couldn't spit out the names quickly enough.

Half an hour later, Di Pietro escorted him to the basement where the employee lockers lined one wall. He made a big show of cutting off the lock from Randy's locker and handing him a bag to gather its contents. Randy shoved a hat, some shorts and a water bottle into the bag and followed the man back upstairs.

"We may be in touch later, but please don't come back," Di Pietro said to him as he showed him out the front door. It was a five-mile walk home, but Randy didn't dare call his parents for a ride.

"That was a bit harsh, no?" Gil asked when Di Pietro reappeared at his office door.

"Hardly. They left the place open all night. They could have burned it down. And I'm going to spend all week chasing down these entitled kids, trying to punish them without pissing off their parents who are members. What a mess."

"Ya, I guess. But they'd want to know, wouldn't they?"

"Ya, for the most part. Depends I guess. Some would appreciate someone else lowering the boom. Others would pretend we were damaging them forever. I have to be careful. But first I need all the names. I might let the kid stew for a couple of days and then go see him and his parents. He might remember a few more names by then."

As he often did after the official part of their meeting was over, Di Pietro loosened his tie, sat back and put his feet on Gil's desk.

"OK Gil, a week ago you told me you were itching to give the tour another try. You didn't exactly say it, but I also got the feeling you were sick of all this," he said, motioning broadly out the office door. "Mornings like this can't help."

"I fall asleep thinking about it every night. This is a great job, you know, most of the time. If I'm back looking for work in two years, there's no guarantee I'll find anything like this, not in the U.S. anyway. I don't want to go work in the Caribbean or chase summer around the globe, working at tennis camps."

"But?"

"Well, nothing I said last week has changed. My old coach is ready to help. Says I'm good enough to do some damage on the challenger circuit, and then who knows? I could get hot and win some qualifiers into the big leagues. I always thought that's where I was headed."

"Pardon me for saying," Di Pietro said, swinging his feet off the desk and leaning forward for emphasis. "You're too good a player to be feeding balls to Howie Fucking Forrester. I don't know if you're good enough to get beyond the challenger level. I'm sure there are some great players there, but if you're asking me – and I know you aren't – I say you have to do it."

Gil nodded and stared beyond Di Pietro, vaguely watching maintenance workers shampoo the beer-soaked carpet.

"What if I told you we'd hold your job here? That you'd sort of be sponsored by the club?"

"I'd say tell me more. It sounds great."

"I've spoken to a few board members, informally, about putting together an agreement that could make things easier. I can't promise anything, but my sense is we can figure something out."

The plan, explained over two coffees in the confines of Gil's office, would make the club Gil's sponsor. It would continue to pay him a nominal salary and hold his job for him. In exchange, he would wear the name of the club – The Racquet Club of Memphis – on his tennis shirt and bag. He would also reimburse his salary to the club, if his winnings in any given year topped $100,000. The agreement would run for three years and be subject to renegotiation at the end of every calendar year.

"You'll know by then, if not sooner, whether it's going to work. And that's about as long as we can hold the job here. Anne is brand new. I'm not sure she can run the whole thing. We'll be looking for someone older, with experience, who wants to work for a couple of years. If you do well and go on to fame and fortune, Anne will be ready by then to take over."

"Jesus Tony, how can I say no to that? You're an answer to prayer. Thank you."

"OK, so you're interested. Let me take it officially to the board on Monday. I think it's a slam dunk, but you never know until they vote."

As they stood to shake hands, there was a knock on the office door. Before either man could get to the door, Howard Forrester walked in.

"You two hiding in here? OK Gil, I'm ready for my hit. You're lucky I was able to reschedule my day."

"You bet Howie. Let's go."

Di Pietro winked as Gil left, 10 steps behind Forrester who was heading for court one. "I think I figured something out about my forehand on the ball machine this morning. Come on, I'll show you."

Chapter 11

Nik left his expensive suits on their hangers, choosing instead a dark, cotton sweater and designer jeans this Tuesday morning. He liked to look good, but on days when he planned to crunch numbers for 12 hours or more in his office, he also liked to be comfortable. Many evenings, he ordered food and changed into a track suit to continue work.

Garfunkel took bets on events around the world, from anyone with a credit card and Internet connection. As a result, the office was open 24 hours a day, 365 days a year. It was a stand-alone building with security befitting a bank. There was no cash on hand, but millions of euros, pounds and dollars surged through its digitally encrypted network every day. Which was why no one worked from home -- or from a coffee shop or bakery or pool hall or cricket match. Everything happened at the office, known to those working there as The Castle because the sophisticated security system had been dubbed The Moat.

Nik spent 10 per cent of his time on the public side of the business, looking over the odds posted on the website, particularly for football matches, which were his specialty and love. He refused to say the word 'soccer' but the word did appear on the website so Americans could bet on the matches across Europe as though they knew something about the game. He also monitored some of the proposition bets Garfunkel, like every oddsmaker, posted regularly to attract attention and give the impression gambling was a harmless, light-hearted activity.

Prop bets ranged from odd to silly to preposterous, but always found an audience.

What color hat would Kate Middleton, the Duchess of Cambridge, wear to the Wimbledon final? Would One Direction reunite and record a new song? Would the singing of the U.S. anthem go over 2:00 at that year's Super Bowl? The stupidest of all was the Super Bowl coin flip. Heads or tails, a 50-50 chance, and yet people studied past flips as though they were indicators of what would happen that year. They knew it came up heads for five consecutive years, ending in 2013. Then it was tails the next four years. And on that basis, they wagered millions of dollars, collectively, on the outcome.

Nik was open with friends and family about the public aspect of his job, letting them believe that was all he and Garfunkel really did. He had perfected a demonstration of how the business worked that was reminiscent of someone selling knives in a booth at the county fair.

"Let's say there are 10 of you and you're gonna bet on the coin flip," he would say to a group of friends at a restaurant or bar. "Let's talk in dollars because so many of our gamblers are American. I collect $10 from each of you. I'm the house. We flip the coin and it's tails. Half of you bet tails, so I give you back your original $10 and the extra $10 you won. Half of you end up with $20 for betting tails, and half lose $10 for betting heads."

"But here's the most important thing. I end up with nothing. I ran the bet and handed out the winnings, but I didn't make any money. Why would I do that? Why would I set up a website and offer odds if I just passed along all the money from the losers to the winners?"

"Instead, let's say you had to bet $11 to win $10 on the coin flip. I collect $11 from everyone, and pay the winners $10 plus their original $11. I keep the extra $1 from the losers to cover my costs. That's how oddsmakers and sports books make money."

Nik could predict who did well and who struggled with math in school by watching the group process his example. What followed was a series of mostly predictable questions.

"OK, but what if everyone, or most of us, had bet tails for some reason. You could lose, right?"

"Exactly, which is why the whole goal is to set the odds so we get roughly half the money on each side. It's easy with a coin flip, but it's more complicated with most games. If Roger Federer is playing some qualifier in the first round, no one would bet on the qualifier to win. So we say you have to bet $100 on Federer to win $1. Still almost no one will bother taking Federer. It's just not worth it. But you might be tempted by the reverse. What if the new guy has the match of his life? What if Federer has a bad day or a sore back? If you bet $10 on the qualifier and he wins, you walk away with $1,000."

That always got people's attention, so he liked to pause at that point in his explanation and order another round for the table.

Freshly served, he answered more questions.

"What about a golf tournament or picking a team to win a championship before the season starts? There are dozens of choices, not just two."

"Yes, but the concept is the same. We want to create enough incentive for people to choose lots of golfers. When Tiger Woods was at his peak, everyone bet on him, but even at his best he won fewer than half the tournaments he entered. We make the odds tempting for other players, so people pick three or four players. Or 10."

"We really only lose big if something like Leicester City at 5000-to-1 wins the Premier League. You can't predict that, so a few people will make a lot of money if they took that bet before the season started. But even then, we can recoup some money because people hedge."

At this point, he usually lost half his tightly packed audience, those who no longer cared about the finer points of betting or were lost in the math. Either way, he was left with a few hard-cores who believed there were getting the inside dope on how sports betting really worked. They all believed wholeheartedly this insider knowledge would help them win more bets in the weeks ahead, and almost without fail it simply enticed them to bet larger sums, which they lost at the same rate they always lost – because most bettors made wagers based on emotions and team loyalty.

Hedging was nothing more than taking what was certain behind door No. 2 instead of waiting to see what was behind door No. 3 – giving up a potentially larger payday in the process.

"Let's say at the beginning of the year, you bet $100 on the Cleveland Browns to win the Super Bowl. Those odds would be astronomical, like 300-to-1 when the season began. But you live in Cleveland and you place the bet just for kicks."

"Then somehow, the Browns are not as awful as usual and by the halfway point of the season, they've won five and lost three. They're still not a favorite to win the Super Bowl, but they are ahead of some other teams and the odds might move to 100-to-1. You could still make a lot of money by betting them at that point."

"Alright, imagine they make the playoffs somehow, squeak in with a record of 9-7. Once they're in the playoffs, their odds get much better, maybe 50-to-1. But you're still sitting there with your 300-to-1 bet of $100, which will pay $30,000 if they somehow get through the playoffs and win the Super Bowl."

At some point, because you have such an enormous payoff potential if the Browns win it all, you might start to bet on some other teams too. When there are four teams left, and your Browns still have to win two games to win your bet, you might bet $1,000 on each of the other three teams. The odds would vary depending on how big a surprise they are to be that far, but you might be able to win a net $5,000 to $10,000 by betting $1,000 on the other teams. So you dip into your potential $30,000 payoff and bet a total of $3,000 on the other teams, just to make sure you win something. If the Browns lose, remember, you only lose $100 that you bet back when the odds were 300-to-1. You're hedging your bet because your long shot has done so well to that point."

"If they got to the Super Bowl, with just one team left to beat, you could argue it would be madness not to hedge. Let's say it's the Browns vs. Dallas. You bet $10,000 on Dallas to win, which might pay $8,000, because they would almost certainly be the favorite. You'd watch the game knowing you were guaranteed to win either $8,000 or $30,000. If the Browns won, you would have lost the $10,000 bet on Dallas, but you'd still clear $20,000. If Dallas won, you'd win $8,000, minus your original $100 bet on Cleveland, and the Cleveland loss wouldn't hurt nearly as much. That's why people hedge. And when they hedge, they place more bets with us and other oddsmakers. More bets equals more fees, equals more profit."

The last few diehards at the table usually nodded very slowly, some stroking their chins like they were in a seminar with Sigmund Freud.

"Is that legal? Hedging?"

"Of course, why wouldn't it be? It's just a matter of when you place your bets. Most of the time, you aren't in a position with a long shot doing that well. Usually you would lose your $100 bet on the Browns in about six weeks when they started the season 1-5 and absolutely stunk."

Forced laughter indicated the study group had run out of

questions. As they got up to leave, some shook his hand, in a sign of something more than thanks. For some, it was the equivalent of meeting the Pope or the Dalai Lama or, decades earlier, Frank Sinatra. It was just cool.

Nik usually enjoyed the attention. Just because he wasn't divulging everything he knew didn't mean he didn't enjoy explaining the basics to such eager bettors. In his office, smashing away on his keyboard, he sometimes imagined these folks and many more like them around the world, hanging on every number he produced, trying to get the better of him by finding events with odds in their favor.

He was careful not to feel too close to them because most of the time he worked on the private side of the business, where he and a carefully selected handful of people did more than guess at the outcomes of games and matches. They manipulated them, ever so subtly, making their bets as close to a sure thing as it was possible to achieve. He felt no guilt about the manipulation. It felt like he was back in his uncle's bakery, crunching numbers and analyzing the system to gain an advantage. What his uncle didn't know never hurt him. There was so much gamblers didn't know about the way odds were set and the factors that went into the bets Garfunkel accepted, that the occasional fixed outcome was peanuts in the overall picture. Or so Nik told himself as he racked up hundreds of millions for the company and millions for himself.

Chapter 12

Not surprisingly, flying from Guadalajara to Mobile was not exactly New York to L.A. Sitting in the concourse at the George Bush Intercontinental Airport in Houston, Svetlana was anxious to board her third flight of the day to get home. The flight from Guadalajara to Mexico City was as quick as it was uncomfortable. The middle leg of her journey was Mexico City to Houston, where she sat waiting for the short flight to Mobile.

The signs should make it clear this place is named after the first George Bush, you know?

The flight from Houston to Mobile Regional Airport – not large enough to be named after a former president or former anything – would be about 45 minutes, getting her home by 6 p.m. But of course, she wasn't going home, not to stay anyhow. She wanted to survey the fire damage but had made other arrangements for a few nights while she got the insurance payments sorted out. Then they would rent a suite downtown and max out the insurance coverage for as long as they could.

The Mobile flight was uneventful and delivered her three minutes early. With no bags to claim, she pulled her carry-on past the luggage carousel and looked to flag down a cab. That's when she noticed the man in uniform holding an iPad with her name handwritten in block letters.

"Excuse me, who are you? I'm Svetlana Ivanov. It seems you're looking for me."

"Mrs. Ivanov, yes. I'm Jerry Baxter. Chief Joseph sends his

regards and asked me to pick you up."

"Who's Chief Joseph? The police chief? Oh, sorry, I should be thanking you for coming to pick me up. But who is he and why would he send a driver?"

"No need to apologize maam. You've been through a lot over the last week or so. Chief Joseph is the fire chief. My boss." He leaned in almost imperceptibly so she could more easily see the row of commendation medals pinned to his crisp, white shirt. A sign of distinction and honor when worn by senior military officials, the version Baxter was sporting, issued by the Mobile Fire Department, did not project the same image.

Looks like a member of the Village People.

"My truck is this way," he said, pointing vaguely toward the parking lot and starting ahead of her at a brisk pace. "The chief would like to speak with you right away."

"Hold on there, Jerry. Is it Jerry?"

"Yes."

"Great. Again, I appreciate the ride, but I've been flying all day and I've made some plans to stay with friends tonight. Plus I haven't even seen our home since the fire. I don't think I could possibly talk to your chief today."

"I could have him meet us at your house. I'll take you there straight away and then wherever you want to go after that. OK? That should work."

When she didn't protest immediately, Baxter punched his cell and reached the chief on the first ring. "I've got her. It's just her, not the guy. Can you meet at the home? That's the only way she'll see you tonight."

"If that's the only way, OK. See you there in 20 minutes."

She was too tired to argue and dozed off briefly on the short drive. As the truck rounded the final corner and ambled down her street, she felt ill. Late March in Mobile meant flowers were starting to bloom and leaves were reappearing on trees. Her street looked picturesque, aside from the burned out hulk ahead on the right, surrounded by police tape – her home.

She let out an involuntary sob as they slowed to park 100 yards away. Before she could get out of the truck, a similar red pickup parked behind them. The driver met her at the curb and introduced himself as Geronimo Joseph.

"My condolences on your loss," he said. "I hope Baxter here was helpful. We sure do appreciate the chance to finally talk with you. Been away, in Mexico I'm told?"

"That's right. My husband plays tennis. He's still there, playing." As she talked, she looked over the man's shoulder to survey the damage. The video of the fire was gruesome, but this was worse. Their home was ripped open for all to see and then left like that. She wanted to wrap a blanket around it, the way rescue workers often did for survivors. Her home had been attacked and then left to fend for itself. She felt sick again and wobbled as she walked past the chief, whose droning voice she ignored, toward her driveway.

It was still strewn with burned wooden beams and sections of roof. She could see the rear bumper of their Acura ILX in the garage. They had taken an Uber to the airport. For whatever reason, she hadn't thought of the car all week. It appeared to be a casualty of the fire.

"This is bloody awful," she whispered to no one in particular.

"Yes maam, it is. Would you like some water?"

"Ah, yes OK, yes. That would be good. Thank you."

The chief handed her a bottle of spring water and finally stopped talking.

Three or four neighbors emerged, having noticed her arrival. She recognized only one of them and couldn't recall her name. Their only friends in Mobile were from Sergei's days at university. They spent no extended time at home, and when they did they kept to themselves.

"Very sorry about the fire," said one, introducing herself as Joan. "Me too," said another, Carla. "Do they know anything more about what happened? I mean, is there an arsonist on the loose?"

Unable to maintain the pretense of caring about the Ivanov loss, Carla had come to the point almost immediately, while pretending otherwise. They all wanted to know what had happened and whether the arson attack was directed at the odd Russian couple, as opposed to being a random attack that might be repeated. It was exactly how people felt when someone was murdered in a part of town they frequented. Hearing the victim was involved with drugs, or gangs – or both – set everyone's mind at ease. At least it wasn't a random attack. We're all still safe.

So too with terror attacks. Better 20 children die in a school bus because a tire blew out or a deer ran in front of the bus, than because of a terrorist bomb. Some tragedies could be processed more easily. And nearly every person on that street wanted, somewhere in their consciousness, to hear the fire was at least partially the fault of the Ivanovs, and not entirely random.

"If you don't mind, Mrs. Ivanov, I have a few questions. We've been waiting all week for a chance to ask you."

"Huh, right. Well, a few maybe. I'm quite tired, and this is very depressing. Can I go in and see if anything is left?"

"It's best if you don't go in just yet. We're still working on the structural integrity, but tomorrow or the next day we could take you in escorted to have a look around. I should warn you, there doesn't seem to be much left or recognizable. Again, I'm sorry."

"Ya, I guess that's to be expected. How did it start?"

"In the basement. We think someone set a fire there."

"Someone? It couldn't just be a bad wire or something like

that. I don't know."

"We're certain someone lit a sheet and tossed it into your basement. It's a very common way to start a fire, and also one that's easy to figure out. It doesn't seem the person was trying to hide the cause of the fire."

She looked away and remained quiet, unwilling to be dragged into whatever conversation the big, fat fire chief wanted to have. He was as subtle as his red pickup truck, and she refused to bite.

"A lot of common arsonists have a signature technique or indicator. This guy wasn't clever like that. Seems to have wanted everyone to know the fire wasn't an accident."

"Huh." Her gaze remained fixed on the horizon.

"The thing is Mrs. Ivanov, we're kind of stuck looking for clues, and are hoping you can help us."

"Are you able to drive me to my friend's house now?" she said, looking past the chief at her driver.

"Did you hear what I said, Mrs. Ivanov?" the chief asked brusquely.

"I'm just so tired. Could you drive me please, now, as you promised? Thank you so much." And with that, she climbed back into her seat in Jerry Baxter's truck and closed her eyes. *That's all for today boys.*

Baxter shrugged at his boss and fired up his truck. The only sound he could coax from his passenger was the address where he could drop her.

The drive took less than 10 minutes and concluded in a neighborhood very much like the one they had just left. They had to stop to wait for a gate to open at the road before winding up the long driveway, where Sally Wilkins was standing on the porch waiting.

During Sergei's four years at South Alabama, Sally had virtually adopted the young Russian couple. While her husband coached the men's tennis team, Sally looked out for the spouses and significant others, especially those coming from other countries who invariably were lost for several weeks or months in the culture of the South.

Tom Wilkins was one of the main reasons the couple had moved back to Mobile, but in Svetlana's mind the coach and his wife were a package deal, and she had wasted no time reconnecting with Sally when they moved back after three years headquartered in Florida.

"I've been worried sick about you," Sally began as she greeted Svetlana with a prolonged hug. "Tom is so bad at texting and keeping track of people. We didn't even know for the first few hours if you were there when it happened. I drove over, but they wouldn't let me get close or ask any questions. Thank God you were away. How are you?"

Only then, as she waited for an answer, did she release her grip and step back. It was as though the hug had popped the cork on Svetlana's emotions. The travel, the house, now seeing Sally – she let it all go in a fit of sobbing on the Wilkins' front porch. It didn't reach the extreme of the night Sergei told her why someone had torched their house, but she churned through most of a box of Kleenex and inhaled two glasses of white wine in less than 20 minutes.

"It feels like it's happening to someone else," she said when she regained control. "I think because we weren't here, it didn't seem real. And then seeing the house today, it really felt like someone's else's tragedy, like it can't be happening to us, you know?"

"I can't even imagine how you feel, to be honest. Come inside and have some dinner. I made that gumbo you always liked. Not too spicy."

"You're the best Sally, the very best. Thank you."

The two ate casually seated at the kitchen island. They avoided the fire topic for a long while, instead discussing Sergei's progress on the Challenger circuit and that year's

South Alabama tennis team. "It has never been as good as it was when Sergei was captain. I know Tom feels that way too."

Inevitably, the fire reemerged in the conversation, which reminded Sally of a phone call she'd received that afternoon.

"Someone named, oh, where's that note? Here, here it is. A man named Nigel Clancy called. He had a funny accent but said he was calling from Florida. Said he works for – I wrote this down because I hadn't heard of it before – the tennis integrity unit. What's that dear?"

"What did he say? I don't know him."

"He seemed to know you were coming home today and staying here. He's flying down and wants to meet with you, and Sergei too, this week."

"I see. Hmm. Well, I hope Sergei is still playing at the end of the week. Did he say what he wanted?"

"No, just said he wanted to meet with you. Sounded friendly enough, if that makes it any better."

"Not really Sally. Listen, I wasn't going to tell you this until Tom was here with us, but if this guy is coming tomorrow, well, I need to discuss it with someone. Without an agent or anything, we're at a loss. So I guess it's you, if that's OK. I mean, I don't want to burden you even more. You're always so kind to us."

"Not at all dear. What's on your mind?"

Chapter 13

"Was it always this good? Why did I ever leave?"

Gil's thoughts were spilling from his brain, forming words against his will. But nothing he said could be understood because his mouth was glued to various parts of a 26-year-old part-time yoga teacher who kept herself in tiptop condition and had encouraged his advances with some suggested activities of her own.

Their evening had started at one of Gil's favorite Ann Arbor bars, HopCat. When he was a student, it was an easy walk from the University of Michigan campus in one direction and his apartment in the other. He could stop there after classes or tennis practice and make his way home with little fuss.

Even three years after graduating, he thought about the place constantly. He had nothing against Memphis and the Racquet Club of Memphis. It was a great town, full of great restaurants and bars, but he didn't expect anything to ever top his college experience. A major part of that experience was in bed with him now, enjoying their reunion as much or more than he was. Samantha went by Sam to everyone, including him.

They'd lasted for one drink at HopCat before she suggested, in a non-verbal way, that they retire to her place, a 15-minute walk or 2-minute drive from the bar. They took a cab and tipped the driver to step on it while they got a head start in the back seat.

It had started even earlier, when she excused herself while

he ordered their drinks. She returned from the washroom with her pale, blue panties balled up in her hand. She sidled up to Gil at the bar and slipped them into the front pocket of his jeans, doing a fair amount of groping along the way.

It was an homage to something she'd done when they had first started seeing each other. Anxious to show he was not a dumb jock, he had invited her to attend a gala opening at the university's Museum of Art. The exhibit was a celebration of urban photography, not some highfalutin investigation of Medieval pottery or Renaissance political upheaval. These were cool black-and-white photos of cities all over the world – art he could understand and enjoy.

She met him there, wearing a sleeveless, black, silk shift dress, with dark blue panels at the sides. It was short, but not too short, its simplicity highlighted with a thin necklace and single bracelet. Her heels were just high enough to draw attention to her firm calves, and when she walked in, the photographs suddenly seemed rather plain and boring.

After an hour or so of slowly making the rounds and considering the merits of Amsterdam vs. Copenhagen vs. London, she excused herself. She returned from the washroom wearing an impish smile and beckoned him behind a pillar with one curl of her forefinger. With her back to the room, she reached into a black clutch and extracted a pair of silk panties, the exact shade of blue to match her dress accents. She handed them to him while maintaining eye contact.

Gil hardly needed reminding, but he was happy to play along as she slipped her underwear into his pocket at HopCat, pushing against him as she did so. They had slept together regularly at school, but the ground rules were clear: She was not leaving Ann Arbor, not for him and not for anyone. Their diverging paths were obvious in Gil's final year, and they had pulled back from each other to some extent, although Gil did remember a fantastic good-bye weekend to celebrate his graduation.

Sporadic emails and texts maintained a connection of sorts, but Gil didn't know what to expect when he announced he would be back on campus for two days to talk to his former coach about giving the pro circuit one last shot. His uncertainty lasted only as long as it took her to return from the washroom and indicate very clearly how she wanted to spend the rest of the evening.

The evening stretched into the early morning, the sex interspersed with bits of conversation that served to catch them up on the last three years. She still enjoyed being spanked, and he still enjoyed spanking her, using a one-hand backhand technique he had perfected in school.

They dozed off just before the sun rose, getting no more than two hours of sleep.

"OK, I've got to get back to my hotel room and change," Gil announced with some reluctance around 7:00.

"Ah, so soon?"

"You know I have a meeting at 9:00, and I can't go in these clothes," he said, slapping her bare ass as he searched for his pants.

"OK, but let's do this again tonight. You have your room until tomorrow, right?"

"I like how you think. Aren't we having dinner anyway?"

"Yes, your coach asked me to join you."

"Ha, is that so? My coach huh? Is that what you call him?"

"Well, when you're not here he's just Daddy to me."

"So I'll see you tonight, at your parents' place for dinner. Keep your underwear on until we get to the hotel, OK?"

"No promises."

Chapter 14

Tom Wilkins arrived home around 9:00 to find his wife and Svetlana Ivanov sitting in the kitchen, their meal long gone, talking earnestly. It had taken half an hour for Svetlana to tell Sally everything she had learned in the previous week about the pressure being exerted on Sergei to fix matches.

Sally knew match fixing happened, but she'd never seen it up close and she'd never seen Svetlana so emotional and scared. She asked Svetlana many of the same questions Svetlana had asked of Sergei, many of which still had no answers. There was no way they could, on their own, staring at text message instructions and demands, figure out who was on the other end of the threats.

The most pressing thing was to figure out whom they could trust with the information, as they tried to plot a course back to normalcy. The Wilkinses were the first people they thought of, certainly ahead of Liz Catalano, the lawyer at the ATP. "I don't think we should tell her anything," Svetlana had said, the moment their phone conversation from Mexico ended.

It took a few minutes to bring Tom up to speed, and then the three of them sat around the quartz-topped island, sipping wine and throwing ideas back and forth.

Tom had some ideas neither the Ivanovs, nor Sally, had voiced.

"You might consider going public. Explain how you've been blackmailed. Show that Sergei never withdrew a cent from the account. Prove you haven't profited from this. In fact, you've suffered terribly. People will sympathize.

Especially if you make it clear you're going to work with authorities to stop this kind of crap."

"And how long do you think Sergei would have to live if he did that?" Sally asked her husband incredulously. "You can't be serious Tom."

"I'm just exploring other ideas. Presumably, the government could offer protection of some kind. Would the crooks be bold enough to do something after Sergei had gone public?"

"Well, we don't know," his wife said. "But why not? Wouldn't that make it easier for them to manipulate others? Wouldn't other players be more scared than ever?"

"Maybe. OK, what else could we do?"

The silence of the kitchen was eerie. The only sounds were the hum of the air conditioning and the rinse cycle of the dishwasher.

"What about this?" Svetlana began. "We hire an investigator, you know, a P.I. They exist, right? He finds the bad guys for us."

"They certainly exist," Tom said. "The university uses them sometimes to look into the backgrounds of athletes before offering scholarships. And even when they hire senior administrators actually. We're just lucky, Sal, they didn't sick anyone on us before we started here."

"Aren't you funny," she replied. "You've got all our bribe money tucked away somewhere, right?" Glancing at her guest, she blanched. "Oh, goodness, Svetlana dear, I'm sorry. I was just kidding. I know it's not funny."

"It's fine, no problem. You have to laugh sometimes. This is crazy, talking about hiring a P.I. and digging around in the criminal world. Excuse my language, but I can't fucking believe it."

"So, Tom, if the university uses investigators, can you get some names? We need to find the right person, obviously. You can't just Google them. Or can you?" Sally asked, half seriously.

"I can poke around, but I'd rather not draw attention by announcing I'm in the market for someone."

"What about that police detective friend of yours, what's his name? You know."

"Gary?"

"Ya, couldn't he recommend some people without needing to know why? You could make something up, about an athlete maybe or a rival school? He doesn't need to know why. Could you talk to him?"

"Actually, I'd rather start with him than ask around at school. Leave it with me."

They were about to leave the kitchen for the comfort of family room couches when the bell at the gate rang. Looking at a screen in the kitchen, Tom could see it was a cop, two in fact. Neither was his friend Gary, and neither appeared to be in a good mood.

The gate swung open slowly when Tom punched in his code, and he watched the car pass through toward the front door. The gate closed on its own 30 seconds later, about the time the cops were parking their cruiser. Tom greeted them on the porch. He was curious but saw no reason to invite them in just yet.

"Evening officers, what's up?"

"Coach Wilkins, I'm Constable Hughes. This is Constable Reynolds. We're sorry to trouble you so late, but we understand someone named, ah…" Looking at his notes in the dim light, he struggled. "Ivanov, I believe is the last name, a woman. Is she here? Is she a friend of yours?"

"Yes and yes. Why? What's happened?"

"It's nothing directly connected to her, but Detective Brison, she asked that we come over and see if she's available to answer just a few questions about something that happened tonight, near her home."

Listening quietly from inside the door, Svetlana joined them on the porch, propelled by her curiosity. "What happened? Something else? Another fire?"

"No maam, no fire. Are you, ah, Mrs. Ivanov?"

"Yes, I am. What's going on?"

"Well, maam, coach, I'm afraid someone has died. We have reason to think it may not be natural causes."

"Good God, who?"

"Ah, a neighbor of yours." Again, he fussed with his notebook, again he struggled with the name. "Do you know someone named, ah, Nester Pid, ah, wer."

"Pidwerbecki? Mr. Pidwerbecki is dead? Really?"

"Yes maam, that's the name. He lived on your street, I understand. Would you be able to swing by the station this evening and talk to the detective? She, you know, we, would be grateful."

"How about first thing in the morning?" Sally suggested, speaking for the first time since the cops had arrived. "Mrs. Ivanov has been travelling all day and is tired. Surely, tomorrow is soon enough." With that, she put her arm around Svetlana's shoulders and gently guided her back into the doorway, indicating the conversation was about to end.

"Ah, the detective is trying to get a start on this tonight. It's important not to let a lot of time pass before we talk to witnesses and such."

"But Mrs. Ivanov is not a witness," Sally noted with slightly more vigor. "Nothing she will tell you will change between now and tomorrow. Please tell your detective we'll come by at 10:00 tomorrow. Good night officers."

And with that, she escorted Svetlana back into the house, leaving Tom to shrug his shoulders and give the cops a sheepish look, as though there were nothing he could do to help them. "I guess we'll pick this up in the morning. Good night guys. The gate will open when your car gets close."

And it did, right on cue.

Chapter 15

Nester Gilbert Pidwerbecki had died as he lived, in his garden, pruning shrubs while keeping an active eye on the comings and goings of his neighbors -- tracking who was visiting with whom, who was fighting with whom, and who was sleeping with whom. His keen sense of observation had failed him, however, when he most needed it.

He neither saw nor heard the person who stabbed him with his own pruning shears as dusk descended on the neighborhood. He was dead before his body fell into the perfectly manicured boxwood hedge he spent part of every morning maintaining. That irony was lost on the coroner who confirmed with scientific exactness what anyone with a functioning temporal lobe could see: The pruning shears jutting out of his back, just below his shoulder blades, were both the cause of death and the murder weapon.

They were – predictably – free of any fingerprints besides Pidwerbecki's.

"The angle of entry eliminates the possibility of a self-inflicted wound," the coroner reported in all seriousness to Detective Angela Brison.

"So, this wasn't the old stab-in-the-back suicide?" she asked with a grin, drawing not so much as a smirk in return from the man in the blue lab coat.

"That's correct detective, the wound was not self-inflicted."

"OK, thanks Jones. Let me know if you make any other breakthroughs."

"Will do."

Back at the station, Brison brought the captain up to speed, leading with the news from the coroner that it wasn't suicide.

"That practically solves the case, doesn't it?" he grunted.

The text, which arrived late the previous day from Hughes and Reynolds, said the tennis woman with the burned down house was coming in that morning.

Sure enough, on the dot of 10, she arrived, with something of an entourage in tow. The South Alabama tennis coach did not register on Brison's radar, so initially she assumed the tennis woman had brought her parents. She half expected them to have Russian accents, but when not-her-mother spoke she sounded the way she looked – a Southern Belle, all polite and formal.

"Detective Brison? A pleasure. This is my husband, Tom, and Svetlana Ivanov. Your officers last night wanted to speak with us, or with Mrs. Ivanov anyway, but this was much more convenient."

"Thank you all three for coming in. Let's find a place to sit down."

She didn't bother specifically inviting the non-parents because it was obvious they would be tagging along at every juncture, possibly into the washroom if Moscow Barbie had to pee at any point during their visit.

"Anyone want a coffee or soda?"

Murmurs around the table suggested they did not, so she put her own mug on the metal surface and flipped open the file folder she had carried in under her arm. It was quite thin and contained mostly just photos of Nester Pidwerbecki – a few in happier days but mostly in his role as a gruesome garden gnome in his lush backyard.

"Just to be clear here, you two don't live in the neighborhood or know the victim, is that right?"

"Correct," Tom said, squeezing Sally's hand under the table.

"So you're friends, or…"

"Tom coached Mrs. Ivanov's husband, Sergei. He was a star on the tennis team until he graduated three years ago and left to play professionally. We've kept in touch, and were thrilled when they moved back to Mobile so Tom could start working with him again."

"I see. Look, Mrs. Ivanov, no offence here, but I've never heard of your husband. You say he's a professional player? Where?"

Svetlana perked up, happy to discuss a topic she actually understood, as opposed to fires and murders. Providing many more details than Brison wanted, she summarized Sergei's career to date, their decision to return to Mobile, and his success that very week in Guadalajara, where he had reached the semi-finals with a win the day before.

"You were in Mexico with him when your house burned down? Sorry, but I'm just establishing a timeline."

"Yes, that's right. I flew back yesterday."

"I talked to Captain Joseph. He says it was definitely arson. Any ideas on that?"

"No, I've told them that. We have no idea. And believe me, we haven't stopped thinking about it all week."

"I understand the victim, Mr. Pidspeckity…, the victim had contacted the fire department. He had some relevant information. Or so he thought."

"Don't know. I talked to him when he was out gardening. Very nice man. It's awful someone killed him. I'm sorry, of course. But I don't know why I'm here or why you're asking about our house."

"He thought he saw the person who started your fire."

"It wasn't *our* fire, OK? It was our house. But it's gone now. I can't even go in and look around. We've lost everything. It wasn't *our* fire."

"OK, sorry. I understand. *The* fire, let's say. He thought he saw who started the fire."

"Great," Sally said, as Svetlana checked out of the discussion. "Who is it? Have you arrested anyone?"

"We haven't. Seems the victim posted a photo on his Facebook account. He thought it was relevant."

"What are you saying? Did he identify the arsonist or not?"

"No, he didn't. It was a video, actually. It's here," she said, punching her iPad. "There doesn't seem to be much to it. It's still on his account. Turns out it's almost impossible to close someone's account if you're not that person. We haven't found any next of kin. If this were really incriminating, I'm not sure how we'd take it down, to be honest. Like I said, though, it seems like nothing, except for the caption."

Svetlana re-engaged long enough to squint and read what her former neighbor had written above the photo: **Is this the arsonist who burned down the Ivanov home? #Mobile #Witness #GetInvolved.**

#GetYourselfKilled, Brison nearly said.

As the video looped a third time, Svetlana stood up. "I don't get it. A truck drives down the street. That's all I see."

"That's all we see too, but we wanted to make sure we're not overlooking anything. Maybe you see something different from the way the street usually looks. Maybe you notice something missing that we aren't aware of. If anything pops into your mind later, please call."

"We will, of course," Sally said. "Now, are you also working with the fire department to catch the arsonist? Maybe it's related to this poor man and maybe not, but it's still important, right?"

"We are liaising with Chief Joseph on that investigation, yes," Brison said. "We want to know what happened in both situations, whether they're related or not. It's possible the arsonist thought this Pidsterdecky fellow knew more than he really did. It's possible there's something we're missing in the video. We can't rule anything out right now."

"Could you maybe rule out that my husband and I are somehow to blame for losing our home?" Svetlana asked quietly, barely lifting her head from her hands. "It's bad enough without this feeling we know something we're not telling you or the fire chief."

"We'll certainly keep you posted on what we find out," Brison said. "For now, that's all I can really promise. Unless you have anything to add, I think we're done here." She gathered the photos and stacked them neatly into the file folder, standing up as she did.

"There's something you're not saying, something you keeping from us," Tom said, standing and looking Brison squarely in the eye. "There's no reason for us to be here. We have nothing to add. What's going on?"

Brison considered her words for a second and then shrugged. "Fair enough. Here's the deal. This looks for all the world like a professional hit. There are no clues, no hints of someone being there, nothing. That itself is pretty rare in Mobile. And it suggests someone pretty nasty wanted this guy dead. We can't figure out why."

"The fire?" Svetlana whispered.

"Could be. It's certainly the most obvious thing. But here's the other problem. Professional killers plan things out. They are meticulous. You don't need to be a cop to know that, right? So, why use the pruning shears? That suggests something much more hasty and unplanned, a spur-of-the-moment attack with whatever was handy. We've got a bunch of pieces that don't add up, including, maam, the fire that destroyed your house, across the street a few days earlier. Maybe they're unrelated, but that would be one hell of a coincidence."

She led the trio down the hall toward the lobby. "Like I said, call if you think of anything. Look at that video again and tell me what we're missing. Thanks for coming in."

Chapter 16

Nik arrived at The Castle at 6:30 a.m., latte in hand, and headed straight for his office. Because so many sporting events took place on weekends, they were the busiest days at The Castle, but at that hour, few people had arrived, so avoiding small talk was easy.

Grabbing one of several remotes from his desk, he turned on the 60-inch flat screen hanging on the far wall, leaving the four smaller screens off for the moment. Green lights danced along the face of the supercharged modem connected to the TV, and within seconds he was watching a local feed from Quanzhou, China. He didn't understand Mandarin and punched mute.

If he had needed to hear the commentary, he could have touched a button on his remote and received an instantaneous translation from one of a dozen translators who worked in a secluded room in another part of The Castle.

Running concurrently with the Guadalajara tournament was another Challenger event, in Quanzhou. The purse was the same US$50,000, which meant none of the players, regardless of how well they did, was going to get rich playing there. Like Sergei on the other side of the world in Mexico, they were desperately trying to collect enough points to move up to the big leagues.

Quanzhou was 12 hours ahead, so at 7:00 a.m. London time, the match would begin under the lights at 7:00 p.m. local time. The tournament was the biggest event every year in the area, so all 12,000 seats would be filled for the final between Gunter Schmidt of Germany and Tobias Madsen of Denmark.

Televised across China, it would draw more viewers than the U.K. had citizens, and still not be the highest rated broadcast that day. Generally speaking, the more viewers of an event, the more people there were betting on it, which is what Nik and his partners at Garfunkel cared about.

There were some exceptions. Regardless of how many people watched World Cup matches live every year – buffeted by time zone considerations -- it attracted more bets than any other tournament, more even than the Super Bowl because there were so many matches. By contrast, the Summer Olympics was one of the biggest viewing spectacles every four years, challenging the World Cup for international viewers. Yet, it drew few bets on anything other than basketball and the men's 100-metre final. There would always be a few people betting on pole vaulting, cycling and the marathon, but in the main, the Olympics just didn't attract much action.

The final of a Challenger tournament in China wasn't about to set any gambling records either, but Nik wasn't interested in the straight up bets people were making about who would win. He was working the other side of the Garfunkel ledger – where the company made most of its profits, running a system of match-fixing Nik knew his father would appreciate, if not love.

There was only so much money to be made taking bets on nobodies like Gunter Schmidt and Tobias Madsen. And it wasn't enough to provide Nik and his associates with the earnings to which they had become accustomed.

Two months earlier, Nik and one of his more muscular employees had visited Tobias Madsen near his home in Copenhagen. The unsuspecting player had gone out for coffee one Saturday morning and was sitting next to a canal flipping through the newspaper on his phone when they approached him. The wording was always different, geared to the player's specific circumstances, but the gist never varied: Sometime in the next few months, you will receive a message from someone you don't know, using a code word you will recognize. It was usually the name of the player's first pet or girlfriend, which had the double effect of ensuring he would remember it and making him understand the people sitting with him had dug into his past and knew a lot about him.

When the player got the message, he simply had to carry out the instructions and all would be well. They weren't asking him to lose the match, just to move the score in one direction or another. "We realize you won't always be able to control things, but we will know if you're trying. You should hit our target more often than you miss."

Like others before him, Madsen listened and grew angry. He had done very little with his life since the age of 8 but hit tennis balls. He was a professional, despite playing at the Challenger level, and he was damned if he was going to fix matches.

"Knep dig selv," he said dismissively. *Go fuck yourself.*

Nik didn't have a translation handy, but it was clear the player was saying no. Without ever raising his voice or touching Madsen, he leaned in and whispered to him. The closing, like the approach, was different for each player. But it always included a specific reference to someone in his life and a promise to share the wealth with the player in the form of deposits in an offshore account.

"Think it over. We'll be in touch," Nik said, lingering for a moment before departing.

His muscular companion had done nothing but observe and intimidate. There were times when he had to do more, however. A year earlier, a basketball player who towered over Nik, reached for his phone and tried to take a picture of Nik and his partner. His plan was to report the incident to league officials. Nik's plan was for his partner to grab the player's phone, smash it on the ground and hold the raging athlete at bay while Nik delivered the closer, showing the player a video of his niece and nephew playing innocently at their daycare in France the day before.

Nik hated having to threaten. He much preferred to cut a deal with the player. The truth was most of them were earning far less than they dreamed of making when they turned pro. They were working in their uncle's bakery. That's why Garfunkel targeted them. Nik wanted a partner, someone who could see the upside in helping out from time to time and earning a bonus that matched or exceeded his legitimate salary. A few players did indeed see the upside. One had embraced the opportunity to such a degree, he pushed for more "assignments" as he called them, and had to be cut loose because he was too keen to throw matches.

He had no idea if it were true, but from reading spy novels, Nik imagined getting a player on his side was similar to the way spies recruited key people to work for them in the world of espionage. He tried to gain their trust and let them justify what they were doing to earn their bonuses. The athletes motivated entirely by threats could never really be relied on and were far more likely to talk to authorities and turn into the equivalent of double agents, trying to snare Nik and his associates. Those who accepted the payments, even if grudgingly at first, usually came to rely on them and found a way to assuage their conscience and fix matches rather deftly.

Today was Tobias Madsen's first assignment and Nik was as curious as he was nervous. Madsen had made it clear he wanted no part of the assignment, but had softened when Nik started talking about the player's mother, Helga, who was battling cervical cancer. In addition to the money, Nik offered to find a spot for Helga in a research project that would include access to very promising experimental drugs – treatments she would not receive in her hometown of Aarhus, two hours from Copenhagen.

Madsen had asked for 24 hours to consider it, which Nik believed was reasonable. When he and his imposing partner left the man sipping his coffee that morning three months earlier, Nik had little doubt he would say yes. And early the next day, he did so, texting a code word to a burner phone tucked into Nik's inside jacket pocket.

A week later, Helga Madsen received a letter asking her to be a subject in a cancer study in Hamburg, Germany, three hours from her home. She couldn't recall applying for it, but she had filled out so many forms and had days when she remembered very little during her grueling treatment. Madsen helped move her to the medical center. The people there had no idea why his mother had been included in the study and welcomed her warmly. On the drive home his mood swung wildly between optimism and guilt.

He did not yet know what he would have to do in exchange for his mother's seemingly random good fortune. And he knew that somewhere in Europe there was another deathly ill person who did not get into the clinic and would never know why.

For several weeks, he was too conflicted to play well. He flamed out of three consecutive tournaments, costing himself more money in travel and other expenses than he made for winning a single match here and there. He lay awake at night, fearful his lousy play would be misinterpreted by the men who had taken over his life. He felt a perverse responsibility to play well for them and for his mother. He dared not discuss anything with anyone, so he kept it in and suffered.

Two months after moving his mother, she was showing signs of improving and his game was returning to form. He won his first two matches in Quanzhou and then moved into the fourth round – the semi-finals -- when his third round opponent pulled out, injured. It was as far as he had gotten in a tournament in months, and that night he got a short text with the magic word: Susu. It was the name of his family dog, a schnauzer, when he was a boy. He texted back and got a longer response, outlining what he was expected to do. It wasn't nearly as bad as he feared.

He was to play the semi-final match straight up. He was heavily favored against a 16-year-old Brazilian who was on the run of his life. The teen had never been to the fourth round as a professional and spent most of the night before the match throwing up from nerves. Madsen almost felt sorry for him as he dispatched the youngster 6-0, 6-2, to move into the final.

He read the second, detailed text several times, committing the instructions to memory before deleting it. In theory, it was quite simple and impossible to detect. In the final, if he won the coin toss, he was to defer the serve, letting his opponent begin. This was a common head game tactic he had actually used from time to time, shifting the pressure immediately to his opponent's serve, hoping to break him right away.

In this case, however, he was to lose the first game. And the second. And the third. And then he was to stall during the changeover prior to game 4. It was all scripted like a Broadway musical, not that he'd ever been in one.

Of course, there was a factor he could not control, the co-lead in the production: Gunter Schmidt. His opponent was oblivious to Madsen's predicament and, of course, would play to win. He was considered the favorite, if only because Madsen had played so poorly the previous two months. But Nik believed his guy was the better player, and just as he had done when picking horses with his father, he was ready to bet heavily on the fundamentals, trusting his analysis above anything else.

Nik figured Madsen would beat Schmidt six or seven times out of 10 matches, all things being equal. So his plan was to bet against the official favorite and back his personal favorite. That was the equivalent of pocket money, however. The path to six or seven figure profits on what otherwise was a little-noticed match was to bet in real time.

Live betting had not existed when Nik was studying the racing form and spending Saturdays at the track with his father. Now it was the life-blood of Garfunkel's success. Instead of picking the winner of a soccer or tennis match and waiting to see who won, gamblers could bet minute-by-minute, wagering on which player would win the next game or current set in a tennis match. They could bet on who would hit the next homerun in a baseball game, who would catch the next touchdown in football and so on, ad infinitum. It was to regular gambling what Fentanyl was to heroine – a much quicker hit with the potential for greater rewards and greater dangers.

Just as drug users could drop dead from one ill-advised brush with Fentanyl, gamblers could lose untold riches in minutes while consumed in a live-betting frenzy, wagering more and more to erase earlier losses, propelled by adrenalin and testosterone to win the next bet, regardless of the epic losing streak they were suffering through.

Live betting worked because oddsmakers and sports books updated the odds in real time, reflecting the results of the game or match to that point. If Michigan fell behind 14-0 to Ohio State, the odds of a Michigan win became much longer. If a $100 bet on Michigan before the game started paid $110 for a straight-up win, it might pay $200 or $250 if placed after Michigan was down 14 points.

In Quanzhou, the pre-match odds favored Schmidt

slightly. But, once Madsen lost the first three games – thereby confirming his underdog status – the odds would move quickly against him. Schmidt would go from slight favorite to overwhelming favorite, Madsen from slight underdog to a long shot beyond all hope. And that was when Nik would pounce.

During the changeover after the first three, one-sided games, he would bet about €1.5-million on Madsen, funneling it through a dozen or more proxy bettors around the world, so his actions were untraceable. It was that kind of sudden bet on an obvious underdog that might attract the attention of the laughable Tennis Integrity Unit, or whatever stupid name it had.

Such a bet before the match might have fetched €1.7-million in winnings, but once the odds swung dramatically in Schmidt's direction, the bet would pay closer to €5-million, so long as Madsen came back to win the best-of-three final.

There were times when Nik and his partners would force their athlete to lose, but that was more likely to draw attention. Most often, they had their athlete fiddle around with moments in the game, creating situations where they could profit by knowing the odds would swing wildly and unexpectedly. Letting athletes try to win also prolonged their usefulness. Most could justify the arrangement if they weren't losing matches outright.

As the final began, Madsen was more nervous than he had ever been. It was one thing to be in a final for the first time all year, with the real possibility of earning enough points to maybe climb to the next level. But beyond that, he knew somewhere the gamblers were watching him, expecting him to carry out their instructions precisely.

He was thrilled to lose the coin flip and hear Schmidt say he would serve. That was the first hurdle and he had side-stepped it completely. Even at the Challenger level, players went through an interminable warm-up session after the coin toss. The 15 minutes had never seemed so long, and his final warm-up serves hit the back wall of the court, nearly maiming one of the young ball kids who had relaxed momentarily.

"Play," the umpire said, at last. Schmidt blasted his first serve right down the middle. Madsen lunged and ticked the ball, the first of four points he would lose quickly to give up the first game. Serving the next game, it wasn't difficult to appear nervous. His first serve nearly short-hopped the net, it was so low. He sliced his second serve wide to open with a double-fault. Aware he had to make things look realistic, he won a couple of serve-and-volley points before hitting a forehand long to lose his serve and go down 0-2 in the first set. Only someone paying very close attention would have noticed Madsen looking relieved, almost pleased, after losing the game.

The third game was very much like the first, with Schmidt serving darts and Madsen flailing around trying to get his racket on the ball.

"Gunter Schmidt looks like twice the player Tobias Madsen is today so far," the TV analyst told the Chinese audience of roughly 70 million. "This could be over very quickly unless Schmidt cools off or Madsen makes some quick adjustments."

Sitting during the changeover, towel over his head, Madsen had trouble breathing. He was relieved his opponent was up 3-0, and that bothered the hell out of him. The competitive part of his brain was screaming in protest. He also knew he was required to turn things around and try to win, something that wasn't going to be as simple as it appeared on paper, or in a text. He wasn't pretending to have trouble with Schmidt's serve. Most of his own bad shots were caused by nerves, and he wasn't sure exactly when – or if – they would settle down and let him play his best.

The moment Schmidt served out the third game to go up 3-0, in London Nik swung into action. Typing on two keyboards, looking at three monitors, he laid bets on multiple continents, going all in on Madsen to win the match. He even placed a few smaller bets on his player to rally and win the first set, although that wasn't part of the plan and wasn't very likely. Nik didn't know how hard Madsen was working to lose those first three games. It was possible he would come out in game 4, freed from the Garfunkel threats, and blow Schmidt off the court. If that happened, Nik would consider it a bonus. What really mattered, however, was the final score of the match. And in that belief, Madsen and Nik were, for the first time, simpatico. Both desperately wanted Madsen to come back and win.

Chapter 17

Gil took a cab from his hotel, the Graduate Ann Arbor, to Coach Ramsey's home in North Burns Park, but not before straightening up his room and making it presentable. During the 10-minute ride, he ignored the driver and tried to organize his thoughts. The night with Sam, the promise of another, and the lack of sleep had short circuited his brain. He could feel his immediate impulses crowding out his long-term plans, but he knew he had to focus on the reason for his visit.

The club had given him a fail-safe chance to chase his dream one last time. He couldn't imagine doing it without Coach Ramsey alongside. Coach had encouraged him and believed he could beat anyone on the Challenger circuit, but that didn't mean he was ready to upend his comfortable Ann Arbor life to travel around the world with Gil.

He had met with Coach that morning, just after 9:00. It felt great to be back at the tennis facility, which had been renovated since he left. Coach gave him a quick tour, grabbed two coffees and led the way to his office. It had not been renovated, which Gil found comforting.

"I'd like to do this, but I'd really love to have you with me," Gil said at last, after they had discussed his plans and the deal the club had offered him. "You're the best coach I've ever had, hands down. I'd be honored if you'd consider it."

"I'm flattered you would ask," Coach replied. "You're one of very few players I would even considering coaching full-time, but I have to be honest. I'm 58. I have a job and life I love. But let me think about it."

Gil nodded and changed the topic. There was no point in pressing. He knew it was something of a long shot, and he was encouraged Coach hadn't said no immediately.

Officially, the coach's daughter was off-limits to his tennis players. Unofficially, once she reached 19 and joined the student population, she made it clear she would make her own decisions in that area. It was discussed for the first and last time during a spectacularly uncomfortable kitchen-table family meeting, where Howard and Beatrice Ramsey laid out some ground rules for their daughter's "extracurricular activity," as he called it.

"Do you mean, when and where I have sex?" she countered, bemused and annoyed.

"Samantha, please," her mother said. "People know you on campus because of your father's job, even before you became a student. We're just trying to protect you and the tennis team."

"Ah, right. Well, what do you want, a list? A schedule?"

"We'd like to make sure we don't read about what you're doing in the goddam Daily, OK Sam?" her father thundered. "Is that clear? Do we have to spell it out for you?"

"Alright, alright, relax. I get it. I don't want to be in the Daily either."

The Michigan Daily was the campus newspaper and delighted in gossiping about the private lives of faculty and their families.

Its best – or worst, depending on your point of view – story had appeared four years earlier, when a student reporter had been writing about school mascots. It was a recurring theme in the newspaper because Michigan was one of the few schools that didn't have a furry creature roaming the sidelines during games. Every few years, the paper would look at all the Big 10 mascots and ask if it was time for Michigan to give in and get one.

With Ohio State coming to Michigan for the annual clash of football rivals, some enterprising Michigan students had created a knock-off Brutus Buckeye costume. While the real Brutus hung out with the Ohio State band at the game, the fake Brutus participated in some less wholesome activities. Using an official-looking Twitter account, the enterprising students posted pictures of their Brutus peeing in the park, drinking beer at a sports bar, and, most notably, having something that resembled sex with something that resembled a dog mascot.

They posted their work just as the football game kicked off, and by halftime it had gone viral. Using the hashtag #DontFucktheMascot, it topped 100,000 views in an hour and was mentioned on the ESPN halftime show, where no one seemed to understand it was a counterfeit Ohio State mascot.

The reporter covering the mascot beat pivoted quickly to investigate Mascotgate, which led to a week's worth of stories in the Daily and more notoriety than any of the practical jokers imagined possible. Despite devoting considerable resources, the university had not been able to identify the students behind the prank, which led to another week's worth of stories about the investigation.

#DontFucktheMascot t-shirts appeared on campus on day two of the saga and were banned from classrooms on day three.

Not surprisingly, the Daily had more website views than ever before or since, and while it continued to do the job of a student newspaper, its editors were always on the lookout for the next story that might rival Mascotgate.

When Howard Ramsey told his daughter he feared a story about her in the Daily, she understood the context perfectly. But she also was determined to be her own person and enjoy her time as a student.

It was into this environment that Gil arrived as a freshman tennis prospect. It took him two months to realize he could ask her out without being thrown immediately off the team. The photography exhibit was the first of many dates, a handful of which included her removing her underwear during the evening in some surreptitious manner.

Gil didn't know what to expect at dinner. It was possible Coach would have an answer to his proposition. It was also possible the topic wouldn't come up. It was possible they would know he had already seen Sam on this trip. It was also possible she had kept it from them. He only knew two things for certain: Beatrice Ramsey would serve an outstanding meal, and he couldn't wait for it to end so he could rendezvous once again with Sam, this time at his hotel.

"Gil Pence, what a treat this is," Beatrice said when she opened the door. She was still hugging him when Coach ambled over to greet him with a bottle of Stella. There was no sign of Sam or her car.

"Come in, come in. Tell us all about life in Memphis," Beatrice said.

"There's not much to tell," Gil said. "Great club, but of course I'm here because I'm thinking of walking away – at least for a while."

"Yes, so exciting. Howie has filled me in. How soon would you start? How does it work?"

Gil was just starting to fade under the pressure of the interrogation when Sam came walking in through the back door. "I thought you'd all be out by the pool," she said, giving Gil a peck on the cheek before issuing hugs to her parents. "Where's the wine? I had Carrie drop me off so I don't have to drive. If I can get a ride from someone," she added, looking fondly in Gil's direction, causing him to blush ever so slightly.

Distracted, Gil happily followed Coach outside to the grill, where he laid on a generous assortment of beef and chicken, closed the lid and took a long draw on his beer.

"I'd like to do this Gil. It might be crazy, but I'm in, if we can work out a schedule that keeps me employed here."

"Fantastic! Of course, yes, what are you thinking?"

Coach's plan felt a lot like the program Gil had been in at college, which suited him just fine. This time around, there would be no teammates or scholarships. He would play for himself and try to earn enough to make it worthwhile. The biggest sacrifice Coach was asking was to base their operations in Ann Arbor, not exactly a professional tennis hot spot.

That meant some longer flights to tournaments, and perhaps a lack of top-flight players to practise with. The upside, beyond working with Coach Ramsey, was the chance to continue seeing Sam Ramsey, secretly or otherwise. Even as Coach was laying out the plan Gil hoped would take him to the ATP tour, part of his mind was jumping forward to that evening, at his hotel, with her.

"I won't come to every nickel-and-dime tournament. I can't," Coach said. "But I'll travel when I can, when I'm not needed here. It's not a perfect situation, I know. So if you decide to go another way and find someone who can be with you full-time, I understand completely. That might be the better option, to be honest. You need to think about it."

"I've thought of little else the last two weeks. I want you, and if this is the way to make it happen, I'm in. Thank you."

Coach removed the chicken from the grill and flipped the steaks one last time, pressing each with his thumb to check their progress.

"Is 10 per cent fair?" he asked.

"Hell ya. Is that enough? Some of these tournaments pay nothing. And 10 per cent of nothing might not even pay for your airfare."

"Oh, you're paying my airfare either way. The 10 per cent is on top of that," he said, smiling. "I don't have to go first class, unless we get to the big leagues. Then we're both going first class, agreed?"

They returned to the house with a platter of perfectly grilled meat and an agreement they would review at the end of the calendar year.

"A toast," Beatrice said, holding up her glass of Chardonnay as the meal began. "To the new team, much success."

Gil gulped his wine and noticed Sam doing the same. The next two hours were going to drag on like math class on a Friday afternoon. At least there was no test.

Chapter 18

In Quanzhou, Madsen had rallied to win the second set, 6-3, after dropping the first, 2-6. He appeared to have momentum as the third set began, dictating play and finding a way to handle Gunter Schmidt's serve. The live odds adjusted to the new circumstances and made him a slight favorite to win.

But Nik's earlier bets when Madsen was a massive underdog were locked in. If he put Schmidt away and won the match, Garfunkel would net €5-million that morning. Equally significant, it would have a new athlete in its stable, able to help the firm work the odds as needed to generate huge profits.

Having made his bets, Nik was now just another spectator, watching to see if his intuition and research would pay off. As always, he thought of his father, remembering the happiest times of his life, side-by-side along the rail, watching their horse charge down the backstretch to win, despite the odds against it. Like most gamblers, he remembered the victories and forgot most of the losses. But it was the camaraderie with his father that he most remembered. Sitting alone in his office, watching a nothing tennis match 12 times zones away, he came as close as he ever could to recreating that feeling.

At the changeover prior to the third and deciding set, Madsen forced himself to breathe slowly. He took 12 bites to eat a small banana, slowing everything down, trying to focus on the match. He was on the verge of his biggest professional victory. He had stage-managed the first set before playing unhindered in the second. It was all there for him now, an honest victory that no one could take from him. He just needed to push through for another hour or so. *Focus.*

Sitting in his chair, 30 feet away, Gunter Schmidt gave himself a banana-free pep talk. For most of the second set, he wondered how the hell he was losing. He had played the perfect opening set, but suddenly in the second, he couldn't touch Madsen. He hadn't played badly; he was still gunning his serves into the corners, but now they were coming back, with interest, and it was annoying the hell out of him. Agitated, he bounced his right leg up and down throughout the changeover. Without a better plan, he decided to hit harder and go for more to win the title. He jumped up and sprinted to the baseline, only to be reminded by the umpire he was at the wrong end.

As omens go, it was an accurate one. The set lasted only 33 minutes. Madsen cruised 6-1, cheered by the capacity crowd as he hit the final shot, a rocket backhand down the line past a diving Schmidt at the net.

After shaking hands with Schmidt and the umpire, Madsen lifted his arms high and soaked up the cheers. He had never played in front of so many people, never won a bigger match, never earned a bigger pay check. It wasn't until he was standing on the red carpet, rolled out quickly by the grounds crew, listening to speeches in Mandarin, that the other shoe dropped -- the gamblers, his mother, the first set. He had done their bidding. They owned him. His honest victory was no such thing. And yet, they cheered. Bittersweet didn't seem to cover it. He wondered, ruefully, if the Chinese had a better word for what he was feeling.

The moment Madsen hit the winning shot, Nik had jumped from his chair and sprinted down the hallway, high-fiving unsuspecting people in the office. It wasn't unusual to celebrate wins at Garfunkel, but few of the recipients of his high-fives had any idea of the magnitude of what Nik was celebrating.

Within moments, his bets would be paid. Garfunkel accounts around the world would be credited his original €1.5-million bet, plus just over €5-million in winnings, from bets placed at the very moment Madsen's odds reached their nadir. It was a brilliant bit of work, the culmination of months of grooming the athlete. That it rarely went so smoothly made it all the sweeter. Few athletes could deliver the first time they were tested.

It wasn't even noon yet on a Sunday in London, and Nik was ready to celebrate. He called his favorite restaurant, The Square, and booked a table for that night, then texted Lola, "5:30, square, wear something super sexy, we're celebrating."

With a few hours to kill, he worked on some files for the next day, which would allow him to show up late Monday morning. He would need to sleep in if the evening went as he hoped. It had been almost two weeks since he had slept with Lola, and he missed her badly.

He had trouble concentrating on run-of-the-mill Premier League football odds and instead replayed the final moments of Madsen's win. He also confirmed all the firm's winnings had arrived, although there was no doubt they would be there. Sports books always made good on their bets. One failure to do so would close their doors within days as gamblers went elsewhere en masse.

By mid-afternoon, he had forced himself to go through the next week's Premier League and also had a look at a few prop bets for the French Open, two months away. He was packing up to leave, already considering what he would order at Square and what Lola would be wearing, when Humphrey Cox walked into his office looking as somber as Nik had ever seen him.

"We've got a problem."

"What? What?"

"Have you heard of a guy named Nester Pidwedspecky, or something like that? In Mobile?"

"Mobile what? Alabama? In the U.S.? No, what about him?"

"He's dead."

"Ah, OK, friend of yours? Sorry Humph."

"No, neighbor of our friend Sergei Ivanov. You know, the homeless guy."

"Uh huh," Nik said, recalling vaguely a report he'd read about another tennis player in the Garfunkel orbit. He was run by Eva Vasquez, Garfunkel's only female partner.

"This guy claimed to know something about the Ivanov house going up and then was found dead in his garden two days later. Our guy may have gone rogue. At the very least, it's a strange coincidence that's drawing a lot more attention to the fire than it was getting. The cops are involved. The idiot tennis integrity dickheads. Could be bad."

"Fuck me sideways," Nik muttered. "Have you talked to Vasquez?"

"She's in Portugal, visiting family or something. Can't reach her. I'll keep trying. In the meantime, we need to find out what the hell is going on."

"Ya, you're right. I guess we should signal our guy, huh? See what he says or does. If he's rogue, that's a much bigger deal than if it's just the Mobile constabulary poking around something we have nothing to do with."

"OK, I'll send the signal. And I'll keep trying Vasquez. I can't exactly spell out the problem in a text, so she's probably just ignoring work for a few days."

"Put Ivanov's code word in the text. She'll figure it out," Nik suggested.

"Good idea. OK, let's meet first thing tomorrow."

"Fine. How early?"

"7:00?"

"Geez, how about 8:00?"

"Alright," Humph said, smiling for the first time. "Say hi to Lola for me."

Chapter 19

No one in Mobile had any idea two professional gambling blokes in England were paying attention to the fire and murder caper in upscale Hannon Park. News trucks were now camped out along the street, allowing reporters to file live updates that boiled down to one thing: Nothing new.

Angela Brison had given up on the coroner as the source of anything resembling a clue. Instead, she began looking for family or friends of the victim. The first question she planned to ask was how the hell to pronounce his name. The neighbors all said it differently, and there didn't seem to be another Pidwerbecki in the city. In fact, most people just knew the man as Nester, which seemed to be the sum total of what they knew about him.

"There's nothing here, just a bunch of flower pictures and some trip he took two years ago," Reynolds reported after spending his lunch hour combing through the dead man's social media trail.

"What trip?"

"Texas, mostly Austin."

"Family there? Did he travel with anyone? Did he have a girlfriend or boyfriend, or just a goddam friend of any kind?" Brison blurted.

"I'm checking. Talked to a detective down there just now. Sent him everything we've got, and he's gonna have a look. It was two years ago, but we should be able to figure out where he stayed and maybe who he saw."

"OK, good. Where's Hughes?"

"He went back to do another door-to-door. Took some help with him. I think they're expanding the perimeter. Oh, also, the guy belonged to a gardening club, and he was going to look into that too."

Brison had just fetched her third coffee of the morning and was heading to her desk, when Mark Fucking Twain walked into the precinct. Dressed in a cream colored suit and matching Panama hat, with a brown leather satchel slung over his right shoulder, the man drew even more attention when he started to speak. His South African accent ebbed and flowed, sometimes overpowered by a New York dialect, picked up during his 30 years living there.

"Good day to you," he said at the front desk. "Where might I find Detective Angela Brison?"

"That's me," she said, intrigued and annoyed in equal measure.

"A pleasure," he said, extending his hand. "I'm Nigel Clancy from the ATP. You know, the tennis folks."

"We get tennis on TV here, Mr. Clancy. I know what the ATP is. In fact, we've all learned a lot more about the tennis tours in the last 72 hours. Let me guess: You have a few questions about the Ivanov fire?"

"I do indeed, detective," he smiled. "Is there somewhere we could talk?"

From his satchel, he produced a stack of papers and fanned them across Brison's desk. "I'm with the integrity unit, to be specific," he said. "You didn't hear this from me, but there's a real problem with tennis and gamblers."

"I see," Brison said, reaching for the pile of papers closest to her. "Match fixing, that type of thing?"

"That's right. At the lower levels, on the Challenger circuit, even college matches, it's happening a lot. And it's bloody hard to stop it, to be honest."

"I see. And you think Ivanov is mixed up in this somehow? Is that what all this paperwork is about?"

"This here is what we know about him," Clancy said, reaching for a different pile of papers. "The rest is some general investigation we've done, things that look fishy. I thought I'd share all of this with you."

"Uh huh, just flew down to Mobile to share with us. How thoughtful Mr. Clancy. Come on, cut the crap, OK?"

"Well, obviously if this fire is connected to gamblers, we want to find out. But, as you'll see in the file, we don't really know what's going on. Cards on the table, I'm hoping you can help us figure it out. I'm going to make the same request of the fire department. We're fighting an enemy we can't see, that almost never leaves any clues. This fire could be a big break for us, or it could be a big, fat zero. That's why I'm here."

The odd couple spent another 30 minutes going back and forth. Brison soon realized the tennis people didn't know much of anything and didn't have much idea of how to conduct an investigation. They had perked up because the fire had been declared arson, but that was about all they had. The file Clancy had dramatically produced was little more than Sergei Ivanov's tournament results and itineraries for the last year. They had his bank records, but they showed nothing unusual. And they had no idea if he and his wife had any other accounts anywhere else in the world. Brison was pretty sure Clancy didn't know how to locate, never mind acquire, such accounts.

Standing up to get more coffee, she ended the meeting by promising to keep in touch with him.

"I'm on my way over to see the fire chief now. And I'll be in town for as long as it takes," he said, as though that would be enough to crack the case and rid the tennis world of match fixing forever. The only thing he didn't do was doff his hat as he left, which Brison actually found surprising.

As she was considering her lunch options, her cell buzzed. She'd almost forgotten Hughes was out doing more door-to-doors in an expanded circle around the fire and murder scenes.

"Boss, the tennis player is back in town. What's his name? The Russian guy."

"He is? Since when. Where is he?"

"I'm sure I saw him near his house, sort of combing through the front yard. When the TV cameras noticed him, he took off. But he wasn't driving the car. Not sure who was. But I got a license."

"I'll bet I know whose it was," she said, tapping her keyboard. "Hang on, ya. OK, it's registered to Sally Wilkins, the den mother coach's wife who was in here with the guy's wife, Moscow Barbie."

"Moscow who?"

"Never mind Hughes. Finish up in the neighborhood and get back here. Have you got anything new?"

"Ah, negative. If people on the same street didn't see anything, no one three blocks away did. We're nearly done."

Brison dialed the fire department and got the chief straight away. Based on what she'd seen of the man on TV, she didn't like him. But they'd never met.

"I'm told this Sergei character is back in town. Any idea when he got back?"

"Are you fucking kidding me?" Geronimo Joseph said, making it very clear he did not. "We've been waiting to talk to him for a week now, and his wife…"

"Moscow Barbie?"

"Ha, ya, that's her. She kept telling us he was playing somewhere in Mexico or something."

"Would you like to coordinate our approach with him?" Brison asked flatly.

"Ah, OK, sure. Is your murder definitely connected?"

"Seems likely, but we're looking at the fire too, so let's get him in here and get him talking. By himself. No handlers this time. And definitely no Mark Twain."

"Huh?"

"Nothing. Oh except, you should expect a visitor this afternoon. A well-dressed man from Florida without one clue about running an investigation. Have fun with him. I'll let you know when we pick up the Russian."

Chapter 20

Dinner, mercifully, was wrapping up by 8:30. Gil had switched from wine to Sanpellegrino around 7:00, even though he found it much too salty. Sam had kept chugging away on the red wine, which he knew would loosen whatever inhibitions she had when they finally got back to his hotel.

After taking one polite bite of carrot cake, he excused himself for the bathroom. Sam winked surreptitiously as he left the table. Alone in the powder room, he understood why. Stuffed into the left pocket of the grey linen jacket he was wearing over his black t-shirt was a thong so tiny he had trouble determining what color it was. That, of course, was beside the point.

The only time she had been close enough to slip her underwear into his pocket was when she arrived and greeted him with a quick peck on the cheek. That meant two things: She had marched into her parents' home with her underwear in one hand and tucked it into his jacket in full view of mom and dad – misdirection that would impress any magician. It also meant she had sat through dinner sans underwear, a fact he found exhilarating, even after the fact.

He splashed cold water on his face, took a deep breath and headed back to the kitchen, determined to get the hell out of there without sitting back down. Sam evidently had the same idea, standing as he emerged and starting the goodbye process with her parents. Gil followed her lead, punctuated by a lengthy handshake with Coach. Their plan was to start formal training the following week, after Gil had cleaned out his apartment in Memphis and made a graceful exit from the club.

"Have a wonderful evening you two," Beatrice Ramsey said, waving from the door as though they were headed to a high school sock hop. Sam waved, then looped her arm through Gil's as they headed toward his car. He opened the door for her, waved one last time toward the house and punched the accelerator in a way that was aggressive, even for a rental.

During the five-minute drive, Sam continued dispensing with undergarments, coaxing her bra out the bottom of her blouse. She stuffed it not into Gil's pocket but into her purse, from which she pulled her phone.

"Selfie," she said, leaning in next to Gil, holding the phone high with one hand and anchoring herself by placing her other hand just below his waist, causing a facial expression seen in very few of the millions of selfies taken around the world every day.

He was happy to see her stow the phone back in her purse as they entered his hotel room. He had treated himself to a suite, celebrating his opportunity to get back on tour, with the financial security of his club job waiting for him. Di Pietro didn't need to know every detail, including those about to transpire.

From the reasonably sized fridge in the reasonably sized kitchenette, he retrieved one of the two bottles of Prosecco he had purchased that morning. To his palate, it was every bit as good as champagne and left him enough funds to splurge on the suite. His allocation of funds seemed to please Sam. After he had sent the plastic cork flying into the sitting room, she grabbed the bottle from him and took a giant swig of the bubbly wine. Most of it spilled from her mouth and cascaded down the front of her blouse. The wet cotton clung to her breasts for only a few seconds before she slipped it over her head and tossed it along the same flight pattern as the cork.

She then took another large swig, allowing most of the wine to pour down her naked torso. "Oops," she giggled. "I need a towel." Looking around, she shrugged, wiggled her hips, and let her skirt fall to her ankles. "This will do," she said, picking up the skirt and wrapping it loosely around her shoulders.

She then ran three steps toward Gil and launched her naked self at him, wrapping her arms and legs around him as he caught her. He carried her to the bed and dropped her from above his shoulders, causing her to giggle and roll around on the king size mattress. Undressing as quickly as he could, he grabbed her by the feet and pulled her across the bed.

"Not so fast mister," she laughed. "What do you think you're doing?"

"Let me show you," he growled, slapping her ass and producing a squeal of delight. Before he continued, he reached for two of the giant pillows that were mostly just getting in the way. As she lay on her front, he put one under her stomach and another under her ankles, forming her ass into a right angle Pythagoras never dreamed of.

Inspecting his work, he grabbed yet another pillow and put it over the back of her head. She grabbed onto it with both hands, and pulled it down hard, a muffler of sorts.

There are many shades of red in nature, but Gil was certain he had never seen anything else the particular shade of Sam's ass after their slapping routine. The sounds escaping from the pillow over her head made it clear how much she loved it. And yet Gil was certain he enjoyed it more. Sometimes he slapped the bottoms of her feet as well, but today he concentrated entirely on her ass, reveling in the sound of his hand hitting her flesh and the guttural reaction it prompted.

He continued for what seemed like an hour, fighting the urge to ditch the pillows and climb on top of her. It was, in fact, only seven minutes before he did just that, causing her to lift her ass even higher as a kind of welcome mat.

At some point in the evening, they uncorked the second bottle of Prosecco and spent some time in the dark on the balcony. When he had nothing left, he faded off, snoring until she rolled him off his back and onto his side. Curling up next to him, she drifted off, but not before deciding she really should go with him to Memphis to help him pack up. She purred lightly and was gone.

Chapter 21

Brison arrived at the Wilkins' unannounced with a show of force. She had no intention of letting the Ivanov fan club control the agenda as they had at the station earlier that week.

At 7:30 a.m., four squad cars arrived at the Wilkins' gate, a set-up Hughes and Reynolds had sketched out for their boss.

"Mr. and Mrs. Wilkins. It's Detective Brison. We met the other day at the station," she said into the microphone on the gate. "We're here to speak with Mr. Ivanov. Please open the gate."

At that moment, Mr. Ivanov was sleeping soundly in the guest room, recovering from a week of chaos and the circuitous travel route he had taken to get to Mobile from Mexico the day before.

"He's sleeping at the moment," Sally Wilkins said into her microphone, noting the phalanx of police vehicles on the kitchen screen. "Maybe this afternoon?"

"Please open the gate Mrs. Wilkins," Brison said, firmly. "We need to speak with him right now." With that, she signaled two junior officers who had come equipped with a battering ram, normally used to knock down flophouse doors during drug raids. It was unlikely to have much effect on the stylish wrought iron gate at the base of the Wilkins driveway, but it conveyed the message that Brison and what looked like 20 per cent of the Mobile police force were not going away.

That's certainly the message Sally Wilkins received. "Go wake him up," she said to Tom who had wandered into the kitchen just as the battering ram appeared on screen. "OK, geez. What are they involved with?" he asked as he left for the guest room.

"The gate has been acting up," Sally said into the microphone, aware it was not a lie detector. "I'll have to come down and open it for you."

"Please do so," Brison replied.

With a fresh cup of coffee in hand, in her robe and slippers, Sally ambled down the long driveway, giving Sergei at least 10 minutes to clear his head after waking up. As the gate swung open, three of the police cars began crawling up the driveway. So too did Geronimo Joseph's bright red pickup truck. When his home phone rang at 6:30 that morning, he had regretted asking to be involved with the questioning, but he didn't dare skip it. He was as curious about Detective Brison as he was about the tennis couple and hoped she looked as good as she sounded on the phone.

The fourth police car stayed at the entrance, lights flashing, blocking the exit route, just in case. It also alerted the neighbors that something was up, which Brison was happy to do. *Anything to shake things up*.

The unlikely group held court in the backyard, where Sally Wilkins, somewhat incongruously, put out a tray of muffins and took coffee orders.

"Nothing for us, thank you," Brison said, short-circuiting Joseph's intention to match a coffee with the banana muffin he had scooped up. "Mr. Ivanov, good to see you. You're a difficult man to track down."

"We've made no secret of where he's been," Svetlana said, grabbing her husband's hand and shooting a non-Barbie look in Brison's direction.

"True, although you did say you would let us know when he was back in town, which I gather was sometime yesterday. Every day that passes makes our investigation more difficult, as I thought I stressed the other day. Anyway, we're here now, and that's great. Chief Joseph, is there anything you'd like to add before we get started?"

Joseph nearly coughed up a muffin chunk in response. It was the first time she had even acknowledged him, and he most certainly had nothing to add.

"Just that I'm happy to speak with Mr. Ivanov too," he said, at last.

"So, we're all happy. Wonderful." Brison flipped open a file folder and turned toward the young couple, ignoring everyone else, particularly the Wilkins who seemed anxious to play some kind of role.

"Sergei. May I call you Sergei?" she began, not waiting for an answer. "Sergei, we've had an arson and a murder in the last week, as you know. It seems possible they're linked, but to be honest we haven't made much progress. We don't even have a motive for either crime. Your wife made it very clear at the station that she has no idea why your house was torched. Do you?"

"No maam," he said, fighting to remain calm, even as his mind raced to the gamblers, the money in a secret account, the texts he'd exchanged and the conversation they'd had with the ATP. "No idea."

"Again, without accusing either of you of anything, that seems very strange, wouldn't you agree?" Brison said. "I mean, you haven't thought of any reason someone might set your house on fire? Are you having any kind of legal disputes with anyone? Anything at all that might help us?"

"Christ Almighty," Svetlana exploded. "If we were walking across the street, on a green light, and someone drove through the light and knocked us down, would you keep asking why it happened, what we had done to provoke it?"

"Only if it appeared the person had targeted you, which certainly is what appears to have happened here," Brison said, without even looking at Moscow Barbie. "We recognize you're victims, but you must understand how incredibly unusual it is for someone to burn down a house without any reason or provocation. We don't have an arsonist running around here. No other homes have been torched, and when the neighbor fellow, Mr. Pisterbeckity or whatever his name is… When he made some sideways suggestion about knowing who did it, he was murdered. So, again, with all due respect, we have to ask these questions."

The tension built in silence until it was broken suddenly by Mark Twain, who strolled through the kitchen, out the back door to the patio. Juggling a muffin with a mug of black coffee, he sat down with a flourish. "Don't mind me folks, carry on."

"Excuse me, Mr. Clancy, who the hell invited you?"

"Ah, that would be me," Joseph said, sheepishly. "I called him this morning after you sent him over to see me the other day."

Brison could feel the meeting getting away from her, the initial show of force waning. "Fine, whatever. I have some specific questions for the Ivanovs."

With that she launched into 30 minutes of what looked very much like a court-room witness interrogation. The court was rather casual, with patio furniture and a pool, but the questions were every bit as specific and unrelenting as any good lawyer would make them.

The only real nugget of potentially useful information she pried out of the Ivanovs was that they had called someone at the ATP the day of the fire and heard back the following day. It wasn't an unreasonable thing to do, but neither they nor Nigel Clancy had mentioned it. And it turned out to be the reason Clancy had shown up in Mobile. Brison had a feeling the mighty Tennis Integrity Unit still wouldn't know about the fire if the Ivanovs hadn't called and reported it.

All of which was interesting but a long way from nailing

down Mr. Green in the library with a rope.

"Alright," Brison finally said. "That's all for now. Oh, unless you have anything Chief?" Absent a muffin in his gullet, Joseph spoke up right away. "Do we have your insurance information yet? You were going to find that and let us know."

"We have it, yes, somewhere here. Can I text it over later?" Svetlana said, dismissively.

Joseph was about to acquiesce when Brison stepped in. "We can wait Miss Ivanov. If you don't mind finding that now, we'll take it with us. We have a lot of loose ends to tie up, including that one."

It took Svetlana a painfully long time to find the name and number of their insurance adjustor. But once she did, the little convoy of official vehicles reversed itself and headed back down the driveway, toward the gate, which somehow was working perfectly and did not require Sally Wilkins to open it by hand.

"Bloody miracle," Brison said to no one as she peeled out of the driveway and headed downtown.

Chapter 22

It took Eva Vasquez two days to respond to the urgent texts from her Garfunkel partners, and when she did it wasn't exactly the answer they were looking for.

"I'm on vacation, idiots. Can't you solve anything yourselves?"

Nik laughed when Humph showed it to him. "If she's not worried, maybe we don't have to be either? Whatcha think?"

"I think she's got a new friend and hasn't paid close enough attention to what I've told her to see what's going on."

In addition to some vague, code-filled texts to Vasquez, Humph had signaled the company's freelancer in the U.S. and heard nothing back. That alone was not cause for concern. He often went off the grid for days, even weeks, at a time. It happened most often after he did a job.

Humph, though, was uneasy. "Everything I see about this murder worries me. We need to know what happened."

Nik hated what he thought of as the blue collar part of the business. Roughing people up, ordering houses burned and pets killed – he steered clear of that as much as he could. But it was unavoidable. Garfunkel had made him rich by getting people to do things they didn't want to do, and that sometimes required more than a conversation and a bag of money.

"We need to bring him in."

"OK, John le Carre, how the hell do we do that?"

"We get Vasquez involved for sure. But I think we set up a dummy job and see what he does. Maybe we fly over and meet him."

"And say what? 'Hey, how's it going? Did you kill the gardener?' If he says yes, then what?"

"We won't go over alone."

"We? What the fuck? I don't know this guy. You had the right idea, getting Vasquez involved."

"I'm worried she's too close to him. We need to meet with everyone asap to chart a course. If it's nothing, OK, no harm done. But if there's a problem with the guy, we need to move fast."

"I still don't know what you mean by moving fast. What exactly are our options?"

"You weren't here when Dunfield happened, were you?"

"No."

Humph recapped Dunfield for Nik over lunch at his desk. There were many details, some of which were lost to history, but Nik only needed the bullet points to understand why Humph was so concerned and why he should be taking the situation more seriously.

Early in the firm's existence, when Nik was at school in Brasov, it had hired an ex-MI6 officer to do help with security and persuasion of athletes. Unsure of what would work and what wouldn't, the firm had largely left it to the new in-house spy to decide how to bring athletes around.

Hiring spies is not easy; you don't get references or traditional resumes. What Humph and the original partners soon discovered was that their spy had been pushed out of MI6 and was supposed to be getting regular care for PTSD. He went to the first two sessions and then dropped out of sight. The therapist had filed a form, but no one had acted on it, and the damaged spy was free to seek employment at Garfunkel.

When a French football star took three payments but had not managed to tilt any matches as requested over six months, the spy showed up at the practice field one morning in full military garb. He fired shots into the empty stands and generally scared the hell out of everyone there, without ever making contact with the recalcitrant athlete or doing much of anything besides attracting a lot of attention and putting a lot of people in danger.

That was bad enough, but when police arrived and found him sitting naked in the goal at the far end of the field, he mumbled the same word over and over as they packed him into a squad car and headed for the hospital: "Garfunkel, Garfunkel, Garfunkel."

It took some adroit work by the firm's legal counsel to convince police the man was simply obsessed with betting on the team and often did so on a Garfunkel account – all perfectly legal, he noted with appropriate deference. Humph had dummied up an account within an hour, with a convincing trail of funds going in and out, to support the lawyer's position.

For months, Humph and his partners came to work every day fearful of a raid, sure the spy would at some point be lucid enough to reveal everything he knew about his short-lived employers. When the man took his own life – or at least was reported to have done so – the firm breathed a collective sigh of relief. The assumption was the former spy could do a lot more harm to MI6 than to Garfunkel, so perhaps they had ended the man's life. Either way, the Garfunkel partners were determined never to leave themselves so exposed again.

The following evening, the nine partners gathered in a boardroom deep in The Castle, in a little-used room known as the Dungeon because it was isolated from the outside world and could not be penetrated by electronic snoopers.

They left their phones outside. No one took notes. The subject was the murder of Nester Pidwerbecki, although few there knew who he was or could pronounce his name.

Vasquez had returned that afternoon and took control of the meeting, vouching for her man in the U.S., but admitting she had not heard from him, despite leaving messages asking for an immediate callback.

"As you know, we use a system of burner phones and black box texts to communicate with our field operatives," she began. "As of 20 minutes ago, I had not heard from him, although I want to stress that could be for a number of reasons, many of which are nothing to worry about. Still, we need to assume the worst and discuss contingencies."

"What's his background Eva?" asked someone at the far end of the table. "Has this happened before?"

"Well, he's certainly been out of reach before, yes. But he's always told us first. So, I guess that is something new."

She detailed his background, to the extent they really knew it. The most salient fact was that he had worked for Garfunkel for nearly four years and performed perfectly.

"He's done about a dozen jobs for us, but never killed anyone. At least not for us," she said. "If you had asked me last week, I would have said he was the person I least had to worry about. He's no Dunfield, if that's what you're wondering."

A few around the table evidently had been, judging by their expressions.

Of course, Dunfield hadn't been a Dunfield until he was. That truth hung over the meeting like an early morning fog.

"OK, options. Let's make a plan," Vasquez said, surveying the room.

Their choices were somewhat limited, given they didn't know where the man was, didn't know what he had done and didn't want to draw attention to their relationship with him. Still, they did manage to form something charitably called an action plan. It began with another push on the snooze bar. They would wait 24 hours to be sure the man wasn't responding to Vasquez's messages.

Then, if nothing had changed, Vasquez and another short-straw holder would fly to Mobile and start searching for clues. Aware of their shortcomings, they would bring in one their own investigators to spearhead the efforts. There was only one actionable item coming out of the meeting: They had to track the man down before he popped up somewhere they didn't expect and did something they couldn't control.

Chapter 23

"I would say they're genuinely worried. If we can believe what we're reading."

The speaker was Morton Reid, executive director of the oft-maligned Tennis Integrity Unit. His audience, sitting at a round, mahogany table in the corner of his office, was small but attentive.

ATP legal counsel Liz Catalano sat to his left, sipping a latte from one of the largest mugs ever produced. And to her left was Nigel Clancy, fresh from doing his Mark Twain impression in Mobile. He sipped no latte of any size.

Reid was based in London at the ATP headquarters but came to Florida periodically to work from the organization's grandly named Americas office. This trip was not on his regular schedule and didn't appear in his official diary.

"Jesus, they've lost control of him. Or so it seems," Catalano said as she finished reading her copy of the notes Reid had produced from his locked briefcase.

"This is genuine? Best we can tell?" Clancy asked.

"Best we can tell," Reid said. "The earlier stuff has panned out. But you're right to be skeptical. Does it mesh with what you saw in Mobile?"

"Sure, as far as it goes. But they don't know what they're dealing with there. The Ivanovs are lying through their Russian teeth, and I think the detective there knows it. But she doesn't have a lot of resources. The fire chief spends most of his time washing his truck."

Six months earlier, Reid had received an envelope from someone who claimed to have inside knowledge about match fixing. It was centered on one organization that appeared to be fixing much more than tennis all over the world. But the source was cagey and had not identified the organization. Nor had the source given a motivation for leaking the information.

Keeping the revelation to himself, Reid had tested the information as best he could. After the third information drop – which dispensed with the envelope and began arriving in untraceable text messages – he had briefed Catalano, looking for advice. If true, it was the biggest break the fledgling TIU had ever received. If not, it set the unit up for an embarrassment that could bury it forever. Reid and Catalano assumed they were being set up, but continued to verify information as they received it. They even went as far as to act on the last batch, suspending two players for a year on what publicly appeared to be a flimsy, circumstantial case.

But the players involved didn't appeal. And their lawyers didn't make a peep about what appeared to be a rather shoddy case – the best evidence yet that the information coming in brown paper texts was accurate.

"Did you get any time with the Russians alone?" Catalano asked.

"No. They were barely accessible to the police. I couldn't tip my hand by showing up and grilling them."

"Fair to say the Mobile police believe you're pretty much an empty hat?"

"The hat was a nice touch, I thought. I'm sure they believe I'm an idiot and the unit here is a joke."

"Perfect. OK Mort, what do we do next? The Ivanovs did reach out to me. It would make sense for me to follow up. If we could turn them somehow, work it from the other end to find these people," Catalano said, holding up the leaked documents.

"Maybe, but right now they have to fear the crooks more

than they fear us. They burned down their bloody house. If I were them, I wouldn't be talking to us or the cops or anyone else. Which is why we've got to clean this up. It's bad enough that matches aren't legit, but we've got players in real danger. How long 'til they kill someone?"

They read through the report another time, in search of a clue they missed the first time. None appeared.

"OK, Nigel, what else did you learn in Mobile?"

With that, he produced three pages of point-form notes. Starting at the top of the first page, he discussed each in some detail, as he had been trained to do in the National Intelligence Agency of South Africa.

Most of the points were little more than identifying the players and offering his initial impressions.

"This gardener fellow, I'd say he died for no reason other than maybe doing a bit of boasting on Facebook. I've seen the video he was flogging. So have the police and most of the good citizens of Mobile. There's nothing to it. Unless it really was a UPS driver who set the fire."

"That's all he did? That got him killed?"

"Sure looks that way, unless it's completely random and not related to the fire at all. Which isn't any better. The guy's dead either way. Anyway, from what I could pick up, the police have tracked down the UPS driver in the video. They haven't released any information, but I assume if it amounted to anything, they would have moved on him. And they wouldn't be sloshing around in the deep end, questioning the Russians with no real idea how they're involved."

When he reached the bottom of the third page, he summed things up succinctly. There was an organization somewhere in the world pressuring tennis players and other athletes to fix matches. They had burned down the Ivanov house but possibly lost control of the person hired to set the fire, who may or may not have killed someone living on the same street who may or may not have known something about who set the fire.

Someone with knowledge of the gambling syndicate was leaking information to the TIU that appeared to be accurate. They had no idea why or whether they were the only sports officials receiving information. Whatever the Ivanovs knew about the identity of the gamblers they were keeping to themselves because they feared, quite properly, for their safety. Despite a thorough examination of Sergei Ivanov's results, they had no evidence he had ever thrown a match or a game or a point.

"Yup, that's where we are," Reid said at last. "It's promising but frustrating as hell. It's like looking for black holes. We know they're out there, but we can't see them no matter what we do."

Chapter 24

The drive from Ann Arbor to Memphis was just over 10 hours in light traffic, which was precisely what Gil and Sam enjoyed as they set off later than planned the next day. The Prosecco-fueled night before had altered their itinerary, a trade-off both were happy to make.

"You might need some help packing things up," she had whispered into his ear around 8:30, roughly five hours after they had finally fallen asleep.

"In Memphis?" he asked. "Oh yes, it's a huge job. I absolutely need some help. Do you know anyone there?"

"Fraid not," she said, rolling on top of him so her breasts hung just above his face. "But I could be convinced to tag along."

"Well, that would be very helpful," he said, lifting his head enough to wrap his lips around her left breast while he grabbed the right and squeezed her nipple. "I should warn you, there might be more of this during the trip. Are you up for it?"

"Ah, yes I think so. I see you are," she said, moving her hand under the cover and grabbing him.

They managed to depart just ahead of the 11 a.m. semi-official check-out deadline, swinging by her apartment so she could pack a bag. By noon, they were on I-75, heading south.

Gil's plan was to sublet his apartment while he was gone. That might be considered bad karma, failing to commit fully to the comeback, but he decided it was trumped by the job being held for him at the Racquet Club. He was all in on the plan, and keeping the apartment did not detract from his enthusiasm or determination. He wasn't exactly sure how to go about subletting the place, but he was pretty sure Di Pietro would help out in some way.

He texted his boss when he arrived and set up a meeting for the morning. "I have someone I want you to meet," he added, cryptically.

During the drive, he had wanted to ask Sam what she had in mind for the next few months. He hadn't even considered asking her to go to Memphis, and now he was wondering if she might tag along at some tournaments as well. But he feared the answer, so he didn't ask.

It was still on his mind when they stopped for dinner in Bowling Green, four hours from Memphis.

"Something on your mind?" she asked as they avoided filling up on bread, waiting for their steaks.

"Lots actually," he volleyed back. "I'm basically quitting my job tomorrow, even though I might get it back at some point. That's a weird feeling. I've been looking at the Challenger circuit schedule, trying to figure out when I'll be in good enough shape to start entering tournaments. There's Sarasota in the middle of April and Tallahassee at the end of April. Maybe one of those. I can't afford to start flying to Europe and Asia right away, not until I start to win a bit."

"What does your coach say?"

"My coach. You're funny. Well, he said we'd figure it out after we start training and see how well I'm doing. I think he's going to set up some matches next week to gauge where I am. It's hard to really know when you spend your time feeding balls to Howard Forrester and friends."

"Ya, that makes sense. Anything else?"

"OK, ya. You. You're on my mind, maybe more than any of this other stuff."

"Is that so? And what are you thinking?"

"Come on Sam, you know exactly what I'm thinking. What are you gonna do the rest of the year?"

"I know, I know, I'm just teasing you. Of course I'm thinking about it. I do plan to go back to class in September, but between now and then… Well, I could be persuaded to stick around and help you and your coach a little bit. Provide some inspiration and rewards, as it were."

"You know I'd love that, but I gotta be honest. I'm doing this for real. It's my last chance. I've gotta get sleep and be fresh first thing in the mornings. I'm not saying never, you know, but, ah, I can't, you know…"

"You can't fuck me until the wee hours of the morning four or five times a week? Is that what you're trying to say?" Sam asked, just as the waiter appeared with her 8 ounce sirloin. He smothered a grin and presented the food with the usual warning about the plate being hot.

They rolled into Memphis around 11 p.m. With no training scheduled for the morning and a civilized meeting time of 10 a.m., they put off their chastity vows for at least one more night. But not before they packed up some of Gil's few possessions.

"Do you ever cook anything? You have one pan and a flipper."

"What else do I need? I can make any kind of eggs in that pan. It's got the high sides, so I can boil pasta in there too."

"Seriously," she said, opening one empty cupboard after another, is this all you have?"

"The club has a fantastic chef. I can get almost anything I want during the day and take-out at night. It's pretty sweet."

"Well, not anymore," she teased. "You're giving all that up."

They retired to his equally spartan bedroom having filled the foyer with boxes. He was going to ask Di Pietro if he could store them in the basement of the club while he was gone. He had no interest in renting a storage locker, even if the new storage facilities seemed more like theme parks than the series of empty cubes they once were.

"We'll deal with them in the morning," Sam said, pulling her t-shirt over her head as she headed to the shower. "Scrub my back?"

Whatever hot water they saved by sharing the shower was wasted by the extra time they took. Eventually, they moved to the bedroom, which featured a box spring, mattress and little else. Like the kitchen, it had a certain minimalist theme while he lived there and required very little packing up.

She woke him before the alarm by sliding down his boxers. As she left for the shower this time, he did not follow her but rolled over, exhausted. And when she emerged, wrapped in the only two towels not packed in boxes, he was lying exactly where she'd left him, naked, except for an iPad propped up on his chest.

He felt odd not going into the club first thing in the morning and instead settled for perusing the online court sheet to see who was playing where that day. As one might have expected, nothing much had changed in the week he'd been gone. The same regulars had booked the same times, and would roll in five minutes ahead, counting the walk to their court as a warmup. Howard Forrester had grudgingly accepted assistant pro Anne Hollings to run his lesson at 8:00, something he would come to accept with slightly less grousing in the weeks to come.

There was no sign of Larry Spangler or Bob Bendheim, both of whom had been fairly scarce since their altercation a few weeks before.

Sam emerged from the bedroom dressed in a Lululemon

tennis outfit that would have melted Instagram. Instead, she would melt the clubhouse, where Gil was about to introduce her to the usual Saturday crowd.

The meeting with Di Pietro was largely a formality. There were papers required to formalize the arrangement of Gil essentially borrowing money from the club and using his far-from-guaranteed winnings as collateral. He also officially resigned from his job, although there was a provision that spelled out how he could reclaim it anytime in the next three years.

"There's a wrinkle here that I couldn't avoid putting in. Read this," Di Pietro said, pointing to a paragraph on the last page. "The executive insisted. Sorry."

The wrinkle was designed to reduce the club's financial risk, and Gil couldn't work up any angst about it. He was still amazed the club was helping him chase his dream. The new clause said if Gil returned to his job having won less than $10,000 total in tournament play, the club could claw back 20 per cent of his salary until it recouped the small salary it had offered to pay him while he was playing and trying to qualify for bigger tournaments.

"It could cost you something in the neighborhood of $25,000, worst case scenario," Di Pietro said. "But that's the worst case, no tournament earnings for a year or so before giving up and coming back here."

"Fair enough," Gil said, signing all the papers as requested. As he was finishing up, there was a knock on the open office door. Sam strolled in and introduced herself to Di Pietro. She uttered a few sentences, maybe a whole paragraph, but the only words Gil actually heard were "Gil's girlfriend."

Sweet.

Having received Di Pietro's approval, they made a couple of trips from the apartment, hauling boxes back and storing them in a room Gil had never seen before. It was dry and had a lock, which were his only requirements, besides being free – which it was.

Taking a break, Gil watched as Sam walked along the side of court one, visible to everyone playing on the club's eight front courts. He watched as every head turned to follow her, women as well as men, several stopping their game momentarily to size her up. The befuddlement made Gil chuckle, and he did nothing to clarify the situation. The moment they were done with the boxes, they tracked down Di Pietro one last time and said goodbye. They gave him the apartment keys, so he could sublet it, likely to the new pro coming to cover for Gil that summer. And they got back on the highway, this time heading north. They arrived in Ann Arbor by midnight. Sam slept at her place; Gil crashed at an Airbnb he had arranged to rent for the next few weeks.

His first practice with Coach was at 7:30 the next morning. He set the alarm for 6:00.

Chapter 25

Not six hours after the Garfunkel brain trust had wrapped up their emergency meeting, the man they had spent two hour discussing suddenly popped up with a single line of text: "WTF is wrong with you?"

He was responding to the barrage of texts, emails and even a couple of voice messages that rained down upon him the moment he turned his phone back on, after two weeks off the grid.

He hadn't read his entire in-box, but the gist was easy to discern. The death of someone whose name he couldn't pronounce near the home he had burned down for them had somehow convinced them he had pulled a Dunfield and was roaming the world, getting ready to bring down the entire Garfunkel empire.

He laughed initially and then became annoyed. *They seriously think I would do that? I'm a fucking professional.* "I'm a fucking professional," he texted as a follow-up to his first missive.

Within five minutes, the phone rang. Vasquez was on the line, talking from her bedroom where she had been packing for the trip to Mobile. "Thank God, I don't have to go there," she said, laughing. "Where the hell have you been?"

"Is this line secure?" he asked.

"Yes. I'm home, and it's routing through our protocol here. You're still using the phone we gave you? We're good on both ends."

"Yes, I'm using your phone. Following procedures like always. It doesn't take much for you to all freak out and assume I've gone nuts, huh?"

"Ya, ya, sorry about that. But there's a murder just down the street and no one can find you."

"You can never find me after a job. That should reassure you. I only took two weeks this time. Glad I didn't do a month like last time. Anyway, whatever. You've got some panicky people over there. Fine. What's with this guy who died? Who cares?"

She quickly sketched out the apparent tie-in with Nester Pidwerbecki and the Ivanov fire, sending him a link to the now-famous Facebook video authorities assumed had sealed the nosy gardener's fate.

He saw what many others had seen – a UPS truck driving down the road, slowing slightly as the driver searched for an address, and then exiting the frame, as a wisp of smoke appeared faintly in the background. He grinned at the smoke, knowing exactly where he had been as the UPS truck rolled by.

A few days later, Detective Brison would know for certain the two crimes were not related. Neighbors had demanded a heightened police presence in the area, and two weeks after Nester Pidwerbecki sniffed his last gardenia, officers in a patrol car noticed a light on in the man's house. Investigating on foot, they surprised one Wilbur Wheaton, a 22-year-old Mobile native with an opioid addiction and a lack of funds to support it.

About an hour into the questioning at the police station, young Wilbur let it slip that it wasn't the first time he had been in the Pidwerbecki house. An hour after that, when Brison had been summoned from a rare dinner out, he broke down and confessed to the murder, having been led to believe doing so would virtually guarantee he wouldn't have to spend any real time in jail. That turned out to be a bit of a fib, and early the following year, Wilbur was sentenced to 25 years for second degree murder.

It was just as reported in the Press-Register -- a senseless murder committed in a panic by a desperate drug addict looking for anything he could turn into cash at his favorite pawn shop. Left unreported was the long-forgotten original theory that the death was related somehow to a nearby fire. That crime had not been solved, not least because Brison lost interest in the case when the murder was solved, leaving Chief Geronimo Joseph to fend for himself. There was little chance anyone could have cracked the case, but Joseph was particularly unequipped and unmotivated to figure it out. He didn't really care for the Russian homeowners, whom he figured were probably responsible for what happened.

Nigel Clancy made one last appearance in Mobile, stumbling his way around long enough to be sure there was no link between the crimes and to realize no one on the city payroll was going to be of any help figuring out what was going on with the Ivanovs.

Two days after Vasquez had talked to the arsonist and cancelled her trip, the Integrity Unit received another secret text from someone inside the unidentified gambling house. "Murder unrelated to arson. Asset resurfaced. Panic over."

It was the shortest note Morton Reid had yet received, but it did the job of confirming what Clancy had discovered independently in Mobile. Reid scratched the fuzz on his chin as he considered the odd web of information he was part of. Leaks from a gambling operation he couldn't identify about an unknown hired gun who committed a crime that was going unsolved by authorities in Mobile, whom Clancy had duped with his bumbling Mark Twain act.

Amusing as it was, it continued to be a major concern. Somewhere in the world, a very professional organization was fixing tennis matches. Reid and his tiny staff had no idea who they were or what matches were being fixed. Their only lead was a fire that no longer interested the authorities in Mobile.

Chapter 26

There were two simultaneous Challenger tournaments running the last week of April. Gil and his modest entourage made their way to Tallahassee, flying coach on American, by way of Charlotte, arriving only two days early to reduce hotel costs.

Training in Ann Arbor had gone well for the first three weeks. By then, Gil was sick of the drills and anxious to play some real matches. The tune-up matches Coach had set up with U of Michigan players were useful as far as they went, but at no time did Gil ever feel he might lose, so there wasn't any real match pressure. And that, as much as the physical training, was what he needed to make his return to professional tennis.

There was also the matter of Sam. She had stayed true to her word and barely allowed him to kiss her on the cheek during those three weeks. However Gil fared at the straightforwardly named Tallahassee Tennis Challenger, he was confident there would be a day or two after when he wasn't training and could enjoy some one-on-one time with her.

Challenger tournaments are to big-time tournaments what amateur theater is to Broadway. They look similar, but everything is scaled down. Crowds and venues are smaller. There are fewer line judges making more questionable calls, none of which can be reviewed by the magical Hawk-Eye computer system. The practice facilities may be off-site, at a college or tennis club. And the prize money is a fraction of what the world's best players divide up at Masters 1000 tournaments, not to mention the four Grand Slams.

A week before Gil began play in Tallahassee, the Monte-Carlo Rolex Masters got underway in Monaco. Matches were played in one of the world's most beautiful tennis settings, and the total purse was over $5-million. It was a 1000 level tournament, one step below a Grand Slam. The next Grand Slam on the calendar was the French Open in late May, where the total purse was just a smidge under $20-million.

In Tallahassee, Gil and 31 other singles players combined were dueling for $75,000, roughly what a first-round loser would receive at a Grand Slam.

The financial disparity explained many things. It explained why Challenger players hung around the tour for a relatively short time: They either collected enough points to move up or gave up the dream. Playing long-term on the Challenger tour was a great way to evaporate a savings account. It explained the desperation of players and their parents who were so very close to their dreams of making it big, but unable to make it over the last, most difficult hurdle. And it explained the fertile ground Nik and his colleagues at Garfunkel had discovered, where players would consider throwing the odd point or game in exchange for a payment that could keep them going for another month, to another tournament, where they might finally get the points needed to reach the pinnacle of the sport.

Nik laughed when he read speculative stories about major tennis stars fixing matches. *Never happens*. With lucrative sponsorships, large tournament payouts and the occasional appearance fee, top players could not be tempted to risk it all for a few more dollars. Even if they could, why risk throwing a high-profile match, when there were so many obscure tournaments all around the world, where no one noticed if a player dumped the second set of a semi-final against an opponent no one had heard of?

Gil, Sam and Coach checked in to the Baymont Inn & Suites, a two-star hotel, less than 15 minutes from the Forestmeadows Tennis Complex, a gorgeous collection of public courts where the tournament had run for 18 years. At $69/night, it was one step above camping. But with free breakfast, free Wi-Fi and a pool, it checked enough boxes for the group.

Creating an anecdote sure to appear in his biography if he ever made it big, Gil booked only two rooms. He convinced Sam to share with her father the night before his matches, otherwise sharing his bed when he had an off-day. The fact that the rooms were side-by-side, separated by a wall that wasn't exactly hurricane proof, meant there wasn't going to be a lot going on, even on the nights she slept with him. If he won a few matches, and they ended up staying a week, it would save about $500.

Coach had been to the Forestmeadows facility before, when he took his team on a pre-season Florida swing five years earlier. It had clay and hard courts; the tournament would be played on clay. Gil had been training indoors on hard courts. The first step on his comeback would be outdoors in the heat on clay. It wasn't exactly like Roger Federer going to Dubai every year to train in the heat and prepare for the exact conditions he would face at the Australian Open. But it would have to do. Everyone playing in Tallahassee had challenges to overcome. Few had Gil's natural ability – or a hot girlfriend sleeping in the room beside him, with his coach.

While Gil searched for the most affordable tournament to enter, the Ivanovs were looking for something that got them far away from Mobile, its snooping police and fire departments, its nosy neighbors and its relentless media attention. Running concurrently with Tallahassee was the

International Di Tennis D'Abruzzo, a cozy tournament in Francavilla, Italy. Like Tallahassee, it was played on clay. Like Tallahassee, it included 32 singles players. And like Tallahassee, its total purse represented a rounding error at the Grand Slams. But unlike Tallahassee, it was a 12-hour flight from Alabama. "That's perfect," Svetlana said, as she studied the Challenger circuit schedule. "From there, we can go to Provence or Rome, bigger tournaments in May. Let's get the hell out of here."

They flew into Rome, rented a Fiat and found the tournament two days early. The first insurance payment from the fire had arrived, so they splurged and booked in at the Villa Maria Hotel Spa. "The money is to pay for housing while we rebuild, right?" she asked him with a wink, as they walked along the hotel's private beach on the crystal blue Adriatic Sea.

They were travelling alone. After several weeks bunking with the Wilkins, everyone was ready for a break. Tom had found some time to coach Sergei, but was consumed with his actual job at the university. However long the Ivanov's European adventure lasted, it represented a bit of a trial separation from Coach Wilkins and his den mother wife. "She's too nice to be human," Svetlana whispered to Sergei one night, as they cuddled, oh so quietly, in the guest room bed. "No one can be that nice all the time. She's a freak."

"I could start looking for a new coach," Sergei said as he slipped his hand under the cotton tee she wore to bed. They had perfected the art of silent sex during the two months after the fire. Like everything else in their lives at that moment, it was becoming tiresome, sapping their spirits.

"Ya, maybe it's time," she answered, returning the favor by slipping her hand into his shorts. "They might be ready for a change too. And then, what's keeping us in Mobile? Let's start over again. Let's not even come back here."

They left the next day for Italy, without raising the topic with the Wilkins. But the goodbyes on all sides seemed more serious than required for just-a-few-weeks away. When they hopped in their cab, the relief on all sides was palpable.

The first change the young Russians made was to turn off the mute button in bed. A long, loud evening of wine-fueled sex announced their arrival at the swanky Villa Maria. It was a release for both of them after two months of fear, shame, anger and scrutiny in a town that no longer seemed like home. They needed a new base, from which to face the one problem they couldn't solve by relocating. The gamblers still had control of them. They needed to regroup and figure out how to escape the noose that was tightening all the time.

But that was far from their minds as they frolicked late into the Italian night. At one point, Sergei stopped to set an alarm for morning. But instead of finding his phone in the kitchen, he found another bottle of wine. It was a screw-top and opened easily – an omen he assumed. He could miss his morning hit. It's not like he had a coach waiting for him on court.

In Tallahassee, Gil woke before his alarm, had the briefest of showers and went in search of the Baymont Inn's free breakfast. What had been the lobby when they checked in the day before had been transformed into what a tired sign euphemistically called the Breakfast Nook. Gil helped himself to some average coffee, picked through the collection of fruit and passed over the basket of day-old bagels. He tucked a copy of USA Today under his arm and headed back to his room, unfettered by other guests or hotel employees.

Steps from his room, he passed Coach, unshaven, about to discover the charms of the Breakfast Nook. "I'll be a few minutes if you want to pop in and wake her up," he said with a smile. "We're on court in an hour."

They had booked the earliest practice time available, a

strategy Coach used whenever he could. It sent a signal to other players who wandered out later in the morning. It also freed up the rest of the day for physio, video strategy or whatever else was needed before a match the next day. Gil was used to early practices from college. Back then, he hated them. Now, he was anxious to get started and was counting down the minutes.

"Morning beautiful," he said, leaning down to kiss Sam gently.

"Drop dead," she said playfully, rolling back under the covers. "Go practise. I'll be here when you get back."

Gil perched on the side of his bed and ate the fruit, along with a protein bar he had packed. He glanced briefly at the newspaper before firing up his iPad. The free Wi-Fi required a password he didn't have, so he shut it off and went to work regripping all his rackets. That was another difference at Challenger events. There wasn't an army of racket stringers looking after the players' needs. At this level, it was strictly DIY. Gil found it refreshing to be stringing and wrapping his own rackets, rather than rackets belonging to club members like Larry Spangler and Howard Forrester. With their swings, a racket strung with twine would produce similar results to whatever hybrid string arrangement they insisted on using.

Gil was sponsored by Head and had six of the company's latest MXG rackets in his bag. For all the attention higher profile players got for playing a sponsor's racket or wearing its clothing, manufacturers sometimes got more bang for their buck by sponsoring club pros. The cost was a fraction of the deals tour players signed, and club pros actually helped influence what racket and equipment members bought. Head had been supplying Gil with rackets, along with clothes and shoes, since he left college. If he won a few tournaments and moved up to the main tour, he would renegotiate his deal, but in the meantime he was happy to get the latest equipment for free.

Coach, shaved but still hungry, drove them to Forestmeadows, where they had court time booked for 7:30. "Tomorrow, we get breakfast on the way," he pledged. The facility had enough courts to schedule practice time as well as tournament games. Not all venues could handle both; often the practice courts were miles away, a fact many a player discovered only after showing up at the wrong place.

Within 20 minutes, Gil had sweated through his shirt and was ripping the ball. He felt liberated – from his club job and from the monotonous training of the previous two months. In two days, he was playing a real match, with real points and potential prize money. Coach's only real job that morning was to make sure his player didn't overdo it, exerting energy he would need in 48 hours.

Sergei woke up naked, with his equally naked wife draped across his torso. It was 9:30, and neither his phone nor the evening's final bottle of wine had beeped to wake them up. No one at the Francavilla practice facility knew how impressive a feat it was when they arrived, together, just after 11:00, in search of a hitting partner for Sergei. That was easily accomplished. A handful of young, local tennis phenoms were hanging around, aching to be asked to hit. Sergei picked a lefty because his first opponent was a lefty. *Who needs a coach anyway?*

They hit for an hour or so, took a break and then returned for 30 minutes of net work, volleying from various positions, hitting cross court and down the line. The kid could play, and after an initial bout of nerves gave Sergei exactly the kind of workout he was looking for. "Thanks Antonio," he said when they wrapped up. "Are you around tomorrow? I'd like to do it again."

"Si," the boy said, taking the €50 Sergei handed him. "Grazie, grazie."

Sergei showered at the courts, then the couple drove the 15 minutes to the tournament site to have a look around and say hello to the handful of acquaintances who had made the same trip as part of a European Challenger swing. What the tournament lacked in prize money it made up for with spectacular, free food for the players and their teams. That wasn't normally part of the Challenger scene, but in Italy the food was always free and plentiful. The Ivanovs ate well and took a little for the road, ensuring they wouldn't have to spend much on dinner. They drove back to their villa on a scenic route, stopping twice to take pictures with the Adriatic in the background. By late afternoon, when they returned to their room, Sergei was ready for a nap.

As he opened the door, he was blinded briefly by the sunshine coming through the balcony door. So he didn't see the man standing to his right, whose fist caught him squarely in the abdomen. As Sergei groaned and doubled over, he saw the man grab Svetlana by the hair and drag her into the living room. He jammed his hand over her mouth to muffle her screams and then slapped her face so hard, she was nearly knocked out.

Every impulse in Sergei's body told him to get up and fight back, but he seemed to be moving in slow motion. As he staggered to his feet, the man produced a knife and held it at Svetlana's throat.

"Quiet now," the man said, in an eerily calm voice. "Please close and lock the door Mr. Ivanov. Thank you. Now come and sit beside your beautiful wife. Good."

When he sat next to Svetlana, she recoiled from him, spitting blood onto the polished bamboo floor.

The man held the knife casually and walked into the kitchen. Opening the fridge, he took a long drink from a bottle of Coke and helped himself to some grapes in a bowl on the counter. He was unconcerned about the time he was taking, the calm in his voice mirrored by his movements.

Sergei flinched when the man reached into an inside pocket, but all he produced was a crisply folded piece of paper. "This is the game plan for the tournament," he said flatly. "Follow these instructions and you won't see me again." He slipped the paper under the bowl of grapes, grabbed half a dozen more and walked directly toward the couple, still seated nervously on the couch.

"Do as we say, OK Mr. Ivanov? We need you to be healthy, to keep playing. Others are more expendable."

As he said it, he ran the edge of his knife blade along the side of Svetlana's neck, all the while maintaining eye contact with Sergei.

When he left, neither of them moved for a very long time. There was no way out.

Chapter 27

Tobias Madsen was an hour from Hamburg, cruising south on BAB7, which connected with E45 in Denmark.

After winning the biggest tournament of his life in Quanzhou, he had spent a few days considering what he should do next. Winners of larger tournaments often took a few weeks off to celebrate, rest and recover. But those players cashed winning checks of six or seven figures.

Madsen had made €12,000 for winning, not enough to finance a month of travel and celebration. Besides, the money was secondary to the real goal of every Challenger player – the points. Winning a tournament gave him a chance to accumulate enough points to move up the following year, but it was not a guarantee. He would have to do well at other venues and continue collecting points to ensure his spot on the ATP Tour.

So he had signed up for two tournaments in France after China. The travel was difficult, but it was better than the alternatives the rest of the month: two tournaments in Mexico. He played the Open Harmonie Mutuelle in St. Brieuc, getting to the third round and then drove 12 hours south to play the following week at the Verrazzano Open, in Sophia Antipolis, near the Swiss border.

He got all the way to the semis at the Verrazzano and used part of the winnings to fly home to Copenhagen. He hadn't been home in more than six weeks, and he wanted more than anything to sleep in his own bed and start the day at his favorite coffee shop.

After three days home, he pointed his black Saab 9-3 south and headed for Hamburg. His only commitment in the next few weeks was the Roma Garden Open in Rome the second week of May. Although entered, he wasn't really committed to going. It was too far to drive, he knew that. Flying to a single tournament, without something the following week nearby as a backup was risky. A first or second round loss would make the trip a money-loser.

He pushed Rome out of his mind and thought about Hamburg. It had been nearly four months since he had delivered his mother to the cancer clinic, the Faustian bargain he had made with the gamblers, which, he had to admit, hadn't been as awful as he feared. He wasn't so naïve to think the Quanzhou tournament would be the last of their demands, but he had been relieved at the lack of communication and threats. He had played both tournaments in France unencumbered by any match fixing demands.

Normally, he would have planned to surprise his mother with his visit. That's what he always did when he returned to Copenhagen, although they both knew she tracked his entries and progress at tournaments and had a reasonable idea of when he might be heading home for a break. There was no such thing as a surprise visit to the Hamburg clinic, where orderliness was next to Godliness in the eyes of the staff.

As he neared the low-slung white building, his memory kicked in and he headed around to the side visitor parking lot. His appointment was for 2:30, and he was nearly an hour early. His Google-assisted plan was to walk a few blocks east to a bakery, with a crowd-sourced rating of five stars, that featured Portuguese custard tarts his mother adored. He bought one coffee and four tarts, the latter placed delicately into a cute, pink box with a white ribbon that served as a handle. He gingerly carried his box to a nearby park bench and set it down next to him. Sipping his coffee, he tried to will time to march more quickly. He had 20 minutes to kill and paced his coffee drinking accordingly.

The greeting he received at the front desk did not match his expectations, particularly given that he was carrying a pink, bakery box, which normally would have lifted the mood of any room he entered by about 30 per cent.

"Herr Madsen, hello," the desk woman said. "Would you please follow me?"

He did so and found himself in a small conference room, alone with his pastries, craving a second cup of coffee. No sooner had he thought it than a different woman appeared and offered him an assortment of drinks, coffee included. He was about three sips in when two doctors, a man and woman, came in from a side door, looking glum, and – Madsen thought – very German.

They shook his hand and took seats together, across the small table from him. Discomfited by their somber mood, he thought fleetingly about passing around the pastries. The pink box sat on the corner of the table, its contents unaffected by the atmosphere of the room.

"Sir, we are terribly sorry to report your mother passed away this morning. About..." She stopped to tap the orange device on her wrist. "About 11:15. We're very sorry."

"Excuse me, what? Why are you just telling me this now?"

"Again, we're very sorry," she said, sounding more annoyed than sorry, and flipping through the chart she held casually in her left hand. "Evidently, we called your home number but we could not reach you."

"I've been driving. I have a mobile. Never mind, doesn't matter now I suppose. Was it from the cancer? I mean, I know she was sick, but, I, ah, thought this was helping," he said, circling his arm in the direction of the hallway and rest of the clinic. "How exactly did she die?"

"She simply fell asleep after breakfast," the chatty doctor said. "Remember, this is an experimental facility, but even so, it doesn't appear her treatments caused her condition to worsen. In fact, they may have given her a few more weeks or months."

"Spent in here," he whispered. He was glad he hadn't offered them a pastry.

"The information we get from all our patients is instrumental in helping others in the future," she said, as though reading from a brochure. "We are very sorry sir."

He froze when they asked if he'd like to see her body. "I don't think so, no." He signed a stack of papers and accepted the clinic's offer to arrange for shipment of his mother back to Copenhagen. It was all covered: part of the fee being paid on his behalf that the clinic assumed was coming from him.

Less than an hour after strolling through the front door with his pink box of tarts, he retraced his steps back to his car, shoulders slumped, mind racing. He had no siblings. His father had died 11 years earlier. There was no one to call, no one with whom he could share the awful news. He sat motionless in his car, door ajar to give him some air.

Suddenly, he thought of the gamblers. They probably knew his mother was dead. They might have known before him. It was another invasion. They had used her to get to him. Sure, it might have helped her, but obviously not for long. She was dead. He had no one. Somewhere in the world, they already knew. They probably knew he had been there. He reached for the pink box on the seat next to him and grabbed one of the tarts. He bit off half, sending custard down his chin. He licked himself clean and finished in two more bites. Then he ate another. And another.

She's gone. I'm alone.

Chapter 28

Antonio returned to the Francavilla practice facility early the next morning, confident Sergei would again choose him to be his hitting partner. He'd hardly slept that night, so excited was he to hit with a real professional player and earn €50.

As players filtered in, heading for the breakfast buffet and then setting up their practice sessions, Antonio searched in vain for the Russian and his beautiful wife. He even turned down a chance to hit with another player because he wanted to be available with Sergei arrived, as he said he would the day before.

"Did your boyfriend dump you?" his best friend Francisco teased him as noon approached and there was no sign of Sergei.

"Shut up asshole."

After lunch, when a coach asked Antonio to hit with his player, the teen agreed halfheartedly. While he waited for the player to arrive, he looked up the draw on his phone. "He withdrew," he yelled to Francisco, who was serving as ball boy on two adjoining practice courts.

"He was probably scared by how well you hit with him," Francisco yelled back. "If I can't beat this little kid, how can I win the tournament, you know?"

Antonio resisted the urge to yell back and simply gave his friend the finger, along with a big smile. His finger was still raised when the coach returned to collect him for his afternoon hit. "You OK?" he asked, neither caring nor waiting for an answer. "Let's go. We're over on 8."

Antonio followed him gamely, immediately transferring his loyalty to this new player, whom he was about to meet for the first time. His only regret was not seeing the Russian's wife again.

As the kid began a mini-tennis warm up on court 8, Sergei and Svetlana were on their way to the airport. They too had hardly slept that night – fighting, crying and trying to figure out what they should do next. Losing their house was awful, but it had happened far away. They felt the loss but not the kind of danger they had just experienced. Svetlana could still feel the cold metal blade against her neck, could still see the dead look in the man's eyes. She also had an ugly bruise on her cheek where the attacker had slapped her nearly unconscious. She was using a scarf to hide the bruise, feeling victimized every time anyone's gaze lingered on her for even a few seconds. They both knew it was a turning point, but they didn't yet know where to turn.

The only thing they really agreed about was that Sergei could not stick around and play in the tournament. They had to get the hell out of Europe. If they couldn't retreat to a home, they could at least retreat to their adopted home country. The last thing they wanted to do was go crawling back to the Wilkins in a town they had come to hate. So early in the morning, when sleep had eluded her for hours, Svetlana pulled up the upcoming Challenger schedule, looking for a safe haven.

"Thank God," she whispered when she saw a tournament the very next week in Savannah, Georgia. It was 500 miles from Mobile and no more difficult to fly into. She tapped a few keys and entered her husband in the tournament before even mentioning the idea to him. She believed the only antidote to his fear, guilt and depression was to play, and this was a way back to the U.S., where he could do just that. Then they would consider everything from whether to come clean with the tour to whether Sergei would continue playing to whether they would stay together at all. As coaches of terrible pro teams sometimes said, there were no untouchables. Everything was up for consideration, and as she lay in bed watching the sun come up over Francavilla, she was considering everything, over and over.

It took the better part of 24 hours to get to Savannah, which, like Francavilla, was an idyllic setting they would have enjoyed had they not been fearful for their lives. The tournament was at the Landings Club, a picturesque Skidaway Island playground for lovers of tennis, golf and being pampered. Having spent almost no money staying in Italy, they again splurged and rented a home that backed onto a golf course. Most importantly, it had a security system, which may not have offered any real protection against the man with the knife but did provide at least the veneer of safety, which was more than Sergei and Svetlana had enjoyed for several weeks.

With the security system activated and a dresser pushed against the door to their bedroom, they slept for nearly 10 hours, trying to overcome a mixture of jet lag and mental anguish. When he woke after 8:00, he slid over and rubbed against her. She recoiled and pushed him away, a reminder of the lingering tension that would be with them indefinitely.

He showered and went out to explore the property. He found a bike in a back shed and peddled toward the golf clubhouse, looking like an adult child visiting his retired parents at their vacation getaway. At the clubhouse, he found coffee and breakfast. He loaded two coffees and several danishes into the basket on the front of the bike and gingerly pedaled back to the rental home, dodging bumps and munching on an apple strudel all the while.

Svetlana was up and dressed when he returned and accepted

his offerings with a formality he hated. They ate together on the screened-in porch, from which they had a great view of a fairway they couldn't identify. Every 15 or 20 minutes a cart would zip near them, delivering a golfer in search of an errant drive. Most found the ball in the rough and kicked it to a more advantageous position. Many then chunked the next shot on a 45-degree angle across into the rough on the other side of the fairway. *I don't get it*, Sergei thought briefly.

Eventually, they got back into their normal tournament routine and planned out the next two days before Sergei's first match. There was practice time available that afternoon, at the Landings Club, so they called ahead to book a time and a hitting partner. Svetlana left Sergei to lounge on the porch, while she locked herself in the bathroom and attempted to drown her worries in the enormous claw foot, copper bathtub.

More out of habit than desire, she climbed into the rental car and went with Sergei at the appointed practice time, wrapping her face in a scarf once again. The swelling was nearly gone, but her skin was working its way through the entire dark portion of the rainbow, mixing blues and blacks in a kaleidoscope of pain.

Sergei found the kid assigned to him, a 16-year-old girl nearly his height, who spent most of her off-court time considering offers pouring in from colleges hopeful she would spend a year or two in their program before turning pro.

As they went off to their court, Svetlana headed for the buffet in search of something healthier than the danish she had picked at that morning. She was happy not to run into anyone she knew, happy she didn't have to explain her bruises or relive the fire yet again with someone feigning concern but really just digging for details to be doled out gleefully at the next cocktail party.

In her junior year at Michigan, Sam had seen domestic abuse up close for the first time in her life. Although she acted like a worldly risk taker, she had grown up in a bucolic home setting. The closest thing to a fight she ever saw her parents have was twice a year or so when her father would leave the house for no apparent reason and just drive around Ann Arbor for an hour or two. While he was gone, her mother would expend vast energy cooking or cleaning, or both.

He always returned with flowers or wine or some other peace offering, and the family ate dinner together as usual. Much later, she realized her parents retired early those nights and completed the family therapy with an evening of make-up sex. She was glad that hadn't occurred to her until much later when she had moved out.

By her third year, she was a residence advisor in the Betsy Barbour Residence. Most of the advising occurred in the first month of classes, when new students were getting their bearings. After that, the job largely entailed making sure everyone knew the holiday schedules and followed the basic rules of the building.

She had come home just after midnight on a Friday in October and was about to turn out her light, when she heard a quiet knock from the hallway. Sam was unprepared for what she saw when she opened the door. Two of the girls from her floor were standing there, one with her arm around the other, giving her physical and emotional support.

"We didn't know what to do or where to go," said Amber Connors, as she held on tightly to her roommate, Peggy Anderson.

"Oh my God, come in, come in."

They sat on the bed, and only then did Peggy pull back her hoodie, revealing a swollen, black eye, framed by a bruised cheek and fat lip. There was a trace of dried blood below the lip, which Sam attempted to wipe away as she held Peggy's face as gingerly as she could.

"Who did this?"

"He said he loved me. He invited me to his family's for Thanksgiving. I'm sorry," Peggy whispered through her swollen lip, before breaking into tears.

"It's her fucking boyfriend, Roddy Kowalachuk," Amber said with disgust. "He's drunk. What an asshole."

"You have nothing to apologize for," Sam said, as she tried to remember what she was supposed to do. The training for residence advisors was fairly relaxed, but there was a handbook. *Where the hell is it?*

After more time consoling Peggy, she called her parents first, then campus police, as required. About 3:00 a.m., campus police went to the Delta Phi Epsilon fraternity, where Roddy Kowalachuk was a member in good standing, and took him to the campus police station for questioning. Before the sun came up, they had charged him with aggravated assault and a handful of other offences.

He was expelled after a short hearing, none of which was in public. His former frat brothers were subjected to 10 hours of education about why it wasn't OK to beat up women, and Sam organized a series of meetings on her floor to let her girls know about the dangers they faced, as unfair as it was.

The entire incident flooded back into Sam's mind as she stood in a line to have her credentials checked at the Landings Club in Savannah, a tournament many of the players in Tallahassee had entered because it was the very next week and only a four hours away.

Gil had reached the semi-finals in Tallahassee, a result that amazed them all. It was his first real tournament in more than two years, and he'd come within two points in a 3rd set tiebreaker from reaching the final. The $3,200 he won covered their Florida expenses and got them two much nicer hotel rooms in Savannah. Not only was the Hampton Suites a significant upgrade from the two-star Baymont Inn, the two rooms were on different floors. Coach was just as happy as Gil and Sam about that arrangement when they had arrived late the night before.

With Gil and Coach off hitting, Sam had gone to check in and pick up the players' package of tournament information – which at smaller tournaments often was a single typed page. There were always coupons and gift cards from local merchants, the value of which usually was minimal.

As she stood in line waiting to check in, she saw a woman at the buffet, loading up more food than she would ingest into her trim body in a week. As she did so, she struggled to keep her blue, silk scarf tied around her face to hide what Sam was certain were fresh bruises.

She fought the urge to march over and ask if she was OK. Instead, she casually tracked her movements out to the patio and then toward the practice court. She appeared to be with a player across the net from a teenage girl who was hitting it every bit as hard as he was. Sitting nearby, Sam became angry imagining this jerk who hit his wife and then no doubt bullied this teenage girl into hitting with him. She listened carefully for anything resembling an abusive comment on the court, but heard only grunts from both sides of the net.

It wasn't difficult to discover the player was Sergei Ivanov, which meant the scarf woman had to be Svetlana Ivanov. Google gave her the background on the destruction of their home, suspected to be arson but never solved. Feeling like a mixture of detective and social worker, Sam plotted to bump into the woman the next day. She couldn't stop thinking of Peggy Anderson's swollen face that night in residence. *I should check up and see where Peggy is now.*

"Just tread carefully sweetheart," Coach said at dinner. "I admire your concern, but it sounds like they've been through a lot. Having someone accuse him of abuse, you know, if it's not true, they don't need that."

"I know Daddy. I'm just gonna see if she wants to talk. That's all."

Gil leaned over and kissed her cheek but said nothing. He still couldn't believe his good fortune to have her following him around the bloody Challenger circuit, sharing a room with her dad half the time, supporting his last shot dream to make it big.

They all had an extra drink after dinner, and then headed for their respective rooms. In keeping with their Tallahassee routine – which had, after all, delivered a semi-final result – Sam would be sleeping in Coach's room, at least at the beginning of the tournament. But she followed Gil to his room to say good night, a task that took nearly an hour and left Gil with a dilemma after she kissed him goodnight and slipped into the hallway.

He remembered once reading that if you flexed a bicep or similar muscle for a solid minute, that would get rid of an unwanted erection. The phrase 'unwanted erection' became his favorite oxymoron, replacing 'jumbo shrimp' in his juvenile catalog of jokes and stupid comments.

The claim flashed through his mind as Sam left the room. There was a much better way to achieve his goal, but the idea of doing so with Sam in the building seemed sacrilegious, or at least a terrible omen. He tried flexing his thighs, which had no effect on any part of his body except his thighs. He was still contemplating his options when he drifted off to sleep. In his dream, Sam stayed and his only decision was in what order he removed her clothes.

Chapter 29

An hour into his drive north from Hamburg, toward Copenhagen, Tobias Madsen pulled off the highway, scrambled out of his car and threw up violently on the gravel shoulder. The mixture of grief and Portuguese tarts overwhelmed his body. On all fours, heaving uncontrollably, he broke down and wept.

Just that morning, he had passed this very spot, happy and care-free, about to celebrate a tournament win with his mother, whom he hoped had stabilized and – who knew? – could be on her way to a miracle recovery.

Now, none of it mattered.

He could no longer ignore the taint of his victory. His mother had died as a guinea pig with no idea why she was there, poked and prodded, drugged and dehumanized. He had convinced himself it was for her benefit, that whatever immoral choices he made were for the greater good, to save his mom's life. Sitting in the sterile office, listening to strangers recite their lines about what happened had shattered the bubble he had constructed around the whole messy arrangement. He'd used her to justify his cowardice.

No more. I will honor her by walking away and playing clean.

Back on the road, he started to consider the practical aspects of what he was determined to do. He couldn't just swing by HR, give notice and resign. Hell, he wasn't even sure who they were or how to contact them.

The memory of being approached in Copenhagen earlier that year was still fresh in his mind. The smaller one did the talking; the bigger one did the threatening. Madsen had no doubt he would be risking his safety if he stopped doing their bidding. He also wondered if his victory in Quanzhou could be revoked for throwing some of the earlier games.

By the time he arrived home, shortly before midnight, he had formulated what could loosely be called a plan. He would wait until his mother's body arrived and he could organize her funeral. Then he would do right by her and set things straight, as best he could. There were some holes in his plan, but he hoped they could be patched over as he went, relying on assistance he hoped he could arrange.

He slept in for the first time in weeks and headed to his new coffee shop for lunch, rather than breakfast. He had to ditch his previous favorite because it was the site of his encounter with the gamblers. He felt bad walking away, but he could hardly go in and explain his mix of shame and anger to the staff. Instead, he found something nearly as good roughly the same distance from his house, in the opposite direction.

As had been his habit at the first shop, he ordered a black coffee to stay and a latte to go. He downed the coffee quickly and carried the latte home, along with two tea biscuits he bought on a whim as he left. The latte was still warm when he sat down at his kitchen table/home office and set up his iPad and Bluetooth keyboard. He took the combo everywhere with him on the road and had no need for a traditional laptop.

Flipping through his contacts, he found the number he wanted and rehearsed, for the 100th time since yesterday, what he would say. It was only 1:30, which meant it was 7:30 a.m. in Florida. No point calling yet. Instead, he inhaled a tea biscuit in two bites and avoided choking by taking a swig from his latte.

When his iPad clock finally read 3:00, he dialed the number. He wasn't sure what to expect, but 15 minutes on hold hadn't crossed his mind. The latte and biscuits were long gone, and he scanned Instagram mindlessly – was there any other way to scan Instagram? – as he waited to be connected.

There were roughly 200 male tennis players who played in at least one ATP World Tour event every year. A few only made it into their country's national tournament by invitation; others earned their way in for a brief time but then fell out of the top ranking as their results faltered.

Liz Catalano knew the names of virtually all those players, along with many of the top players on the Challenger series, but when her assistant told her Tobias Madsen was calling, she didn't know if he was a tennis player or the prime minister of Denmark. His bio was easy to pull up, and she quickly discovered he had just won a tournament in China and was sitting at his highest rank ever in a burgeoning career, spent almost entirely in Europe and Asia.

That was all she knew about the caller when she punched line 3 and began speaking to him, feet up on her desk, sipping a latte herself.

"Mr. Madsen? So sorry to keep you waiting. This is Liz Catalano. How can I help?"

Madsen stammered for the first minute or two, prompting Catalano to send a quick text to her assistant: "Do we need a translator for this?"

"No," came the answer instantly. "He speaks perfect English."

Soon, he started to prove it and got to the point.

"I'm being blackmailed to fix matches. I'm calling you because I want to clear my name and catch the bastards who have done this to me. Can you help?"

Even across an ocean, Madsen could tell he had finally captured her full attention.

Swinging her feet down from the desk and frantically signaling her assistant to come back into her office, Catalano asked Madsen to repeat what he had said. He did so calmly and again fell silent.

"Do you plan to be in Florida, or anywhere in the U.S. in the next week?" she asked, looking at the Challenger series schedule as she asked and realizing he almost certainly did not.

"Ah, no. Sorry. I'm entered in Rome in two weeks, but I may not go. My mother passed away yesterday. There's a lot to do."

Sweet Jesus, what a mess.

"My condolences Mr. Madsen. I'm very sorry to hear about your mother."

"Tobias, please. Yes, it's heart-breaking and also part of this whole story I need to tell you."

"Where are you now?"

"Copenhagen."

"And you'll be there for a few days. I mean, of course, your mother's funeral. When's that?"

"I'm not sure, but in the next three or four days, I imagine. I'm still waiting for her body to arrive. I have to make arrangements. It won't be a large event."

While he spoke, Catalano and her assistant communicated silently, examining her schedule for the week. They managed to open up 48 hours, beginning the day after next, a Thursday.

"I'm going to get on a plane tomorrow and be in Copenhagen Thursday morning, Tobias. Please email my assistant the details about where I can find you and what you decide about your mother's funeral, alright? I won't be able to stay long, but I want to speak with you directly, OK?"

"Yes, yes, that is very generous of you. I will send all the information, yes."

"And Tobias, one more thing. Do not talk about any of this with anyone else. That's very important. Agreed?"

"Yes, thank you again. See you Thursday then."

Chapter 30

Sam's illusion that she was some kind of world-class detective was shattered with five words, whispered from behind her: "Why are you following me?"

She whirled around to find Svetlana Ivanov, her faced shielded with an orange scarf, still hiding the bruises Sam was so determined to investigate.

"Ah, I'm not. Not really. I mean, well. You know. I just want to, ah, talk to you."

"Why? Do I know you?"

"No. I'm Sam Ramsey. I'm here with one of the players and my father. He's a coach."

As she talked, Sam could see herself from above, stammering and acting like an idiot teenager. She had rehearsed her comments repeatedly, but not once did she imagine the conversation starting with Svetlana giving her the slip and circling around to confront her.

"Could we move over to a table with some privacy? Just for a moment?" It was the first sensible thing she had said, spontaneous and honest.

The Russian was intrigued, if nothing else, and had nowhere to be. "Ya, OK. Let me just get a coffee."

"Oh, let me do that. I'll get two. What do you want?"

"Thanks. I'll get my own. Just wait at that table there, alright?"

"Right, yes. OK."

Sam headed to the corner table, buffered from prying eyes and sensitive ears by what might charitably be called a decorative plant grouping. At one time – 1986 – it would have been considered stylish, but now the artificial ferns and miniature palms simply looked like a dusty museum piece. No matter, it provided the perfect oasis for the conversation Sam planned to have.

It was day three in Savannah and Svetlana had enjoyed a second consecutive night of deep sleep. Feeling somewhat better, she had dropped Sergei off to practise and gone into the city that morning, poking around in cute tourist traps, occasionally catching a glimpse of her scarfed head in a shop window.

When she returned to the Landings Club and the tournament, it hadn't taken long to notice the blonde who was trying very hard not to be noticed. Svetlana moved from court to court and wandered out to the putting green attached to the golf course. The blonde followed at a distance, seemingly unaware of her conspicuous beauty and clumsy surveillance skills.

Convinced it was more than her imagination, Svetlana ducked into the women's locker room and immediately out the courtside exit, giving her shadow the slip without any difficulty. As Sam tried to casually survey the club for her subject, Svetlana had come up behind her and ended the cat-and-mouse game by confronting her.

"Who are you exactly?" Svetlana said, setting down her coffee at a seat across the table from Sam.

"Yes, let's start over. I'm so sorry for scaring you, if I did."

"Go on."

Relaxing ever so slightly, Sam launched into a three-minute recap of her background, her reason for being in Savannah and her concern that perhaps Svetlana was in danger, judging from the injuries she was hiding.

Aside from tugging at her scarf when Sam got to that part, Svetlana did not react during Sam's soliloquy. She sipped her coffee and stared straight ahead, giving no indication her brain was in overdrive, calculating how to respond and whether to trust the blonde.

"I'm not really sure what I expected by approaching you," Sam said, wrapping up. "And again, I'm sorry for sneaking around. But now you know why. I guess what I'm really wondering is whether you need help. Do you?"

It wasn't so much that she trusted the blonde. It wasn't so much that she was touched by her out-of-the-blue concern. It certainly wasn't that she expected this stranger to provide any meaningful help. But at that very moment, with the images of her bruised face reflected in the store windows and of the dresser pushed against her bedroom door, the weight of everything finally exceeded her emotional and physical strength. It was time to let go. She would trust the blonde.

"Can we go somewhere less public to talk? I know it sounds paranoid, but I never know who's watching."

An hour later, Svetlana arrived at Sam's hotel room. She hesitated before knocking softly on the door, aware she could be walking into a trap. It made no sense, however, for the gamblers to lure her in that way when five days earlier, they had dispatched a thug to confront Sergei and her directly. Anything was possible, of course, but she thought the odds were in her favor. *I'm due for something good to happen.*

Sam had spent the hour rounding up snacks and tidying the room she was sharing with Coach. The unexpected arrival of the cleaners while she was prepping caused her to jump. She dismissed them with a nervous smile and went back to doing their job for another 40 minutes before she heard the quiet knock on the door.

Svetlana entered the room the way a nervous kid enters a haunted house, looking in all directions at once, expecting something bad to happen at any moment.

"We're the only ones here," Sam said, softly. "Would you

like to sit on the balcony?"

"Sure," came the response, as Svetlana continued to survey the room, clutching her bag like a toddler's stuffed animal.

"Drink?" Sam offered from the kitchenette.

"Sure."

She poured two ginger ales over ice and headed for the balcony, which was mostly shaded by early afternoon.

Svetlana followed, her guard still up. She sat with her back to the corner of the balcony, able to see into the apartment and also down three floors to the ground.

"My husband didn't hit me. He never would," she began. Her hand shook as she took a sip of her ginger ale. "It was someone else."

"Someone you know?"

"Not exactly. Look, this is complicated and also dangerous. I just met you. Do you really want to know?"

Sam reached out and took her hand. "Tell me whatever you want to tell me. If I can help you, I'd like to, but you have every right to keep things private if you want. Are you in danger now? Did it happen here?"

Svetlana pulled her hand back, took another shaky sip of her drink and slowly unwrapped the scarf from her head. Placing it on the table, she looked Sam directly in the eye. "It happened in Europe. We came here to get away, but we can't really get away. They burned down our house. They attacked me. It's awful."

The final words were barely audible as she began to sob. Face in her hands, she pulled her knees up to her chest and continued crying.

Among the frenetic preparations Sam had made, Kleenex was not included. She pushed her chair closer and made an awkward attempt to hug this stranger she had met just that morning.

Eventually Sam got up, found some Kleenex and refilled

their drinks. In fits and starts, Svetlana told the story of how her life and marriage had been attacked and infiltrated by faceless thugs who made money by blackmailing her husband. She held nothing back, the momentum of the story taking over before she could consciously decide whether to reveal everything.

"The worst part of it all -- and it's all really bad -- is that I can't trust my husband anymore. He kept this from me for so long. How can we fight back if we're divided?"

Sam's response was just as honest. "Holy shit. What a fucking mess."

Unguarded for the first time in months, Svetlana laughed at her response. And laughed some more. They both laughed in convulsions, erasing the last remnants of any tension. That's when Sam opened a bottle of wine and Svetlana texted Sergei: "I'm shopping and won't be back til later. Take cab home. Meet you there later."

Chapter 31

The last time Liz Catalano had packed so quickly for a trip was when she booked a last-minute romp in the Dominican with a college boyfriend. All she really needed then was a couple of bikinis, a dress and flip flops. Even then, she over-packed for what turned out to be a long weekend spent having villa sex during the day and beach sex at night.

The moment she hung up with Tobias Madsen, she popped in to see Morton Reid who was still at the Florida office.

"I came here for a bunch of sponsor meetings this week. I can't miss them, but I can have someone from London meet you in Copenhagen," he offered after she had sketched out everything Madsen had just told her.

"I think that would spook him," she replied. "Let me start one-on-one and see where it leads." She had no desire to include a stranger in the process, someone she neither knew nor trusted. "If he checks out, we can figure out our next step."

"Jesus Liz, this is huge. It could be the biggest break we've ever had."

"I know, I know, but if he senses we're anxious, who knows if he cooperates? It had to be a tough thing to call and admit he's being pressured. Plus, don't forget, his mother died, just, well yesterday, his time. In the last 36 hours anyway. What a shitty week."

"Alright, see what he has to say. But let's at least send some security with you. We don't know if he's on the level or if he's being watched," Reid said. "You have no idea what you're walking into."

"That would certainly spook him, me showing up with a henchman. Come on Mort, relax. We'll meet somewhere public. I'll be very careful. I won't have a big ATP name tag or anything. No one will even know who I am."

They went back and forth for another 15 minutes. She convinced him to let her go alone, and then they agreed on the topics she would discuss with Madsen. It wasn't difficult to hone in on what mattered: They needed to use Madsen to work their way up the ladder to the faceless gamblers who were fixing matches worldwide, raking in millions of dollars for their efforts.

A last-minute, first-class ticket to Copenhagen from Jacksonville, via Chicago, cost more than Madsen had netted for his victory in Quanzhou. Catalano decided not to share that information with him.

She headed to the Copenhagen Admiral Hotel immediately after landing, texting Madsen from the back of the cab. She wondered about his desire to meet at the Tivoli Gardens, but agreed right away. *It's your meeting pal.* She spent 20 minutes comatose on the bed, freshened up and headed down to the bar. She had time for a splash of white wine before the 7-minute ride across town to Tivoli.

Reading about an amusement park built in the 1840s, she had expected something antiquated, but Tivoli was like a little piece of Disney smack dab in the heart of Copenhagen. More importantly, for her purposes, it featured a dozen or more restaurants and thousands of tourists who looked a lot like her. The perfect place to meet.

She had Madsen's photo on her phone and had sent him her own mugshot. The meet was for 1:30 at Fru Nimb, billed as a classic Danish open face sandwich restaurant. It was a step above the many, nearby fast food joints; they could sit at a table with the right mixture of privacy and public protection.

Madsen had arrived an hour early, wearing sunglasses and feeling both silly and fully justified for being cautious. It hadn't occurred to him until later that using his home phone to call New York might be risky. Could they be listening? He'd wrestled with that unknowable question for hours while trying to sleep, mixing that what-if with elaborate scenarios of what would happen after he spilled his guts. In some scenarios, he was a hero for blowing the whistle. In others his career ended. In others his life ended.

He scouted the perimeter of the restaurant using what he imagined was a professional strategy, moving around and casually surveying his surroundings. He was bored within 20 minutes and wondered how real spies maintained their concentration. Just before 1:30, he walked into Fru Nimb, and found a table in a corner of the main room. The décor was French, as interpreted by Danes – elegant and crisp, white tablecloths and beech wood chairs. And of course, lots and lots of open face sandwiches. One small part of his brain noted the fabulous smells of the place, but only fleetingly.

He recognized Catalano the moment she walked in and stood up to greet her. His plan was to pretend they were friends catching up over lunch. That made sense to him at 3:30 that morning as he tossed and turned, mapping out every detail of the meeting. But as he stood, he realized she wasn't in on the plan and might find it odd if he hugged her like an old friend would do. And so, rather than commit fully, he leaned in awkwardly and managed only to bump heads with the woman, who looked confused and apologetic.

"Shit, sorry," he said, sitting back down quickly, relieved to see a smile forming on her face, just below the area he had smacked with his forehead in a new and painful form of greeting.

"So much for icebreakers," she laughed. "Very nice to meet you Mr. Madsen," she said, extending her hand for a more conventional greeting.

"Tobias, please," he said, shaking her hand without inflicting any further damage on her person.

"It's Liz. First let me say how sorry I am, our entire office is, about your mother."

"Thank you. Yes, it was a shock. She had cancer, but I had reason to believe she was getting better, or, well, at least not getting worse."

"And secondly, I want to thank you for reaching out about the other thing. I'm here because we want to help."

"Alright, yes. I'll get into all of that. But shall we order first? All I've had today is coffee. I've been walking around out there for the last hour."

"I'll bet your coffee was better than the stuff they had on the plane. Yes, let's order. Looks like maybe a sandwich of some kind?"

The banter between them was friendly and genuine even as each one sized up the other. At some point, Catalano would have to make a judgment about his claims and decide whether she could trust him. So too would Madsen have to decide whether to trust her, and by extension the ATP office. He really hoped he could because he didn't have a Plan B.

She wanted to plop her iPhone down on the table between them and hit 'record,' but didn't dare. "Tell me about how you got interested in tennis, if you don't mind. When did you think you might be a professional?"

He had just come to the part about turning down a partial college scholarship at some school Catalano had never heard of, when their food arrived. She had ordered the creamy chicken salad with mushrooms and bacon. He had opted for the more athlete-friendly organic eggs and prawns on crisp rye.

Credit the organic eggs or his growing comfort level, at a certain point in the conversation, he decided at some subconscious level to hold nothing back. He might lose his career, but holding back now would be even worse. And so he told her everything, ending with his vomiting on the highway three days ago, unable to absorb the despair that surrounded him.

An hour or so in, when they gave in and ordered dessert, Catalano decided he must be telling the truth. It was too raw to be anything else. *This is going to work. Thank God.*

Chapter 32

Nik blanched as he read the monthly reports. The firm was still ridiculously profitable, but things seemed to be getting a little tattered around the edges. He read about the enforcer's visit to rough up the Ivanovs and how they had fled Europe the next day. Erratic behavior like that was exactly what could alert the authorities, regardless of how inept they had been to that point.

The TIU had suspended a couple of Garfunkel's lesser players in the last two months, giving Nik a bad feeling. There didn't seem to be much of a public case against the players, so what exactly had the TIU acted upon? It wasn't any clearer in May than it had been in March, and it continued to worry him.

Evidently, he wasn't the only partner concerned about the suspensions. The report included the suggestion that information about Garfunkel's operations was being leaked to authorities, possibly the TIU. There was no actual evidence to support the suggestion, but it was the first time Nik could recall it ever being mentioned. The report urged caution and reminded partners of the security measures they should be taking at all times. Nik assumed he wasn't the only one who cut the occasional corner.

As much of a concern as Sergei Ivanov was, he was Vasquez's problem. She had recruited him and tried to win him over with generous payments. When that didn't work, she had ratcheted up the intimidation, but from where Nik sat it didn't seem to be accomplishing much, other than drawing headlines about houses burning down and players dropping out of Challenger events in Italy.

Nik's problem was Tobias Madsen. He only ever cooperated because of the cancer treatment his mother was receiving. They would have to find a new lever, and Nik was determined to avoid the conspicuous, mob-style violence some of his colleagues and partners seemed to prefer, if not enjoy. But he wasn't flush with other ideas.

He cued up the recording of Madsen winning in Quanzhou. The joy on his face was pure, unsullied by the circumstances. He thought back to the player's reaction when they'd approached him in Copenhagen. Sometimes athletes reacted to the gamblers' demands with a mixture of fear and grudging acceptance. What could they do? Madsen, though, had been resolute in his defiance. Nik wondered if Madsen realized how badly he'd wanted Mrs. Madsen to go on living at the treatment center? Her death was bad news for everyone.

Sitting in his office, thumbing through reports, Nik stared hard at Madsen's joyful face, frozen on the screen. He looked at the reports he had on his mother's death and the procedure to ship her body back to Copenhagen – all being financed by Garfunkel, in keeping with the original set up at the clinic. For a second, Nik remembered the days after his father had died. Madsen was older than Nik had been, but he appeared to be dealing with the loss all by himself.

The file didn't include every detail of the player's life, but it painted a full picture. The thing missing from Madsen's picture was a companion of any kind – a best friend, a girlfriend, a boyfriend. Not even a dog. His cancer-stricken mother seemed to have been his best and only friend in the world. The problem was still rattling around in his head when it was time to leave for dinner. He hadn't seen Lola in more than a week, and texting, regardless of its x-rated nature, was a weak substitute.

They met at Square, as they often did. She was waiting at the bar, when he walked in 15 minutes late. It wasn't that he had forgotten, but the sight of her staggered him slightly. He'd never been with a more beautiful woman, not even close. Which made the whole thing bittersweet because he never forgot their relationship was based on a lie – a series of lies, actually, flowing from one big lie about his job. Like all his friends, Lola only knew about the legal side of Nik's work at Garfunkel. But she knew it in more detail than anyone else in his life. She'd grown up in an Everton household, an allegiance that stretched back several generations in her family.

If you grew up in Liverpool, you had to choose. And sometime back more than 100 years, one of her grandfathers had chosen Everton Football Club over Liverpool Football Club – maybe because Everton had been formed in 1878 and was a founding member of the Football League 10 years later. Fresh-faced newcomer Liverpool hadn't arrived until 1892.

She followed the Toffees as religiously as her friends followed singers and movie stars. Her family couldn't afford tickets to many games, but she remembered the few times she'd been to Goodison Park much the way a devout Catholic would remember meeting the Pope. The grounds were as hallowed to her as any in Vatican City.

It was her love of Everton football that prompted mutual friends to set her up with Nik three years earlier. He was smitten from the start, amazed by the combination of beauty, brains and football interest. She found Nik fascinating but was put off by the clinical and cynical way he viewed sports. Setting odds on football matches robbed them of what she most loved, the passion. His was an antiseptic calculation about tendencies and advantages, with no real consequences for losing. Sure there were financial consequences, but she was suspicious of anyone who could watch sports so keenly without engaging emotionally. Two months after their 3rd anniversary, she saw the same thing in his approach to her.

There was no doubt he loved her, but he'd never really opened up with her. He was holding back, and she'd started wondering which came first: his oddsmaker job or his careful and reserved nature, the chicken or the egg. His nature seemed to mesh perfectly with the job, but she wanted something more, something deeper from him in their relationship. She was 26 and ready for the next chapter. She doubted he was.

At dinner, they barely spoke. While she considered macro relationship issues, he stewed over Madsen. Both were so deep in thought that neither even noticed the waiter, standing awkwardly, unable to gain the attention of either one.

"Excuse me, if I may, would you care for drinks to start? Sir? Madam?"

She answered first, but not quickly, and ordered wine for both of them. She drank her first glass in three gulps and looked at him with laser focus. "Where are you Nik? What's going on?"

She asked two more times before he came back to the table and heard her words as anything more than background noise.

"Huh? Sorry. What?" He sipped wine he didn't remember ordering. "What were you saying?"

"I was asking where the fuck you are right now. What's up?"

"Oh, sorry. It's work stuff. Trying to solve a problem, you know."

"Actually, I don't. I don't know much of anything about you or your work, and lately it's been getting worse. What the hell is going on? Is it us? Are you not happy with this?" she asked, swinging her index finger back and forth between them. "I'm afraid to ask, but I need to know."

"No no no, not at all," he said, at last tuning in to her frustration. "It really isn't. I love you baby. Honest. It's just. Well there's a lot at work that's on my mind. I don't want to trouble you with it."

"Wish you would. Wish you would tear down some of those barriers 'cause they seem to be getting higher, and I don't know how to react."

It wasn't the first time she'd hinted at the issue, but it was the first time she'd been so direct about it – direct and in public. He felt a pain in his forehead and rubbed his temples.

More than once he'd considered telling her what was really happening at work, but the risks always outweighed the rewards by a huge margin. The truth would turn her into a mafia wife of sorts, saddled with at least cursory knowledge of wrongdoing and complicit in it. He couldn't do that to her. But if she decided to leave... He couldn't have that either. Whenever he'd looked ahead 10 years, he imagined a family with her and some kind of unspecified solution to the mafia problem.

"That's it," he exclaimed, like Archimedes in his bathtub. "I love you. I'd do anything for you. That's the pressure point."

She watched him spin and wondered, briefly, about the symptoms of a stroke.

"I'm OK, honest. This problem, I just figured out the solution. I don't want to lose you. I'd do anything for you. So would he. I mean anyone in that situation, right? We need to create that situation."

On TV, she'd seen some con artist preacher 'speaking in tongues', receiving, rather conveniently, a message from the all-powerful creator of the universe that his gullible followers should send money his way to keep his vital show on the air. She didn't like the vibe on TV, and she certainly didn't like it when her boyfriend sounded the same way across the table from her in public.

"Nik, quiet. What are you doing?" She squeezed his palm as though he were a doll and there was a volume switch sewn into his hand. "Please stop talking. Honey, please."

He finally stopped, motivated mostly by the look of terror on her face. He hadn't noticed the eyes of those all around them at the high-end lounge, watching like he was Meg Ryan, sitting across from Billy Crystal.

"Let's go somewhere more private," he said, his voice returning to normal. "I can explain all this to you. All of it, and more. Let's go."

She followed him at a speed walker's pace and hopped into the back of the cab he hadn't hailed so much as commandeered by stepping into traffic and holding out his arms.

Chapter 33

Charging her phone in her room, Catalano wondered briefly if she was spending more on mobile charges than on her hotel room. *Whatever, it's all worth it.*

Her lunch meeting with Madsen had stretched well into the afternoon. As the crowds around them dwindled and Fru Nimb emptied, they left Tivoli separately having agreed to reconvene for a more private meeting that evening. He left the park at 4:00 and planned to stop at the aptly named Funeral Copenhagen before dinner.

He felt a wave of relief as he left Tivoli and headed for the bus stop. He wished he had told someone sooner but dismissed the self-criticism right away. *I did what I could. It was worth it to help mother.*

Funeral Copenhagen was an oddly bustling place with visitors milling around looking for the proper family members to visit and console. The office portion was closing at 5:00, although there was an evening of visitations lined up for half a dozen grieving families. Madsen found the office with 15 minutes to spare and learned his mother's body was due to arrive the next morning.

"We're tracking her every day," the depressingly cheerful woman at the desk said. "It's much easier to cross borders in Europe when you're alive than when you're not," she said, without a hint of sarcasm. "We're assured, tomorrow. Have you decided on the ceremony and visitation?" she asked Madsen.

"No visitation," he answered back, flatly but firmly. "The rest is simple. We will have a private ceremony and that's all.

Could we do that tomorrow afternoon?"

"Earliest would be the next morning," she countered. "Assuming, of course, things go as expected tomorrow."

"Yes, let's assume that, shall we?" he said. "So the next morning, first thing, we can do a very short ceremony. I have a priest in mind."

He spun and left the office before she had a chance to protest. Then he texted his boyhood friend, Anders Jensen, and confirmed the ceremony for the morning after next. Surprising friends and family alike, Jensen had become a Lutheran priest after studying philosophy at university.

Madsen hadn't known his high school buddy to go to a church of any kind, aside from Christmas Eve, under protest, with his family. They'd lost contact when Madsen moved to Spain as a teen to focus on tennis exclusively. He knew his friend had gone to Aarhus University but that was the extent of his knowledge. It wasn't until Facebook kept asking if he knew someone called Anders Jensen who looked like a version of his friend, 40 lbs. heavier with a full beard, that he was aware of his old friend's new life.

It was an enormous imposition to ask someone he barely knew anymore to travel three hours to Copenhagen to conduct a private funeral that would last about 15 minutes. But in the days following his mother's death, Madsen found himself caring a lot less about what people might think of him. It was a similar spike of courage that prompted him to call New York. True or not, he convinced himself his mother would approve of what he was doing. He even imagined his actions, taken together, were a kind of tribute to her life. He knew it was an infinitely more important tribute than any words he might utter at her ceremony in two days.

Jensen texted back almost immediately. "Be there at 8:30. Thinking of you, brother."

Taking reassurance from wherever he could get it, Madsen

pocketed his phone and strode toward the bus stop once again. The day was going as well as he could have hoped that morning, when he feared the exact opposite. He went home, showered and changed his clothes quickly, before taking a cab to meet Catalano.

She was already at Musling Bistro when he arrived just after 7:00. It was one of his favorite restaurants, the place with the best seafood in a city of great seafood. Plus, it was next to the Torvehallerne food market, which meant lots of people around, just in case the gamblers were watching. *It's not paranoia. It's just smart.*

Walking across the spacious dining room, he immediately noticed how different Catalano looked. That afternoon, she'd worn jeans and a hoodie, an innocuous outfit perfect for mom errands on a Saturday morning. Now she was wearing a black dress that disappeared mid-thigh, black suede boots and about 5 lbs. of silver jewelry. He forced himself to look straight ahead as they greeted each other for the second time that day, this time without smashing heads or inflicting injury of any kind.

"You look lovely, Liz," he said flatly, like he was observing the weather or a football score on TV.

"Thank you very much. I've felt groggy since I got here. Nothing better than a long hotel shower and some fresh clothes to get going again."

They ordered wine and studied the menu.

"You were going to the funeral home after our lunch, right? How was that?"

"Bloody awful, to be honest," he blurted, committing to the answer more than he planned. "I mean, of course right?"

"I lost my mother six years ago. I remember how painful it was. Were you close?"

After days of dealing with her death by himself, the opportunity to talk to someone about it, fueled by the wine, prompted Madsen to deliver a soliloquy of Shakespearean length, if not eloquence.

Catalano was happy to listen. It was the decent thing to do, but it was also further proof of the man's sincerity. She needed someone willing to be open and honest about the gamblers. This was their man.

When they had drained the final drops from their decaf lattes, they got up to leave. "We can share a cab," he suggested. "Which way are you heading?"

"Ha, beats me. Which way is the Admiral Hotel?"

"Yes, I know it. I can drop you first. It's on my way home. Or it can be anyway."

The bustling food market was quiet for the evening as Madsen surveyed the street for a cab. There were a few on the next block and he tried to get their attention by waving and whistling. As he gesticulated, he noticed a car parked closer, on the other side of the street, with a man sitting alone behind the wheel. The city was in the midst of a fight with alternate cab companies, demanding minimum training and standards of their drivers. In the meantime, many drivers operated in a grey zone, taking rides unofficially and undercutting traditional cab rates by 50 per cent or more.

All of that flashed through Madsen's mind when he saw and dismissed the car. He didn't think about it again until it pulled out directly behind them after they'd climbed into the back seat of the cab he'd managed to flag down. He wouldn't have noticed, except he was sitting on the same side as the driver and could see everything behind them in the expanded rear view mirror affixed above the standard mirror.

He watched for a few minutes without saying anything. Catalano was scrolling through messages and the driver was oblivious. Finally, after the car had followed them on a 4th turn, he couldn't help himself. "That car," he said in Danish, motioning with his thumb, "is following us."

The driver glanced into the mirror and shrugged. "Let's see." With that, he pulled over next to the bike path that snaked through the entire city, right blinker flashing. The car behind them slowed slightly but continued down the street. It was a Mercedes, but Madsen could not make out the licence plate. *What am I going to do with it anyway?*

Catalano was deep into her phone, oblivious to the brief stop. The driver pulled back into traffic and grinned into the mirror at Madsen. He didn't mind the odd diversion from his mind-numbing job. Initially, he thought the diversion would be listening to the couple, obviously on a date, talk on their way home. But they didn't talk or cuddle or show any interest in each other.

Madsen returned the grin, ruefully.

"Wait, isn't that him again?" Into the wide mirror emerged a familiar set of headlights, pulling out from a side street, hanging back two or three cars. "I'm sure it's him. Right? You see him, don't you?"

The driver's smile disappeared as he squinted and peered into the mirror. "Could be," he grunted. "Why would someone be following you?" Still in Danish, he added, "Someone's husband maybe?"

Madsen ignored the comment and kept his eyes on the mirror. "What did he say?" Catalano asked him, shoving her phone into her purse and engaging. "Is that car really following us?"

"He was joking, never mind. Ya, it looks like it is. You didn't bring anyone with you did you?"

"Like who? No."

The hotel was another 10 minutes away. During that time they decided to both get out there and see if the mystery car made any other moves. The driver was not the least bit surprised when both hopped out at the hotel, a change of plans he often witnessed couples make late at night.

The hotel was on a one-way street. The driver pulled over across the street from the hotel entrance, as close as he could get amidst a sea of cabs and other vehicles. Madsen was about to suggest she slide over and exit from his side, next to the sidewalk, when she disappeared out her own door. As her foot touched the ground, the heel of her boot slid on the cobblestone and she lurched forward, rolling her ankle. She hit the ground hard and was lying perpendicular to the curb, her head halfway into the left lane of traffic, groaning in pain, reaching for her injured ankle.

Madsen circled behind the cab and was about to help her get up, when headlights behind them suddenly illuminated Catalano. The driver stomped the brakes and swerved to the right, clipped the fender of a car in the center lane, and avoided Catalano by the width of a tire. As Madsen bent over to help her, he saw the plates of the car that had nearly killed her. The Mercedes. Again. A third time.

Chapter 34

Sergei found it nearly impossible to concentrate on his first match in Savannah. He had slept very little the night before, having the same dream on a loop, with just enough variation to be jarring. Each time, he was on the court, playing some faceless opponent when a crowd started to gather at one corner of the court.

Among the group were police and security people, sometimes with guns drawn, sometimes on horses. He could never figure out why the cops were on horses, but that was the least of his problems. Within minutes of their arrival, the officials in the corner walked onto his court, sometimes during the point, sometimes as he was about to serve. For some reason, they never waited for the changeover when he was seated under an umbrella, sipping Gatorade.

They not only came out to get him, but handcuffed him in front of a crowd at least 5x as large as the real center court stadium could actually accommodate. Without knowing anything, the crowd booed him lustily as he was frog marched off the court, into a waiting cruiser parked, inexplicably, on an adjoining court with lights flashing, interrupting another match. Those fans booed him as well, as the cops stuffed him into the back seat.

Sometimes, the people grabbing him were not cops, but gamblers. They wore dark suits and black dress shoes that dug into the clay and ruined the court. No one stopped them from grabbing him and tossing him the back of their giant black Lincoln. Sergei tried to scream, but could no longer speak English. His cries came out in Russian, which no one could understand and further turned the American crowd against him.

Svetlana watched from the VIP section but did nothing. In some versions of the dream, she was sitting with an old boyfriend, laughing and pointing at him.

He woke multiple times, sweating, unsure of his surroundings each time. And each time, it took him at least 10 seconds to remember where he was, what had happened that evening and why he was sleeping on the couch of a rented house. The last two points were related, but it took him even longer to recall that.

Svetlana had returned late from what she initially told him was a shopping trip. But she had no packages and couldn't name any of the stores she had been to. She was also drunk, or so it appeared, when she came crashing in the house around 10:00, looking for money to pay her driver.

"Where's the car?" he asked. "Are you OK?"

"Yes, I'm fine. I'll get the car tomorrow. It was easier to leave it."

The conversation became more convoluted and unclear from that point, until Sergei held up his hand. "Stop lying to me, alright? Just tell me where you've been. I was worried."

"*You* were worried?" she said, at a level just short of a scream. "*You* were worried? That's great. You ruin our lives and destroy everything we have. We're attacked, and now you're worried?"

It was half an hour before she emerged from the bathroom, her voice quieter, her mood subdued, if not apologetic.

"The pressure just got to me," she said, sitting next to him on the couch and resting her head on his chest. "I had to let it out. I had to tell someone."

"Uh huh. Who?" he asked, cautiously.

"A woman I met. She's here with another player, ah, I'll

think of his name. Anyway, she's great. Listened to our whole story. It was such a relief to tell someone, not to keep everything, here, between us."

"And you trust her? You told her everything?"

"Everything I could remember, which I think was everything."

"But we don't know…"

"Look, Sergei, I trust her OK? I had to tell someone. She's empathetic, or I think so. I never really know what that word means. But she listened, that's all I'm saying. She seems concerned about us and wants to help."

The conversation went long into the night, until both were too tired to continue. Svetlana headed to the master bedroom and closed the door behind her. His options were a guest room full of undersized bunk beds or the spacious couch in the main room. He ripped sheets off two of the bunks and set up the couch. But he couldn't sleep.

His opponent, a 19-year-old wunderkind, had less weighty matters on his mind as he ripped groundstrokes down the line and came in behind them to put away easy volleys. His biggest concern was a zit forming on his forehead and a text from his girlfriend asking if she could bring a friend to the party that night.

After losing the first set 6-1, Sergei's pride kick-started his brain. He finally noticed the kid struggled to return serve on the backhand side. And he was so close to the net in search of put away volleys that he could be lobbed with ease. Once the kid got tired of being lobbed and stayed back, Sergei delivered a few well disguised drop shots to further frustrate him. The last two sets weren't particularly close -- 6-3, 6-2 -- and the kid looked bewildered as he shook Sergei's hand at the net.

It was the start of an encouraging run that landed Sergei

in the semi-finals, his best result in months. He lost but was happy with the state of his game: the only good news in his life it seemed.

Gil did not fare as well. The high of returning to competition the previous week in Tallahassee had worn off. His relative lack of conditioning started to nip at his tired legs when he had to play a third set. He squeaked by a player older than him but lost decisively in the second round. The payday would cover travel expenses, but that was it. The few rankings points he got barely moved him up the overall standings.

"This is gonna happen," Coach said, encouragingly. "Keep working. It'll come." With that, Coach hopped a flight back home where his paying job beckoned. For reasons no one could explain, Savannah was the last Challenger tournament in North America for more than two months. There were multiple tournaments every week across Europe and Asia, but nothing in North America until Winnetka, Illinois, and Winnipeg, Manitoba, in mid-July. That left Gil with some logistical challenges he had yet to address. All along, he planned to see how he felt about his play, his fitness, and his relationships with Coach and Coach's daughter before deciding how much time to spend in Europe.

As always, it was about money as much as time. If he were honest, he had to admit his level of play was better than he expected it to be. After not playing any serious tennis for three years, he was on an equal footing with most Challenger players and better than many. He'd really hardly started to train, so was sure his results would improve. Like all players at that level, he spent a lot of time calculating what kind of results he needed to qualify for the main tour the next year. It was impossible to know for certain because so much depended on how others performed, but generally anyone who could win two Challenger tournaments and finish high in another three or four would qualify. He was sure he could do that. But he had to go to Europe.

Sam returned from dropping Coach at the airport and moved her luggage to Gil's room three floors down. With Coach gone and Gil done in the tournament, there was no reason to keep both rooms – and certainly no reason for Gil and her to stretch their abstinence pledge into a second week.

Gil's plans to wash away his disappointment with an intimate evening were thwarted when Sam began talking about her meeting the day before with the Russian woman, Svetlana. He had a vague memory that she was going to reach out to her and offer help, but he forgot exactly when that was happening. He certainly didn't think to ask how it went.

"I think we should have dinner with them, maybe tonight," she said, as she was hanging up her dresses and blouses. "They're in real trouble and I told her we'd try to help."

Gil sighed imperceptibly as he got comfortable on the bed. There was no point objecting or suggesting an alternate schedule when Sam was locked in like this.

She recounted the entire evening for him, including her bungled attempts at playing spy. When she got to the part about gamblers attacking their house and then beating her up, Gil got up and cracked open a beer. When he came back, he sat at the table, listening like he was in school again.

"So you two got drunk last night after all this?" he laughed. "I guess you hit it off. I thought you were asleep in Coach's room."

"I do like her, but more important I believe her. And I think we should see if we can help. At least hear the whole story from both of them. See if they need anything. Have you ever played the guy or heard of him?"

"Heard of him? Ya. I think he was a college hot shot a year

or two after I graduated. Not sure what happened. Why he didn't get to the main tour. Maybe he got injured and took a club job hundreds of miles away from his smoking hot girlfriend. Nah, no one's that stupid right?"

"No way," she laughed, as she reached for her phone and started texting. "Let's see if they can have dinner tonight. We're not sticking around much longer, are we? He's still playing. Sorry. What's the plan anyway?"

Gil grabbed Sam from behind to reveal his short term plan, but she wasn't interested. "Not now. We need to set things up with them. If they can't do it tonight, is tomorrow OK? Are we sticking around?"

"Sure, let's stay a couple of days and relax. We need to figure out Europe anyway. We can do that sitting by the pool, right?"

The ding of her phone interrupted her answer. "OK, they're in. We're meeting tonight."

Chapter 35

Lola was intrigued and terrified in equal parts as the cab careened around the last corner and approached The Castle. She knew where Nik worked, but she'd never been there. When she had imagined visiting, early in their relationship when it seemed like a natural progression, she pictured something during daylight hours. Something less frenetic, like meeting for lunch and waiting in his office while he finished a phone call, maybe meeting a few of his colleagues who wandered by the open door.

"We've heard so much about you."

"All of it good, I hope."

She craved relationship small talk; she wanted the validation of being presented as Nik's girlfriend among the people with whom he spent virtually all his time.

That wasn't on the agenda as the cab screeched to a halt at the fortified front door.

"Come on, let's go," he said, pulling her out of the car and simultaneously paying the driver in one motion. "I want to show you my office."

"Right now? This late? What's gotten into you?"

"Just come in, OK?"

With that, he kissed her cheek and looped his arm through hers. His security pass opened the front door and then a secondary door below a conspicuous video camera.

"No retina scanners?" she joked.

"They're inside," he said flatly.

"I was joking."

"I wasn't. Come on."

183

He dispensed with any kind of tour, nodding to anyone they passed, still pulling on her arm as though he were kidnapping her. She was amazed by the number of people still working at 10 p.m.

"We have people here 24 hours, remember?"

"Ya, you told me, but I thought you meant like the janitor and a few people just to keep an eye on things. This is like a whole night shift."

"Exactly. Come on, my office is down this hall."

A six-digit code opened the frosted glass door to his office, which she noticed right away was bigger than his apartment. It was an office the same way Italy's winding, mountainous Stelvio Pass was a road. The floor was covered with a dark wood she could not identify. The desk was the size of her car and featured ornate carvings around the entire surface. There were flat screens covering the wall opposite the desk and three additional screens fanned out, u-shaped, on the desk.

The leather on the sofa was softer than anything she'd ever sat on. The coffee machine looked more like a Transformer and sat on its own pedestal, next to a kitchen sink and stainless steel fridge.

"No wonder you spend so much time here," she cooed, sprawling on the sofa. "It's amazing."

Like hosts who take their out-of-town visitors to local attractions they've long since taken for granted, Nik enjoyed seeing his office through Lola's eyes. Her enthusiasm reminded him of how excited he had once been about the office. Earlier that day, it had been nothing more than a place to get more bad news.

An hour before their dinner date, his European fixer called him directly. That almost never happened, so when he saw the number his shoulders slumped. Locking the door, he flipped the speaker button and listened to a frantic recap of events in Copenhagen.

"Jesus! Did they see you?"

"Not sure, but it's possible. It all happened so fast. I did get the pictures you wanted."

"Oh great, way to go. Well, send them over. You were supposed to keep a low profile. We need him to go about his business, not to think someone's following him or, Jesus, trying to kill him."

Nik had dispatched him the day Madsen's mother died. Faced with such a tragedy, surely Madsen would reach out to close friends. If Nik could figure out who they were, he might find a new way to keep the player motivated and on board.

"Just hang around in the background, get pictures of anyone he meets and generally observe him for a week or so, at least until his mother's funeral."

The instructions couldn't have been more clear. How could someone who was so effective when they initially targeted Madsen turn into a bumbling amateur a year later?

The pictures showed up in his secure mail app 10 minutes later. Nik was so agitated, he ignored them initially.

When he finally opened them, he shrugged. They showed Madsen at two restaurants, each time eating with a woman. The first woman was a bit frumpy, older than Madsen, an aunt maybe. They appeared to be meeting at some kind of theme park. *Oh, ya, read the note. Tivoli, yesterday afternoon.* The second woman was just short of stunning, dressed in black, drinking wine and seeming to enjoy herself. Madsen, too, seemed happy in the evening shots. There was no record of a girlfriend in any of Nik's material on the player.

There were a few blurry shots of Madsen and the black dress coming out of the restaurant and getting into a cab. And then a few blurrier shots of the back of the cab driving through traffic.

Scrolling down, Nik found clear enough shots of both women to run them through the firm's facial recognition program. Garfunkel had paid a substantial sum to acquire the technology, primarily to use at the casinos it owned around the world. A handful of sharps were banned from gambling at Garfunkel properties, simply because they were so good at beating the system in one game or another. If the Garfunkel brain trust couldn't figure out how they were beating the odds so consistently, they just banned them from their casinos. There was no constitutional right to enter a casino. Persistent sharps, banned from other casinos as well, would disguise themselves to sneak in. The software was very good at looking through a heavy beard and sunglasses.

Nik loaded the best two photos of the women and clicked 'Go'. Somewhere in the cloud, a mainframe whirred while Nik waited. After five minutes, a ding indicated the software had matched one of the photos. Nik waited to hear a second ding and continued working on over/under totals for that weekend's crop of Premier League fixtures. He had worked his way through the entire schedule and was about to tackle the crappy MLS playoff matchups, but there still was no second ding. Even if the system couldn't match a face, it dinged with a report.

He had to leave in 15 minutes to meet Lola on time. So he closed his laptop, on which he conducted legitimate Garfunkel business, and focused again on the facial recognition. At first, he didn't understand what he was looking at. When it dawned on him, he could only sit in stunned silence, staring at the screen. He felt a wee bit nauseous as he read the same name under both pictures, a single match as far as the software was concerned: Elizabeth Catalano, legal counsel, Association of Tennis Professionals (ATP).

"Humph, got a minute?" he texted his fellow partner, sitting four offices down the hall. "Come in here, fast."

It took Humph one minute to arrive and about 20 seconds

to grasp what Nik was showing him. "Holy shit. That's a problem."

Nik had left Humph sitting in his office, mouth agape when he dashed out and headed to the restaurant. Arriving late, his head was still there, the challenge of motivating Madsen now compounded by his meeting with an ATP lawyer.

"Show me what you do in here."

Lola's voice snapped him back to the present, where his girlfriend was lying provocatively on his sofa, waiting to hear why they were there.

He sat next to her and she rested her head on his lap, looking up expectantly.

"Lola, I love you. I really do. I want to tell you about my life, my job, but if I do that, you…well…you might not like everything you hear. I've been scared about that for a long time now."

"Well, now you're scaring me. Just tell me, OK?"

Nik started by talking about his father and their mutual love of betting on horses. He'd never divulged much about his childhood, glossing over his nifty system of skimming cash from his Uncle Fritz and hiding it in trees and random bank accounts. This time, he told her everything, explaining how he stole from his uncle and how he used the money to invest in Garfunkel.

"You were a pretty smart kid," she said, admiringly. She also hoped that was the sum total of the bad stuff he had been afraid to tell her. Hope as she might, she was pretty sure there was more.

For the next 15 minutes, Nik revealed more about Garfunkel's inner workings than he ever had to anyone. There were partners who knew less about what Nik actually did for the company than Lola would when he finally wrapped up his presentation.

He was terrified she would bolt from the office and never

speak with him again. Call the cops maybe. If she did that, she would become a problem the firm had to address. Nik wouldn't take an active role, but he knew her life would be ruined, if not ended, if she reported what she'd just learned to the authorities. His terror was alloyed, strangely, with relief. Whatever happened, part of him was just happy to no longer be keeping the secret, no longer screening her from so much of his life.

She sat up half way through his explanation, pulling back but still listening intently. When he stopped talking, he sat beside her and reached for her hand. She kept it firmly on her lap and looked straight ahead, saying nothing. He could not read her.

"Did you know that's what this place was when you invested?" she finally asked.

"Uh huh, ya."

"And it's running the way you thought it would. I mean, you're doing what you always planned?"

"In general, ya. I didn't know a lot about how things would work or what we'd have to do to keep it going. It was all new to me."

"I'm going to ask you something, and you have to be honest. No screwing around, OK? I need to know this."

He leaned forward, feeling light-headed. "OK, promise."

"Have you ever killed anyone?"

He laughed briefly, until he noticed she wasn't smiling. "No. No. I swear to you I have never killed anyone. I couldn't. I hope you know that."

"OK, not personally, but have you made it happen, like in a movie or something? I can't believe I'm asking you this."

"No. Again, no. We try to persuade people."

Although he was determined to be honest, he decided not to mention that Vasquez had arranged to burn down Sergei Ivanov's house as a means of persuasion. *Why confuse things?*

"OK, that's good I guess. I think I believe you. I want to, I know that," she said. "What about all this? If the police knew about what you're doing, would you go to jail? Is it that kind of thing or is it more like being behind on your taxes, or something white collar like that?"

"Well, you never know until it happens, but I think it's safe to assume jail. Probably for a while. We're definitely breaking the law. Which is why I've never told you this stuff. I don't want to make you complicit."

"I'm not complicit," she said defiantly. "I haven't done a thing wrong."

"Of course not, but now that you know, if things went bad, if police were snooping around, you could be in trouble. Again, that's why I wanted to keep you out, to protect you in a way."

"You lied to me to protect me?"

"Well, sort of, ya. I didn't really lie to you, but OK, I know, I didn't give you the whole truth either. That's absolutely true. Yes, no doubt."

As he stammered, she leaned against him once again, pulling him close.

"I'm not saying it's OK that you're breaking the law. I'm not, OK? But honestly I'm thrilled you finally told me. You've never opened up like this." Pulling him tighter still, she whispered, "I love you. Can we fuck on this sofa?"

Chapter 36

The answer was an emphatic yes. By the time Nik had walked the 10 steps to lock the door, Lola had removed her blouse and skirt. Her lace bra and panties were the same jet black as her 4-inch heels, a detail that popped briefly into Nik's mind as she walked toward the door and wrapped her arms around him.

Together they removed his violet tie and unbuttoned his shirt. She handled the pants alone, releasing his belt and zipper so they fell to the ground. Despite looking ridiculous, his dark socks juxtaposed with his pasty white calves did not slow them down. For all its softness and beauty, the leather sofa was cold on bare skin, and their skin was nothing but bare.

Nik found an afghan in a drawer and spread it hastily on the sofa. Lola looked at it with bemusement, then reached down provocatively and ripped it off, as though removing a table cloth while leaving the dishes and glassware in place. She flapped it once like a bedsheet before spreading it and herself on the ground. Facing down, she lifted her ass in the air and looked back over her shoulder to see the look on Nik's face.

It was a look of animal excitement, and he wasted no time joining her on the floor. They spent the rest of the evening consummating what amounted to a new level in their relationship. They weren't exactly Bonnie and Clyde, not yet, but they reveled in their newly shared secret and eventually worked their way onto the sofa after all.

Nik had spent all night at his office many times, but never like this. At 6:00 that morning, they woke to the sound of someone trying to open the locked door, nose to the frosted glass. The cleaning staff worked early in the morning, between shifts and had never been stymied from entering Nik's office.

"Good morning," Lola purred, rolling back on top of Nik and bringing him back to life with her right hand. "How are you feeling?"

The cleaners moved on and it was another 20 minutes before Lola allowed Nik to fire up the Transformer espresso machine. While he tended to it like an American dad grilling on the 4th of July, she jumped into the shower attached to his office. When she emerged, wrapped in a towel, they sipped their coffees and slowly got dressed, smiling like newlyweds the whole time.

She turned down the Jordan's Frusli raisin and hazelnut bar he scrounged from his desk, the only food he could offer. Instead, she had a second coffee while they waited for the car he summoned. When it arrived at the fortified front door, he made something of a show of escorting her downstairs, past dozens of interested onlookers, and conspicuously kissing her goodbye. As her car departed, he walked back toward his office, for the moment unconcerned about Tobias Madsen, the ATP lawyer or whatever bare knuckles stunt Vasquez and her henchmen had perpetrated on some unsuspecting athlete in the last 48 hours.

Chapter 37

Catalano's decision to stay in Copenhagen for the funeral was made simpler by the condition of her ankle after her fall. Despite the best efforts of hotel staff to help her ice it, the joint had swollen to twice its normal size by the next morning. She winced as she put her weight on it getting out of bed. There was also a bump on the back of her head, where a cobblestone had stopped her fall.

She recalled falling and seeing headlights whiz past, but much of the next hour was a blur. Madsen had walked her into the hotel and summoned help from worried staff. She remembered waking at some point in the night to discover the bag of ice taped to her ankle had melted and soaked one corner of the bed.

Half asleep, she kicked off the bag and pushed herself over to the dry side of the King size bed. She also remembered taking a lot of Advil.

As she leaned on the wall for support, she saw a note Madsen had left on the bedside table – essentially a business card. He had left his name, phone number and address.

It was next to her phone, which she had not remembered to charge. With its last 8 per cent of power, it alerted her to 46 emails and texts that had arrived since dinner. On her way back from the bathroom, she hobbled over to the desk where her laptop was plugged in and ready to go.

She punched '7' on the hotel phone to order breakfast, then dragged a chair over and situated it next to the desk. She managed to lift her right leg onto the chair so it stretched out and took the pressure off her ankle. Then she opened her computer and started to consider the possibility someone had tried to kill her the night before. She'd never had a thought like that, and her whole body went clammy as a result.

Her next thought was almost as depressing. She wouldn't be able to play tennis the following Wednesday as planned and probably for some time beyond that. *If I can't play, I might as well be dead.* She laughed at herself and scrolled to the starting point of the messages.

A handful were from Morton Reid, still in Florida and anxious to hear about her meeting with Madsen. She started to type, then ditched the idea and lifted the hotel phone. For a moment, she considered whether her phone could be bugged. Hell, someone could be hacking into all her communications, but what could she really do about it?

"Mort? I know it's late there, sorry."

"Uhhhhh, Liz?" The voice on the other end cracked.

"Oh, you were sleeping. I thought I might get you before you went to bed."

"At 1:30? Whatever. Forget it. What's up?"

It took her almost 10 minutes to recount both Madsen meetings and the strange way her evening had ended. Reid didn't catch everything the first time as he struggled to wake up.

"Geez Liz, that's scary. Are you alright?"

"My ankle's not great, to be honest. But I'm OK otherwise," she said, choosing not to mention the throbbing neck pain she had started to notice since waking up. "I'm gonna stay for his mother's funeral tomorrow and then figure out what's next. I have a few kernels of a plan rolling around in my head. I need today to think more about it. Then I'll call you again. Maybe after 8 a.m. your time."

"Alright, send me anything else you think of. I'll bring Nigel up to speed and see if he has some ideas. The one thing I can think of right away is that you need some protection over there. You're clearly in danger."

"I'm only here another day or two. If that car had wanted me dead, I'd be dead Mort. I know that sounds dramatic, but I'm really OK. We can't risk spooking Madsen."

A knock at her door divided her attention, and she quickly said good bye and hung up. "Coming, coming," she yelled while she gently stood up and dragged her leg along to open the door.

"Morning maam, your breakfast."

She set up shop at the desk once again, replacing her laptop with the tray of coffee, eggs and pastries. The coffee tasted great and helped wash down three extra strength Advil. She was two forkfuls into the eggs, when there was another knock on her door, locked but no longer bolted. It was the kind of quiet, probing knock she knew from spy movies, the kind the bad guy uses before reaching into his coat for a device that magically picks the lock and allows him to open the door with an ominous gloved hand.

She pulled herself up once again, relying as before on the wall to keep her upright. Armed with a fork and a furrowed brow, she limped to the door and looked out the fisheye peep hole.

Another knock. Something was covering the peep hole. She tensed and reached for the bolt.

"Liz? Are you in there? It's Tobias. I don't want to wake you, but I brought you some food."

He lowered the bag of danishes from the peep hole, revealing a distorted view of his smiling face. For a split second, Liz thought of watching tennis matches televised from outer courts, where there is just one wide angle camera and all the images are distorted. Then she opened the door, invited Madsen in, turned to walk ahead of him and tripped over her boots, askew by the door where she had left them the night before.

"Damn it, my ankle."

Chapter 38

No one needed to tell Gil that Sergei Ivanov was Russian. At 6'2" with straight blonde hair, he looked like the villain from an 80s action movie. On the court, he could be menacing when things were clicking. As Sam prepared the room for guests, just as she had done the day before in a different room for a girls-only meeting, Gil found Sergei on YouTube.

"He was a real prospect," he yelled out in Sam's general direction. "South Alabama is a good school."

When she didn't respond he tried a different tack.

"Ya, good school. Probably one of the best coaches in the country. Better than anyone in the Big 10, that's for sure."

She smirked and continued arranging fruit, cheese and crackers on the fanciest paper plates she had found at Harris Teeter an hour earlier. There was beer and wine in the fridge. She cracked open a bottle of Blue Moon, took a sip and walked the bottle to Gil on the couch.

"I guess that's why you got in to a Big 10 school, huh? Their standards aren't quite as high."

"What an awful thing to say about Ohio State," he smiled as he took the bottle from her.

To an outsider, the banter would have appeared normal, but they both knew it was masking their nerves. Gil was just nervous in general about what was about to happen. Sam was doubly nervous, unsure of how the meeting would go and also about Gil's reaction to what she recognized as a rash decision to get involved in something that was none of their business.

Gil's nerves were not calmed when YouTube took him

to a related video of the Ivanov's house going up in flames two months earlier. "Hey babe, if we had a house and it was burning down, do you think our neighbors would stand around taking videos or maybe try to put it out?"

The Ivanovs were due at 6:00. Showing up early for a party is less popular than double-dipping chips. But with the tension building, everyone would have been OK had they done so. The chances of that were low, however, given their own machinations prior to the meeting.

Sergei understood his wife needed to confide in someone. He could see a difference in her already from the day before. But he was terrified to share their secret with anyone, especially a complete stranger. It might even be worse than a complete stranger. Gil Pence was a very good player taking his last shot at making the Tour. Would he hesitate to sabotage an opponent to reach his goal? *Who knows? Had Svetlana thought of that before she invited these strangers into our world?*

Svetlana was the only one of the four who was more excited than nervous. She had high hopes that something would change if they confided in Sam and Gil. That was as far as her thinking had gone, but it was enough to make her hopeful. She checked again that the wine she found that morning at Harris Teeter was cooling in the fridge. She put an empty bottle beside her purse to remind her to grab the cold bottle on the way out.

At last it was time to make the 10-minute drive to the Hampton Suites, cold wine bottle in tow. At the door, the women greeted each other like sisters at a reunion, introducing their new boyfriends to each other.

"You changed rooms?" Svetlana asked, confused.

"I was staying with my father, ah, his coach. It's unusual, but sometimes I stay away to, you know, keep him focused on his tennis."

They all laughed nervously, most especially Sergei who thought that was a terrible idea.

When everyone had drinks and had admired Sam's work with fruits and cheese, Sam kicked things off by recapping events of the previous day, including her bungled surveillance work.

"Sergei," she said, wrapping up. "I know you've just met us. Here's what I want to get across. If we can help you in some way, we are willing. That's all."

With that, she lifted her wine glass. "To new friendships and creative solutions."

"I will drink to that," Sergei said, draining his beer and fetching another.

They ordered pizza and talked about the paths that delivered them to this point in their tennis careers. With little else in common, Gil and Sergei bonded over the frustration both had felt in not fulfilling what they considered to be their potential. In college, both fully expected to become full-fledged ATP players, winning tournaments and sniffing around a Top 20 ranking. As different as their lives had been, the failure to reach those heights was something they shared.

They had been expectations, more than dreams. Coaches, friends and family acted as though it were just a matter of time before it happened. They worked hard and never took it for granted, but the shift in their mindset from expecting, to hoping, to now -- taking one last shot -- was difficult.

"OK, you were injured," Sergei said, four beers into the evening. "That is bad and set you back, for sure. But did anyone ever burn down your fucking house?"

Without thinking, Gil laughed and shot back, "Not yet."

More so than the assortment of fruit and cheese, served on little napkins featuring old ladies uttering wine puns, the exchange broke the remaining tension and set the tone for a night that stretched well into the next day.

Well after midnight, Sergei mentioned the money his faceless blackmailers had deposited in a secret account.

"And you've never touched it? Never even looked at it?" Sam asked, amazed.

"Nope, never."

"Until tonight," Gil said excitedly. "Come on, let's have a look."

"I don't even know how to access it, off-hand."

"I do," Svetlana said quietly, from the opposite couch.

"What? We agreed, never ever."

"I know, but when that madman attacked us, I realized we were never going to escape this. We need to get ahead of them somehow."

"And so you went into the account? Why? How does that help?"

Sam and Gil sat stone silent, barely breathing, and exchanged a look that said, *Maybe we shouldn't be here for this.*

"I needed to know where we stood, with everything. The money is a part of that. If they're going to take our house and maybe take tennis away from us, what have we got? I had to know. I had to look."

Sergei had stood up halfway through her answer. He continued pacing when she stopped talking. Three pairs of eyes followed him, back-and-forth, into the kitchen and down the hall, into the common room and back into the kitchen.

"Fuck, fuck, fuck," he muttered endlessly. While Svetlana continued to watch him, Sam and Gil shifted their attention to her, wondering if she would respond to what looked very much like an emotional breakdown occurring in Suite 502.

After three minutes that felt much longer, Sergei stopped pacing and leaned on the kitchen island, palms down, arms outstretched. He was doubled over and breathing deeply, trying to gain some composure. She approached him gently and wrapped her arms around his right arm, pulling herself close. He neither welcomed or rejected her, and they stood like that, breathing in unison, oblivious to the other couple on the couch.

She whispered in his ear and stroked his head, like a mother comforting her child after a nightmare.

"I don't know what to do," he said, finally, before breaking into tears and sobbing in great bursts on her shoulder.

We really shouldn't be here for this.

There was nowhere for Sam and Gil to escape, no right moment to evacuate and give them the privacy they clearly needed. Instead, they sat dead still, to the extent that Gil's left leg went to sleep under his crossed right leg. But he dared not shift his weight.

At long last, the Russians worked their way to the other couch, no longer two people but one emotional mass of arms and legs, moving awkwardly across the room.

Sam pushed a box of Kleenex across the coffee table between them and caught Svetlana's eye. Her unspoken question was whether she could do anything to help. Short of firing up a time machine and taking Sergei and Svetlana back to his days in college, before they even knew what match fixing was, there wasn't much Sam, or Gil, or anyone, could do.

It was nearly 1:30 and Gil was having trouble staying awake. It didn't help when Sergei's breathing revealed he had dozed off, lying on the couch where Svetlana had left him when she slipped into the bathroom.

"Let him sleep," Sam said, when Svetlana returned.

They all slept – Svetlana on the couch opposite with pillows and blankets scrounged from various closets in the room; Sam and Gil in the bedroom, their evening ending in a way they could never have predicted.

Chapter 39

There was no official title of founder at Garfunkel, but a vote of the original partners would have chosen Eva Vasquez unanimously. Those votes would have come in part from respect for her hard work and in part from fear of not voting for her.

Nothing in her background hinted at where she had landed in her 40s. As a teen, she hated sports and loved boys. Three decades later, she was consumed with sports and slept exclusively with women. In university, she imagined herself teaching or running an art gallery. Studying art history seemed like a useful step in those directions.

She had worked briefly at an art shop after graduating, but quickly moved on to other interests, among them gambling. The art shop was pivotal to her future in one important way: That was where she met Amber Rosecroft.

Rosecroft was 10 years older than her, married and wealthy. Twice a month, she came into the art shop where Vasquez worked and would spend half a day looking at various works, discussing various artists and arranging to buy and trade various art. Some of it went to her home in London; some of it went to her vacation villa in France's Loire Valley.

Vasquez soon began looking forward to the mornings Rosecroft would spend in the shop. It had taken only a few months to realize her job was boring and repetitive. Most customers, or clients as she was instructed to call them, knew nothing about art and thought of it the same way they thought of gold bullion. It was just a sexier investment.

After one particularly intriguing morning spent discussing

the merit of Jeff Koons' kitschy balloon dogs and other objects, Rosecroft invited Vasquez for lunch. They met around the corner from the gallery. Vasquez considered the meeting an extension of her job and expected the conversation to center on art. By contrast, Rosecroft was looking for someone interesting and smart in whom she could confide the various dilemmas of her life, none of which her rich, elitists friends would understand or even acknowledge.

In short order, after their salads were gone but before their pasta arrived, Rosecroft had laid out the artifice of her life. Yes, she was married, but her husband paid her no attention and was having multiple affairs. She was 36 and was 60 per cent sure she wanted to have a child. Her husband's indifference had pushed her to try other options, one of which was sleeping with women.

"They don't judge," she said quietly over the table.

The lunch ended only because Vasquez had to return to her job. The next week, they met for dinner and had no time constraints. Four hours of conversation led to dinner the following week, this time in a hotel dining room, after which they slipped upstairs to the room Rosecroft had booked, using a false name.

They continued meeting every month or so, being careful not to behave differently when Rosecroft visited the shop.

If the relationship was cathartic for Rosecroft, it was pivotal for Vasquez. She hadn't acknowledged her own roiling uncertainty about her job, her future and her sexuality. She felt clumsy and embarrassed the first night in the hotel, but Rosecroft set her at ease as no man ever had. The relaxed manner in which she undressed and invited Vasquez to do the same was a stark contrast to the exhilaration of trying something new, something she had dared only wonder about before.

After about six months of this pattern, they agreed to spend a Saturday together. Rosecroft suggested they take the train an hour outside London to Newbury Racecourse. They could watch the horses, have lunch and make a day of exploring the town. On the train, they sat together, facing rearward, with no one across from them. Vasquez slipped her hand into Rosecroft's, under a scarf, and squeezed it gently.

Rosecroft had ridden horses as a child and knew almost as much about them as she did about art. This was a surprise to Vasquez who didn't recall her ever mentioning horses before. Knowing nothing about what she was doing, Vasquez placed three bets and won enough money on the third to cover the two losses. The winning hardly mattered. Short of sex with Rosecroft, the sensation of picking a horse and then cheering madly for it was the most liberating thing she could remember doing.

With two races left on the schedule, she watched in amazement as people started to filter out the gates, toward their cars.

"Where are they going? Aren't there more races?"

"They come all the time," Rosecroft answered, without condescending. "They'll be back next week."

"We won't be," Vasquez said, laughing as she sprinted to the betting window to place bets on the final two races. With people leaving, she moved even closer to the track and screamed as loudly as she could for the entire two minutes of each race.

She lost but was smitten.

They ate at Valle D'oro, an Italian spot not far from the station, and caught the 10:00 train back to London.

"We have to do that again," she said as they kissed good night in a quiet corner of Paddington Station.

"Yes, we will," Rosecroft promised.

They never did.

Over the next four months, their schedules never meshed with the race schedules. They continued to meet for dinners, often skipping the restaurant foreplay and heading straight to their hotel. Neither ever invited the other to her home, Rosecroft because she didn't want to create suspicion and Vasquez because she was embarrassed by the modest flat she was renting.

One evening, Rosecroft suggested they meet in the park at midday. On the bus, scrolling through dozens of NSFW selfies they had taken of themselves, Vasquez was giddy. She had no idea it would be the last time she ever saw or talked to Rosecroft. She certainly had no idea her life would change forever after that day.

The moment she sat on the park bench next to her, Vasquez noticed the change. Her independent, carefree lover was reserved and disconsolate. Later Vasquez couldn't remember all the words Rosecroft had used in the next 15 minutes. But she remembered the gist of the situation: Her lover's husband was being transferred to Japan. And she was going with him.

Instantly, Vasquez saw Rosecroft for what she really was – not a risk-taker, not a free spirit, not independent at all. She played those roles within the safety of a larger edifice around her. She didn't dare leave her husband and risk being poor, or even middle class. She didn't dare acknowledge her interest in women, in Vasquez particularly. She apologized over and over, but her words suddenly were hollow.

Vasquez felt like a diversion, a plaything for a society woman who never really loved her. But amidst her grief, Vasquez felt sorry for her. Her freedom was limited and doled out by a man she didn't love, controlling the money she valued above all. She would never have children. She would never control her own destiny.

They hugged after an hour or so, and Vasquez found her

way back to the bus stop. She turned to look back at the woman on the bench and saw a diminished figure, a pathetic woman for whom she suddenly had little respect or affection.

She deleted the pictures on the way home, clicking yes to ensure they were erased from her cloud account as well. She removed her from her contacts list and deleted their texts. Because their relationship had been secret, she didn't have to comb through dozens of social media settings pages to remove her. By the time the bus arrived at her stop, she had deleted Rosecroft from everything but her memory.

After a few weeks, the pain of losing a companion had been replaced by a fierce determination to never allow herself to be boxed in the way Rosecroft had been. Vasquez wanted to be truly independent, reliant on no one and fully in charge of her own life. That's what she took away from her year with Amber Rosecroft – that and a fascination with gambling on horses that soon spread to other sports and events, leading her to create a whole new world, one she could control.

She stayed at the art shop only long enough to create a new plan. It included working a second job at a PR firm, planning and hosting charity events and galas. It wasn't too far removed from her work at the art shop; indeed, she saw some of the same people in both spheres. She even recognized some of the most prominent gala goers from descriptions Rosecroft had given, as they giggled in bed and laughed at them. She moved into an even smaller, less expensive flat and saved more than half of her income from the two jobs. She also took on private jobs, consulting with the rich and clueless about their art collections.

Whenever she could, she researched the gambling world. She started with horses but quickly moved into other sports. She found a bookie and pestered him with questions. When he told her to sod off, she found another who had more patience, partially, she knew, because he thought if he answered her questions he might eventually find his way into her bed. She let him believe that while she squeezed him for every nugget of information he had about sports gambling in Britain.

When there was nothing left to learn from him, she bought him 12 bottles of Harvey's Sussex Best Bitter, his favorite beer, and attached a note.

"Thanks for everything Carl. You're a great teacher. And just so you don't think you missed out on anything, I like girls. Love, Eva."

She left them on his doorstep early one morning and disappeared from his life. She wanted neither a long goodbye nor a bunch of questions about what she planned to do next. A decade later, when the Guardian did a story about the rise of British sports books and their influence around the world, he saw a quote from someone named Eva Vasquez. He'd never known her last name, but he figured it had to be her. "Cheers to you, Eva," he said under his breath at the pub that night.

In that decade, she and four partners had built Garfunkel into a medium-sized sports book. It was not big enough to sponsor a stadium or Premier League football club, but it was profitable immediately and employed a cadre of programmers to make sure its online presence was first rate.

From the start, however, the public part of the business was a front. Garfunkel had been designed, from the ground up, to fix matches and shave points. That was the real profit center. A low profile for the legal side of the business was essential.

The arrangement could be compared to a legitimate investment advisor who was running a Ponzi scheme behind a curtain of legitimacy. Except Garfunkel's scheme was not destined to collapse of its own weight. In fact, it continued to grow every year, as the same programmers who made the website hum found new, more complex ways of capitalizing on fixed matches all over the world.

And under her leadership, Garfunkel had become very good at squeezing athletes to fix matches. For all the trouble Tobias Madsen was causing Nik, he was just one of about 100 athletes the company could rely on to lose a game or influence a score when needed. In addition to tennis and European football, they played everything from basketball to American football, cricket to darts. Yes, darts. It was impossible to tell if a player missed a treble-20 and hit the single-1 – known as a nail – to lose a leg and ensure the underdog bet won big.

Garfunkel had so many athletes under its control, Nik might very well have jettisoned Madsen if he couldn't find a new lever after the player's mother died. But the meeting with a WTA lawyer changed all that. He could not ignore Madsen, and he had to let the partners know what was going on. He wasn't looking forward to Vasquez's reaction.

Chapter 40

The conference room dwarfed the trio sitting at one end of its enormous, oval-shaped table. It wasn't even the largest conference room at the ATP headquarters in London, but it provided both privacy and a secure video link system.

Morton Reid and Nigel Clancy had flown back to London a day early to meet with Catalano. She was now sporting a heavily wrapped ankle and a cane. Happy to take the shorter flight to London, she would rest up for a couple of days before flying home to Florida.

"How bad is it?" Reid asked, as she sat down and slung her leg onto one of the 21 empty chairs circling the table and struggled to get comfortable.

"I've cut down the Advil quite a bit, so I guess that's a good sign," she joked. "The physio who wrapped it for me was pretty sure it's just a sprain, but I'll get it checked when I get home."

Clancy only nodded, anxious to get into the substance of the meeting. He and Reid had gone over Catalano's lengthy recap of her time with Madsen, so there was no need for a play-by-play account of her exploits. She stressed her belief in Madsen's sincerity and determination to help – one factor she wasn't sure her report brought home.

To illustrate her point, she connected her laptop to the giant screen on the long wall of the room and up popped Tobias Madsen, from Copenhagen. Three days had passed since his mother's funeral, and the inherently unflattering Skype image did nothing to hide the strain on his face. His voice, however, was strong and boomed through the half dozen speakers embedded in the ceiling of the room.

"Hello Tobias," Catalano said. "I'd like to introduce you to Morton Reid, head of the Integrity Unit, and our associate, Nigel Clancy."

"Hello," he answered. "Thank you for setting this up."

"We are the ones who should be thanking you, Mr. Madsen," Reid said. "Liz told us about the ordeal you've been through with tennis, and then your mother. We're very sorry about her passing."

"Yes, thank you. It's been a challenging time, that's for sure. Please call me Tobias."

"Tobias, we'd like to ask you about some possible approaches we could take to catch these gamblers who've been threatening you," Clancy said, pushing his chair closer to the laptop camera. "Liz told us you're anxious to help us do that."

"Most certainly. I want to get this behind me and resume my career. So, yes, the answer is yes."

"That's good to hear," Clancy said. "Let me start by asking if you have a way of signaling your contact. How do you communicate?"

The question prompted a lengthy recounting of the day Tobias was approached by the gambler and his menacing partner. Much of what he said was in Catalano's report, but the trio let Madsen finish his story. Clancy, in particular, was looking for inconsistencies.

"You're our only link to this kind of gambling organization," Reid said, stretching the truth slightly. There was no need to tell Madsen about the leaks the TIU was receiving from a gambling organization they hadn't identified. He certainly was the only player who'd ever offered to help catch the bad guys.

"We'd like to do whatever we can to entice them to reach out to you again."

"Well, I think I know how you can do that," Madsen answered, flatly. "Put me in some big tournaments. Get me some sponsor exemptions to tournaments with bigger purses. Of course, yes, that would be good for me, but I'm quite certain that would bring them out of the shadows. They couldn't resist using me again."

"I was thinking about something along the same lines," Clancy said. "Where were you thinking?"

"How about the French?" Madsen asked without cracking a smile.

"The French *Open*?" Reid choked. "We can't do that. You have to qualify."

"Yes, I know. So how about the quallies? You could get me in those, right? Or a wildcard? That would put me right in the main draw."

"If we could do that, you think they would contact you?" Clancy said, less worried about the logistics than Reid.

"That tournament is less than a month away," Reid said, more worried about the logistics than Clancy.

"I know, but we have to do something soon," Madsen said. "I'm in limbo here."

"Alright," Catalano said. "Let's say for argument's sake we can do this. Or at a big tournament later in the summer. I dunno, maybe Wimbledon."

"Wimbledon?" Reid moaned. "Seriously?"

"Let's say we somehow make it happen," Catalano continued. "Then what? How do we snare them? We can't just get him in the tournament and then watch as they cash in on more illegal bets."

"You're right," Madsen said. "They would only get involved if they thought they could manipulate me. Or someone else in the tournament. Let's be honest, they might have other athletes in the French or Wimbledon. I'd have to agree to their demands, then do the opposite, so they lose big and are angry. That might flush them out."

"Or get you killed," Catalano added.

"He's right," Clancy said. "Whatever tournament we choose, what we're talking about is using Mr. Madsen here as bait. It's imperative we are organized and ready for them to keep him safe and to catch them when we get the opportunity. It feels like our best chance ever to catch some of these guys."

"It feels like a chance to get Tobias hurt, or worse, and to deliver millions of dollars of payoffs to the gamblers," Reid said, depressed by his own pessimism.

"You would get the police involved too, right?" Madsen asked.

"Ah, we haven't talked about that yet," Clancy said, quickly placing his hand on Reid's knee to discourage him from correcting his lie. "We'd certainly look into that."

Madsen had asked the very question the trio had debated hotly by phone the night before their meeting. Reid wanted to get Interpol and local authorities involved in their investigation. Clancy was dead set against the idea, believing the more widely they distributed information the more likely the gamblers would be tipped off.

"We shouldn't trust anyone right now," he said. "Gamblers are always one step ahead of the law; several steps ahead of us. The only success we've even had with this unit is because someone leaked us information, no doubt for their own purposes. On our own, we've come up with zero. They're always ahead of us. That only happens if they have contacts who tip them off. We can't let this information go beyond the three of us. That's the only way to finally surprise them."

It had been a persuasive case the previous evening. But when the plan evolved to luring the bad guys into the open at Roland Garros so they could be caught, Reid felt thoroughly unqualified.

"How can we use him as bait without having dozens of cops positioned to help if something happens?" he asked when Madsen logged off and left the meeting. "Never mind keeping him alive, which we must do. How about catching the bad guys? How are the three of us going to do that?"

Clancy stood and began walking the long oval around the table. He grabbed an apple and chomped on it between sentences. If there had been any doubt about which person in the room had worked in National Intelligence for South Africa, it evaporated before he had exposed the core of the apple.

"To catch these guys, we need them to show up, in person, at a location we know about," he started. "We need Madsen there to get into a big tournament and then tell them to fuck off when they lean on him to throw his match. Maybe he demands a meeting, maybe he's so belligerent they come to see him. Either way, that's when we move, not during the tournament when they're watching their millions ping through a dozen countries into some account we can't touch or even find."

With each declaration, the volume of Clancy's voice rose. Apple pulp flew from his mouth as he reached a crescendo, slamming his fist into the giant table. His wry detachment, so effective in Mobile playing the role of stumblebum, was gone.

"Uhhh," Catalano began, breaking an awkward silence. "What about this? What if he agrees to throw a match but doesn't? Somehow fakes like he's gonna follow their orders but double-crosses them? That would get their attention."

"Are we just trying to think of ways to get him killed?" Reid asked. "Come on, that puts a target on his head. You've got the Russian couple, what's their names, whose house burned down? We haven't found one connection with gamblers, not one. He seems to be squeaky clean, but that is goddam suspicious. If he's not even involved with them and his house burns down, what could happen to Madsen? We have to think about that. And don't say 'collateral damage' OK? I'm not alright with that."

"I wasn't going to say that," Clancy said, tossing Reid an apple. "I was going to say we should ask Madsen which approach he prefers. If he's OK double-crossing them, it has the added benefit of hurting them financially, at least a little bit, which is OK by me."

"Whatever way we do it, we're dangling him out there," Catalano said. "Reid's right. We need to protect him."

"We will," Clancy said, his voice calm once again. "We most certainly will, but we'll handle things ourselves. I know some people we can trust to keep a secret."

Chapter 41

The first thing he noticed was the color of the clay. Yes, it was red -- as advertised, as he'd always seen on TV. But in person, it was deeper and more vibrant. Contrasted with the forest green of the court walls and surrounding seats, it seemed almost alive. The care and management of the clay suggested it was indeed a living, breathing entity. Before, during and after matches, crews worked feverishly to revive the surface with a loving mixture of water and grooming, as though each court were a thoroughbred about to run the Kentucky Derby.

He was standing along the sidelines of Court Suzanne Lenglen, wearing his player's I.D. as much out of necessity as pride. Every 20 steps an official of some kind stopped him to ask who he was. When he indicated he was a player in the tournament, reactions ranged from surprise to indifference. After several such interactions, he tried a new tact, just for fun.

"I'm Tobias Madsen, defending champion of the Quanzhou International."

That drew just as many blank stares, although one fan who overheard him immediately asked for a selfie – which he happily gave.

This was as close as he was going to get to the Lenglen court. Scanning his surroundings, he couldn't believe this was only the *second* largest court on the grounds. It held 10,000 fans, but Court Philippe Chatrier held nearly 15,000. Despite his player's I.D. and Quanzhou title, he would not be playing on either of these courts. After enjoying a free espresso in the player's lounge, he wandered to the outer courts and was still charmed by the atmosphere. The red clay received no less attention from the grounds crew and was no less impressive.

He had arrived as early as he was permitted, four days before play began. After checking in and getting his improbable player I.D., he was assigned a practice court. The ticket, printed in French and English, made no sense to him: Lagardere Racing Club, 10:30 a.m.

With so few practice courts at the rather crowded Roland Garros venue, tournament organizers assigned practice sessions at nearby facilities. Despite its name, Lagardere was one such place, the furthest away, requiring a cab ride of at least 10 minutes to get there.

Madsen laughed. Even at some racing club, he would be the least recognized player. He practised every morning, hitting with eager volunteers, and returned to the main venue every afternoon. He soaked it all up and wished his mother could have seen him there, maybe even sat in one of the green seats and watched him play. In his imagination, his mother was young and healthy, as she had been when she signed him up for tennis lessons and pushed him to practise and improve.

As always, when he thought of his mother, he thought of the gamblers. They crowded out the good memories like a tumor pushing against his brain. There hadn't been a day since they first approached him that he didn't think about them for at least a moment. Some days, it was a fleeting thought that he could dispense with quickly. Other days, it was his central focus, a spiral he could only break with a sleeping pill and 10 hours in bed. He knew the dangers of working with Catalano and company to help catch them, but he had no choice. He could not continue living under the pressure, guilt and uncertainty.

Since Quanzhou, there hadn't been a lot of contact. But

then again, he hadn't played a lot of tennis. Burying his mother and meeting with the tennis cops had taken most of his time. In mid-May, he had entered a Challenger event in Bordeaux. His French Open wildcard wasn't official just yet, but either way he needed to play again. Bordeaux would either be a tune-up for Paris or simply another chance to gain points toward someday getting to Paris on his own, following the legitimate path.

No sooner had he entered Bordeaux than he heard from them. Once again it was an untraceable text, this time telling him to play his first match straight up but lose the second set of the next match. It was a bigger tournament with bigger names than Quanzhou, so the gamblers couldn't wait for him to reach the finals to bet on his fixed match. The second round would do.

As it turned out, they couldn't resist the third round either, this time telling him to lose the 7th game in each set, regardless of the score or match situation. He hated being forced into it as much as ever, but he was also relieved they were still using him. If they bit in Bordeaux, they would pounce in Paris.

As the 7th game of all three sets approached, Nik swung into action, live-betting against Madsen, even when he was serving and leading in the set. In fact, that was the ideal time to bet, when everyone else betting game-by-game assumed Madsen would hold serve as he had done most of the day. The odds against him losing his serve stretched longer with every game he held, so by the 7th game of the third and deciding set, with Madsen leading 4-2, Nik bet the equivalent of €8-million around the world, that he would lose the game.

The odds were 4-to-1; the logical bet was that Madsen would hold serve and go on to win the match. By going against Madsen, Nik collected €20-million when the player inexplicably double-faulted twice in the game and hit two forehands just wide.

Oblivious to the forces working against his opponent, the young Austrian across the net was encouraged by Madsen's terrible service game and made a final push to win the match. He held his serve to draw even, 4-4. Then he broke Madsen again – this time without any double faults – and controlled his nerves long enough to serve it out, 6-4 in the third set. His best result ever.

The following day, when the French Open wildcards were announced, few people took notice of the name Tobias Madsen. There was one young Austrian player, however, who did a double-take when he saw the list. "Hey, I just beat that guy. He can't serve with the pressure on. Why'd *he* get a wildcard?"

The answer went to the highest levels of international tennis. As Reid had suggested, the French Tennis Federation was not inclined to hand out a valuable wildcard slot to a middling player on the Challenger Circuit, even if he had vanquished his opponents in Quanzhou that summer. Furthermore, the members of the committee in charge of running qualifier rounds and inviting wildcards did not appreciate being overruled by the higher-ups in their own Federation.

"Your interference is an outrage," wrote Rene Cortous, the proud and heretofore independent head of the selection committee, in an email.

The official answer was that the Federation was swapping a spot in Paris for a spot in New York later that year at the U.S. Open for an aspiring French player. Although it was against the spirit of the selection rules, that kind of trade was common among tournament organizers. But in this case, Cortous pointed out with vigor, the player was Danish. Why would the Americans make a deal to get him into the draw?

The answer – that it was part of a multi-country deal

involving several players – was accompanied by another message: The matter is closed.

Chapter 42

The morning after their impromptu sleepover in Savannah, Gil and Sam had breakfast with Sergei and Svetlana. After 10 minutes of stilted conversation, Svetlana broke the ice.

"That was awkward last night, huh?"

"Noooo, not at all," Gil joked. "That's our typical evening to be honest."

"Look, I'm sorry," Sergei said, between sips of coffee. "As you saw, the pressure of all this is getting to me. But there's no reason you have to see it up close like that."

"It's a weird life, huh?" Sam said. "I mean, we're all out here because we have to be, but mostly everyone wants to be somewhere else. You're all competing with each other at the tournaments and for a chance to move up. You can't have friends."

Gil caught her eye and smiled. He knew where she was going and he was, as always, amazed by her instincts and generosity. His initial reaction was to avoid the Russians entirely. Whatever was going on could threaten his tennis dream and their lives, potentially. But Sam insisted they offer some form of help. It was a humanitarian gesture, and he couldn't say no. But he still feared the consequences of being dragged into a situation about which they knew nothing.

"You've got the other person, but that's not enough," Sam continued. "It puts a strain on the relationship. You need friends out here. Not just the person you're sleeping with."

"Or next to on the other couch," Svetlana added, prompting a reluctant smile from Sergei.

"Even when things are going well, you need friends," Sam

said. "And let's face it, things are not going well for you right now. Let's all have dinner again tonight. See where it goes. I think it could be good for all of us."

They ate at Cotton & Rye, snagging a private booth and shooing away the server whenever he attempted to give them the bill. When they were the last people in the restaurant, they finally settled up. The Russians treated, still drawing down their insurance settlement.

By the end of the evening, the quartet had hatched a plan of sorts. At its most modest, it laid out a schedule of tournaments Gil and Sergei would play in the months ahead, allowing the couples to travel together some of the time.

At its most ambitious, it dared to imagine they could unshackle Sergei and Svetlana from the grip of the gamblers, delivering justice and writing a happy ending to their tale of woe. The details of the ambitious part were somewhat hazy, but after their evening of seafood and wine, they firmly believed they would sharpen the plan as they travelled together that summer.

"To us," Sam said, lifting her glass as they prepared to leave. "We can do this."

"I'm not sure what *this* is," Gil added. "But I'm willing to go along to find out."

They toasted themselves and planned to meet up 10 days later in Heilbronn, Germany, site of the annual Heilbronner Neckarcup Challenger tournament.

"Heilbronner?" Gil joked. "I hardly know her."

"What?" Sergei asked.

"Ignore him," Sam said. "He thinks he's funny."

Ten days later, while Madsen was throwing games in Bordeaux, Gil and Sergei played in Heilbronn. Both won their opening match with ease. The women kept each other company watching both matches and spent time together while their men practised or took advantage of the complementary massage service – an upgrade from many Challenger events.

Gil nixed Sam's suggestion they all travel together to Venice, their last stop on the Challenger circuit before they decamped together to Paris to watch a few days of the French Open.

"They're great, but let's not push it, OK? We can meet them there, that's enough, isn't it?"

"Ya, sure. I get it," she smiled. "We'll meet them there."

Venice was a disaster from the moment they arrived – separately. The title sponsor, a chemical manufacturer, had dumped the tournament two months earlier when it declared bankruptcy. Local organizers had found a way to keep it going, but the solution relied largely on volunteers to run almost every aspect of the event. Prize money was halved, although the ATP would still award the original number of points, meaning it was still worthwhile for hungry players.

But the free massages and gourmet food choices of Heilbronner were nowhere to be found. There was great food – it was Venice after all – but the players had to pay for it themselves at the city's many restaurants and cafes.

Whether it was the disorganization or excitement of heading next to Paris, neither Sergei nor Gil played their best. Gil got to the second round, largely because his first round opponent was a local player whose parents were instrumental in keeping the tournament afloat after the sponsor disappeared. The kid was 17 and the best player at his club in Bologna, 90 minutes away. Being the best tennis player at a Bologna club was like being the best bobsledder in Jamaica, and Gil dispatched the teenager with ease, 6-0, 6-1, in 75 minutes.

When it was over, Gil was surprised to see a photographer charging toward both players as they shook hands at the net.

They had taken a routine photo after the coin toss, prior to a match. That was de rigueur, even at the Challenger level. Gil had never seen it done after the match, but he obliged and stood next to the kid while the photographer crouched and aimed. The kid held up his fingers in a V-for-Victory sign and didn't need a reminder to smile.

It was only later that someone told Gil the photographer had been hired by the kid's family to record the moment for their family photo album. It was the high point of the kid's tennis career and would remain so in perpetuity.

Sergei flamed out badly in the first round, matched up against a legit player and never focused enough to perform. "I couldn't do anything out there today," he told Svetlana as they were walking back to their hotel.

"I noticed," she said with a grin. "Does that mean you have some energy left for me tonight?"

It was a rhetorical question that he answered by tapping out a text as they continued walking. "Hey brother, on yer own for dinner tonite. Early nite here."

Gil saw it later and made his own plans for the evening, some of which bore a striking resemblance to what his new "brother" had in mind. *No wonder we're getting along so well.*

Chapter 43

"What do we know about her?"

There were still two empty seats at the Dungeon table when Eva Vasquez began the meeting with the only topic anyone there was interested in.

"And why the hell is she in Copenhagen meeting with this player? One of your players, Nik."

The last of the 9 partners found their seats as Nik began to speak. Vasquez's tone had caught him off guard, but he could certainly understand it. Having an ATP lawyer, one apparently working for the Integrity Unit, meeting with a Garfunkel athlete was a threat to everyone in the room. The Integrity Unit suddenly seemed less laughable and pathetic.

"Her name is Elizabeth Catalano. Goes by Liz. Apparently, some people call her the Queen. She was a New York lawyer who joined the ATP a few years ago as a legal counsel," he began. The partners were all looking at her photo, one of several items in identical blue folders at each seat. "She seems to have some connection with the Integrity people, but that part is not as clear. She's 47, divorced, no kids. Plays a lot of tennis."

"And?" Vasquez interjected. "What the hell is going on with her?"

"All we know for sure is she met with Madsen -- that's Tobias Madsen a player we've been using for a year or so – in Copenhagen last week. She stayed for three days and went to his mother's funeral. There's no suggestion they're romantically linked, although you never know. Madsen doesn't seem to have sex with anyone, not even himself."

"At one point, I thought we could find him a girlfriend, or boyfriend – plant someone to gain some leverage. But he's so uninterested in finding someone, that went nowhere. As far as we can tell, he's never trolled a dating site or gone on a date of any kind."

"Honestly, this could all be nothing," Nik continued. "The guy performed perfectly in Bordeaux. We haven't found a new hook since his mother died, but it could be enough to have the Quanzhou result hanging over him. It's his only big win, and if there was a hint he had thrown games, it would destroy him. The point is we made more than €20-million from Bordeaux."

"I don't know about you, but I am not willing to hope it's nothing because we don't have all the facts," Vasquez said. "Why *don't* we have all the facts by the way? I thought you had a guy in Copenhagen."

"Yes, we do. He's reliable. I don't know if we can get what we need by simply tailing them though." Nik decided to skip the part where his guy nearly ran Catalano over outside the hotel. "How about getting the hackers into this?"

The silence that greeted his question lasted several seconds until Vasquez nodded almost imperceptibly in Humphrey Cox's direction.

"We thought of that," Humph said. "One of the first things we did, last week when Nik here discovered they had met. Turned up nothing."

"I didn't realize you were doing that," Nik said, pulling up just short of annoyed.

"You had other stuff on the go. No point distracting you," Humph responded, weakly.

"Really? You thought I'd be distracted? One of the things I was doing was trying to figure out what she was doing in Copenhagen. Just like you, as it turns out."

"Relax," Vasquez said. "I told Humph to go ahead. The

plan was to get into her phone and emails, his too. You are in contact with the guy. If we got into his life, we could have seen your stuff. These guys follow every path, every trail. It was better if you didn't know."

"Hold on, did you hack into my phone?"

"No, we didn't. But we were prepared to if the hackers gave us a reason to. Turns out they didn't get shit. Couldn't even get into her phone. Someone did everything right to seal it off from prying eyes. And his phone, it's like you said, the guy has no life outside tennis. Either that, or he runs a double life we haven't detected. He's so boring, I'm not ruling it out."

"No harm done, I guess, but I'm not crazy about the secrecy. How often are the hackers poking around in our lives?" Nik pressed, surveying the table for support.

"About as often as a fucking ATP lawyer flies to Europe to meet with a player making us €50-million this year, OK? Jesus, give it a rest."

The meeting followed a more familiar pattern thereafter, with each partner reporting on the results from his stable of crooked players, some willing participants, some token protestors, and a few actively defiant. The Ivanovs fell into the latter category, still resisting pressure to throw matches, even after an encounter with the knife-wielding persuader in Italy.

"Maybe it's time to move on, cut our losses," one previously mute partner said, after Vasquez had summarized the Ivanov circumstance. On a handful of occasions in the last decade, they had cut bait with an athlete who resisted all attempts to corrupt him and moved on to a less obstinate target.

The look on Vasquez's face suggested this would not be one of those times. The harder the Ivanovs pushed back, the more determined she was to break them, like a cowboy who refuses to let a wild horse get the better of him.

Nik was not alone in thinking Vasquez had taken an unnecessary risk in burning down their house. Sending some muscle was not uncommon, but when that didn't appear to work either, it was hard to make the case for continuing. There was no risk of emboldening other athletes to push back; no one knew Garfunkel was leaning on the Ivanovs.

We should have walked away months ago.

When the meeting wrapped up after nearly two hours, Nik couldn't get out of the building quickly enough. His dinner with Lola was already late. The good news was he could be more open with her about the reason. He wasn't about to give her a copy of the minutes of the meeting – not that there were any; nothing was recorded at Dungeon meetings – but he could honestly explain he was meeting with the partners to discuss the secret part of the business. If she didn't understand completely, she had a much better idea than ever before.

As the partners filed out, some making arrangements to meet for drinks before heading home, Vasquez gestured with her index finger, pulling Humph back into the room. After he had relocked the door from the inside, she poured two whiskies and sighed. "What are we gonna do about him?"

Partners were not expected to be single or celibate, but neither were they permitted to share sensitive information with the people – always women as it turned out – they slept with. The hackers had been more successful than Humph had let on in the meeting, but it was another information program that was causing the two partners even more concern.

"She knows a lot. Too much," Humph said, flatly. "We could keep monitoring things and see if that's as far as it goes."

"Do you think that's likely?" she asked, rhetorically. "I like him too. He's a goddam savant with the numbers. But this…"

this is a real problem."

As the Garfunkel partnership expanded, a few years after Vasquez created the company, she began to worry that the firm's secret was known by too many people. All it would take was a slip by one of the partners to the wrong person, after a night of drinking, and the cops would be there the next day. Or at least, that's how she viewed it in her darkest moments. She even wondered if someone could utter something in his sleep that would reveal their secret.

So, six years earlier, Vasquez had installed a series of bugs throughout the building. Unbeknownst to most of the partners, she could listen to anything that was happening anywhere in the building. Ten years in without a whiff of scandal or police interest, the system was largely ignored. But it was always on, filling the cloud with every sound made in the building, 24 hours a day, every day of the year.

When the hackers had looked at Nik's phone, they'd followed the trail to Lola's phone, where one phrase set off an alarm. Amid an avalanche of words, "bribing the player," jolted the algorithm and produced a report. Every year or two, the system recognized a series of potentially damaging words. It had always been harmless, the equivalent of a room full of monkeys and typewriters banging away all day, occasionally forming sentences.

This time was different. A partner's girlfriend had typed "bribing the player," in a message to the partner, revealing a casual awareness of Garfunkel's secret, the very phenomenon Vasquez had always feared.

So the hackers went further and summoned the recordings from Nik's office whenever Lola had been on the premises. That was an easy thing to do because the first of her few visits was just a couple of weeks earlier.

If they felt uncomfortable listening to the private

exchanges between a partner and his lover, the hackers hid it well. They simply created the expected report, forwarded it as ordered and moved on to their next project – which could be anything, including hacking into a player's social media or getting an early look at a scheduled match so one of the partners could get a jumpstart fixing it.

Vasquez and Humph did feel squeamish listening to the recording, so they reverted to the transcript right away, getting to the alarming parts about five pages in.

"He's explaining the whole operation to her," she said, in disbelief. "He's not naming players, but he's confessing to throwing matches. My God."

"If she went to the police…" Humph's voice drifted off. "Or just blackmailed us… She has so much power over him. Over us. I can't believe he told her."

Humph was selling his disbelief hard while thinking about the times he'd been with a woman, failing by his own standards in bed, and decided to impress her by telling her who was going to win that night's football match or basketball game. He'd never been as brazen as Nik, but he was sure he'd said enough to cause a lot of trouble if any of the women had decided to pursue it.

Vasquez's mind was free of such doubts. She had never breathed a syllable of anything revealing to anyone, friends, family and lovers included. Knowing things others didn't know was a powerful aphrodisiac; diminishing that power by giving away some or all the information made no sense to her, and she struggled to understand the temptation in others.

"We should talk to him."

"And say what? We bugged your office and heard you betray us. Also, your girlfriend giggles during sex."

"Maybe there's a way to warn him without saying how or what we know."

"He's a goddam genius Humph. He'll see through anything like that. And then what? Is there a chance he walks out? Even if it's just a 10 per cent chance, we can't risk it."

"I guess that's true, but isn't that a chance no matter what we do? And we have to do something, right?"

"Fraid so."

Neither would say what both were thinking. In the end, neither did. Instead, Vasquez nodded slowly, swirling and staring at the remains in the bottom of her mug. "I'll look after it. Not a word Humph. Not a word."

Chapter 44

"Are you sure you're at the right café? They have a dozen on every block. Everyone in Paris either works at one or visits one daily."

"I'm at the right place. Stop asking me questions."

Two days before he was to play his debut match at the French Open, the last thing Tobias Madsen wanted to be doing was sitting in a café waiting to meet with the gambler. But that's exactly what he was doing, understanding he wouldn't be in the tournament at all if he hadn't agreed to a plan that included this very meeting.

He put his phone on the table, screen-down, to avoid more texts from the organizer of this caper. He and his crew were stationed near the café, in various locations and guises, all monitoring the text chain Madsen was now trying to ignore.

His phone buzzed again. Then again. He gave in and flipped it over.

"New location. Strada Café, 15 mins."

Like every message he received from the gamblers, it was anonymous.

"He's moved the location to Strada. Where's that?" he texted his handlers, double-checking he wasn't replying to the gambler's text by accident.

"You're 10 minutes away. Go east on Rue de Temple."

Madsen had no idea how to do that, so instead he paid for his coffee and headed outside. When he was far enough away from the first café to feel comfortable asking for directions to another café, he did just that, using the French he'd learned as a boy in the Danish school system.

Street light poles displayed posters celebrating the French Open, with pictures of players Madsen would never get to play. Despite the stress, he grinned at the posters, and nearly approached a group of tourists who were standing below one featuring Rafa Nadal, the greatest champion in tournament history. *I could tell them I'm in the tournament, offer a picture.* He was still thinking that, when his phone buzzed yet again, this time indicating a call.

"Madsen, what the hell are you doing?"

"I'm walking to the new place."

"I told you how to get there. Why are you going that way? You're going to be late."

He ended the call without responding, but doubled his tempo and left behind the tourists who were unaware of how close they had been to an actual French Open player. He looked behind him once in a while, curious to see who was following him. The good guys obviously were if they knew what route he was taking. Were the bad guys following too? Would they sniff out the good guys?

Who am I, Jason Bourne?

The fact that he wasn't became very clear moments later as he neared the final block before the Strada Café. A man he never saw coming suddenly appeared beside him and grabbed his arm, in a subtle but firm manner. Before Madsen realized what was happening, the man steered him into an alley, into the side door of a building and down a flight of stairs.

"Who are you? What are you doing?" he asked, trying his best to sound confident and indignant.

"Relax Mr. Madsen. We're just making sure everyone is safe before we all sit down to talk. Could I see your phone for a moment?"

Madsen had no intention of handing over his phone, but his hand reflexively pushed down into his left pocket in response to the question. "Thank you sir," the man said, as he pickpocketed the device, removed its SIM card and slipped it into his coat pocket instead. "You won't need that during the meeting. But you can have it back when we're done, OK?"

Madsen could feel sweat forming on his forehead. His ears were turning bright red.

Definitely not Jason Bourne.

"Where'd he go? What happened?"

Half a dozen people, all dressed to blend in, suddenly were speaking into their lapels and listening intently on earpieces, confounded by the disappearance of Tobias Madsen. When the last of them had walked past the unannounced meeting place, observed by a man and woman who were even better at blending into a crowd, Nik appeared before Madsen and offered him a café au lait.

"It's not that we don't trust you Tobias, but we don't like to take any chances. You might have been followed, without even knowing."

As Nik began to talk, memories of their meeting in Copenhagen flooded into Madsen's mind. He'd almost forgotten what the man looked and sounded like. It had been one brief conversation a year earlier. He remembered the man's menacing sidekick from that day too and was relieved not to see him anywhere.

"First, let me assure you, you're in no danger. We'll give your phone back when we're done. Actually, we're very impressed with how you performed in Bordeaux. That was very good. Congratulations."

Madsen was in a fog. He'd wanted a meeting like this since the first time they'd forced him to throw a match. He'd planned the insults he would hurl at them as he declared the arrangement over. He'd rehearsed his threat to turn them in to some unspecified police force more than 100 times. In the best versions of his scenario, he punched one of the gamblers right in the nose before walking away, his dignity restored.

But now, his mind was in quicksand. His arms were limp. He could hardly control his bladder. Nothing was going as he'd planned. And this man just kept talking, barely above a whisper, in complete control of everything. *Where the hell is my backup? Where are the good guys?*

"It's quite an accomplishment to get into the French Open Tobias. I must admit we were surprised by that. Perhaps you were as well?"

At last he paused, waiting for Madsen to say something.

"Ah, ya," was all he could muster. *Fuck!*

"Right, so that got us to thinking about how that happened. Obviously, we understand you got a wildcard, but why? With all due respect, the Quanzhou Open isn't exactly Rome or Indian Wells, right? You know tennis better than I do, but that's my impression. You don't just win a Challenger tournament in China and pack your bags for Paris."

"I don't know. Fuck you." *Yes, said it. Ha, take that you stupid, awful man. Ha.*

"Listen, Tobias. You might not like me, but you have to admit I've been nothing but honest with you. And honestly, I understand why you hate me, hate us. I get that. Go ahead and swear at us. Get it out. When you've calmed down, you'll assess things and see it's really the best thing for you to continue working with us."

"My mother is dead. You killed her."

"Be reasonable Tobias. We didn't kill her. We helped her. That's the best clinic in Europe. Could you have gotten her in there? Of course not. We were happy to make that happen, and as I said, you've done very well for us. I'm sure you don't believe it, but we appreciate what you've done."

"I don't want your appreciation. I want my fucking life back, OK? you asshole." *That was good. That felt good. Don't think I should punch him though.*

"We could trade insults all day, I suppose, but that's boring, and you have a practice session later at the racing club, don't you? So here's the point, and I think you might even consider this good news."

"I seriously doubt it."

"Suit yourself. First thing is we have no plans to spoil your Quanzhou win or the points you've racked up at other tournaments. That's between us. Always will be so long as you don't get any stupid ideas in your head, alright? That's the first point. Second, we're taking a pass here in Paris. Think of it as a goodwill gesture. You're free to compete and do as well as you can. Win the goddam tournament for all we care, OK?"

"I have no chance of doing that, as you very well know."

"What we know is it's a little suspicious that you're in this tournament at all, which leads me to my third and final point. The best speeches make three points, don't you think? They always did that in church when I went as a kid. Three point sermons. So boring. Are you a religious man, Tobias? Never mind. The third point is this. If you ever make a move to work with the authorities or report any of this or even breathe a hint about matches you've influenced, we will indeed end this arrangement because you won't be in any shape to continue playing tennis. Is that clear? I told you I have been honest with you, and that is the most honest thing I've said here."

Madsen's small supply of courage evaporated as quickly as it had appeared. He had to fight hard to avoid crying. "I, I have to go."

"I'll assume that means you understand," Nik said, holding out his hand, palm up, behind him and receiving Madsen's phone from the phone snatcher. "Here's your phone Tobias, as promised. I think it's best if you get another SIM card.

They're easy to find at a mobile shop."

He took the phone, grudgingly, and fumbled to pocket it. "Why? Why me? That's all I want to know."

"A fair question Tobias. It might help you to know you're not the only one. There are many others. Others who are rewarded handsomely. They resist much less. You should think about that. We share the wealth, if you're willing to accept your share."

"I'm never taking your dirty money. You said I could go, so I'm leaving. Va te faire foutre."

The third man in the room, the translator if needed, had been silent until that point. He laughed at Madsen's final outburst and didn't bother to translate it.

Thirty seconds later, Madsen was outside on the busy street, feeling lightheaded. He looked back at the building where he had been and tried to memorize its appearance. Without thinking, he turned on his phone to take a picture of the place. *It worked.* Then he noticed the Wi-Fi symbol at the top. There were a dozen signals from shops all around him. He could connect to those as well without a SIM card.

When he finally connected, messages poured in, all variations on one question: Where are you?

He messaged back, reporting he was OK. "They're here. They grabbed me. Meet me at Strada. I can see it from where I am."

His Wi-Fi quit as he walked the rest of the block, but he connected again as he approached Strada. More messages scrolled in, some indicating missed calls. Many had a stupid red exclamation mark beside them, as if he needed that to know a message about his whereabouts was a high priority.

"Tobias!"

He heard his name being shouted just ahead. He didn't recognize the woman signaling him, but walked toward her anyway. With her were two equally nondescript men. All three seemed more relieved than happy to see him.

Instead of going into Strada, they led him around the corner to a white service van, where the rest of the team was camped out, frantically trying to locate Madsen using a combination of cellular triangulation and live surveillance camera feeds. Looking at one screen with a map of the area, he pointed out the building where he'd been. "Don't bother going back," he said flatly. "They're long gone. They knew everything. They're not even taking the bait. This is hopeless. I'm screwed."

Chapter 45

"We're screwed," Nigel Clancy whispered to no one in particular when the call ended. "Madsen's OK, but we're screwed."

He was sitting in Morton Reid's spacious living room. Catalano was sprawled on the sofa, her ankle nearly 100 per cent.

Reid lived there alone, 30 minutes from his London office. Catalano noticed the remaining vestiges of his ex-wife's design choices throughout the house. In the five years since they split, Reid had not so much as repainted a wall. He got rid of the photos in which she appeared and moved on, burying himself in his ATP work.

When the organization created the Integrity Unit, he was at the top of the short list to run it. He jumped at the chance to reset his career without leaving the ATP or London. When he was in Florida, he stayed at one of those hotels with a kitchen and dedicated TV room – euphemistically called a suite. It was fine for short bursts, but he always looked forward to getting home.

Clancy and Catalano had delayed their flights back to the U.S. when the trio had hatched their plan to dangle Tobias Madsen in front of the faceless gamblers in Paris. Clancy had rounded up a team of his former colleagues, all with years of experience in the intelligence service in South Africa.

The spies-for-hire came up with a plan that everyone agreed was clever because of its simplicity. Unsure of who would show up to meet Madsen or what the person or persons looked like, they coached Madsen to meet with them and stonewall them while they surrounded the place. Rather than burst in and make a big show of arresting them, the idea was to tail whomever showed up, leading them higher up the gambling hierarchy to the brains behind the organization.

"Won't they expect us to do that?" Reid had asked.

"If Madsen is convincing when he demands a meeting, they won't suspect anything," Clancy reasoned. "They don't know he's talking to us. They have no reason to think anyone will be watching."

Like a president in the situation room watching a covert operation to free hostages halfway around the world, the TIU trio had camped out at Reid's house, waiting for news from the meeting. They didn't get the live video feed presidents get in every movie. Instead, they got some sporadic texts that stopped coming moments before Madsen was to arrive at the new meeting place.

"They changed the location," Reid said, immediately ditching his plan to resist panic. "That means they know we're watching."

"No, it doesn't," Clancy said, firmly. "They are being cautious. It's an expected strategy. They would do that whether they suspected something or not."

Despite his apparent confidence, Clancy too worried when the texts stopped arriving. He dared not call to ask what was happening, and he was confident in his team's ability, but still…

"This is awful. Can't we do something?" Reid said, after about 20 minutes of no texts or updates.

"Sit tight. They're good at what they do," Clancy said, trying to convince himself as much as anyone else.

At last Clancy's cell buzzed. "Uh huh, Uh huh. Fuck. OK, conference in 30 minutes as planned."

"What do you mean, we're screwed? What happened?"

Reid shouted at a suddenly pensive Clancy.

"They grabbed up Madsen before he got to the new location. No one saw it happen, and they couldn't track his signal. They're heading back to their hotel and we'll get more information in half an hour. But the bottom line, we missed our chance."

"But you said Madsen's OK?" Catalano added. "That's good news, at least."

"Who wants a drink?" Reid asked. "Besides me, I mean. Jesus, I can't believe this."

Exactly 30 minutes later, Clancy's laptop screen filled up with the faces of Madsen and the leader of the failed operation. Even over the spotty Skype connection, Madsen's despair was obvious.

He described in all the detail he could remember what had happened over the previous two hours. He was sure it was the same gambler who initially approached him in Copenhagen. He didn't recognize anyone else. Yes, he would work with their sketch artist, for all the good that would do. Yes, he still wanted to play in the French. "It's the first match I can play clean in a year, so yes, I'm playing."

The team leader didn't have much to add. They had scoured the area where Madsen had been grabbed and found nothing. No evidence, no witnesses, not even a surveillance camera they could hack into.

Madsen then explained, in somber tones, how the gamblers would continue to pressure him after the French. "They said the wildcard thing was suspicious, but they never actually said they thought I was talking to the cops. In fact, they basically said they'd beat me up or worse if I did. So, why the hell did I contact you? Why did I agree to any of this? Maybe I should just accept their money and survive. What other options do I have?"

His last comments stung Catalano, who felt responsible

for dragging him into the mess. She liked and respected him after her time in Copenhagen, and although he was already in deep when he called her, she had raised his hopes of finding a way out. And right now, she had nothing more to offer.

"Tobias, I'm truly sorry," she finally said. "We aren't giving up on you. I promise."

"Thank you Liz. I don't blame you. But things seem a lot worse than ever. I can't believe I woke up this morning thinking this could be the day I got my freedom back."

Chapter 46

Gil hadn't exactly forgotten about Memphis and the support he was getting from The Racquet Club, but it wasn't top of mind either. He had the club logo on his bag and shirts, and every once in a while another player would ask about his arrangement. But generally, he didn't give it much thought.

Halfway along the 12-hour drive from Venice to Paris, Gil got an email from Tony Di Pietro. He was surprised, only because they had just emailed the week before, only the second time they'd communicated since he left the club. He'd given him a rundown of his success to date, thanked him and the club profusely for their support and mentioned he and Sam were heading to the French Open.

"There's a group of club members going to the French during the first week of the tournament. Can you spend some time with them?"

"Of course," he typed back without hesitation. "Send me the details." He owed Di Pietro for 100 reasons, not least his role in securing the club support. And how big an imposition could it really be?

"It's eight of them, led by your old pal Howard Forrester," came the reply the next morning. "I've given them your cell number. They'd like to have dinner with you somewhere at Roland Garros, and have you show them around, maybe introduce them to a few players. And they've also packed their rackets…"

The next line was a collection of mischievous smiley face emojis.

"We've booked two courts Tuesday afternoon at Club de Lutece in your name. They'd like you to hit with them, you know, run a bit of a clinic for the afternoon. I said you'd be fine with it, since I knew you would be there."

"For crying out loud," Gil said, as Sam drove the car and he read the message. "They want a bloody clinic. Howard Forrester is coming to Paris so I can feed him balls and watch him launch them over the fence."

"Oh, I'm going to be there for that," Sam sputtered, through tears of laughter. "This is the price you pay for that sweet deal with the club. Serves you right Mr. Bigshot."

"How am I a bigshot? I can't believe they've tracked me down for a lesson."

"Maybe they're also coming for the Open, just sayin'. Might not be all about you."

"Ha ha, OK. But Tuesday afternoon. Wait when are our tickets? Not Tuesday afternoon, please, please."

He scrolled down to another email and sighed with relief. "OK, we've got all day Monday and just Tuesday morning. So I guess it will work."

"Oh, you were doing it either way my friend. And you have to make an effort too. They have to go home happy."

"Sure, sure, but not so happy they tell all their friends to meet us at Wimbledon."

"Oh, are we going to Wimbledon?" Sam asked with a wink.

Gil sulked for the next hour, while Sam simply smirked in his general direction. They arrived in Paris – actually near Paris – Saturday night and found the Hostellerie du Prieure, in Saint Prix. The town was just north of the city, where rooms were half as expensive. They'd booked a room for Sergei and Svetlana as well.

"I'm famished. Let's clean up and find some fabulous French food," he said as they wheeled into Saint Prix. Gil was at the wheel now and feeling much better.

"They're coming tomorrow," Sam said, reading a text from Svetlana. "They're taking the train."

For reasons no one can explain, the French Open starts play on a Sunday, rather than the traditional Monday. As a result, a handful of players are bounced each year before most of the world even realizes the tournament has begun.

There weren't enough Sunday matches to make it worth going, so the two couples planned to spend all day Monday at the tournament. It wasn't clear whether Sergei and Gil could breach security and get somewhere near the players' lounge by showing their Challenger Tour credentials. But they had them packed just in case.

Gil noted wryly that no one from Mobile was coming to the tournament and expecting Sergei to give a lesson.

"We're not getting any money from Mobile either you idiot," Sergei shot back, as the four of them reconnected Sunday evening over dinner.

With no tournament play of their own for several weeks, the conversation was more free-ranging. Although the women had spent a lot of time together and seemed to bond almost immediately, the men were closer to strangers than friends. As always, the talk eventually gravitated back to the Ivanovs' predicament. Time apart had kindled some new approaches, and they batted them around for much of the evening.

As supportive as Gil and Sam were, they couldn't really understand the depths of despair their new friends felt. So to them, the ideas to outfox the gamblers felt like Danny Ocean rounding up a crew to pull a heist and even the score with a casino titan who wronged a dear friend. They threw out ideas with little connection to reality, and for much of the evening Sergei laughed at their naivety.

"This isn't a spy novel. You know that, right?" he asked as they were settling the bill and saying goodnight. "Whatever we do, it has to work. We have to win. We can't swing and miss because the backlash will hit us, not you. You weren't there in Italy when he had a knife at Svetlana's throat. You just don't know what it's like." His eyes watered and he pulled his wife closer.

There wasn't much to say in response. Instead they all exchanged hugs and somberly headed back to the hotel.

"Let's not leave Paris without a concrete plan," Sam said, before drifting off.

Perfect weather and the prospect of a full day at the French Open lifted everyone's mood as they waited for the train early the next morning. By 9:00, they had passed security, giddy as grade schoolers walking through the gates at Disney World. The fact that the guys' Challenger credentials were completely useless didn't dampen their spirits one bit as they worked their way around the grounds, watching matches on outside courts, and soaking in the atmosphere.

Gil dared not say it, but he couldn't help wonder if he might be playing there next year, if he kept going the way he had been so far. Sam was certainly wondering it, but also decided not to say it.

Sergei's dream was more complicated. He wanted more than anything to qualify for a Grand Slam, but his more immediate goal was simply to break free and play for himself with a clear mind. He could barely remember what that felt like.

Wandering around after a spectacular lunch – croque-monsieur on a terrace next to Suzanne-Lenglen Court – they walked out as far from the center of action as they could, to court 18, which stuck out all by itself at the pointy end of the pie-shaped property, separated from the outside world by a small hedge and fence.

There were no more than 50 people watching the match between two players neither Sergei nor Gil had ever heard of. They had to listen to the umpire say the players' names and then scroll through the French Open app listing all the participants to figure out who they were watching.

"The guy in the red shirt is Clement Charest," Svetlana said, holding her phone so they could see his official tournament picture. He was one of a dozen French players who'd received wildcards into their home tournament.

"The other guy is from Denmark, Tobias Madsen," she continued, again holding up her phone so they could see him. "He's a wildcard too."

Wildcard or not, there was no denying the high level of tennis they were playing. Both men were contesting every point, lunging and sliding, doing everything they could to return one more ball, one more ball.

"My God, we've got work to do Sergei," Gil whispered. "These are wildcards, and they're absolutely killing it. In theory, there are 126 other players here who are better than them. Wow."

They stayed long enough to see the Dane take the first set, 7-5. Both players left the court after the first set, during which time the few people watching evacuated for other matches on other outer courts. A grounds pass on the first two days of a Grand Slam was every tennis fan's dream situation. There were matches being played everywhere, and you could switch from one to another, like you were using a TV remote and calling up whatever match you wanted to watch.

When Madsen returned to court 18, which was a 5-minute walk from the washroom where he'd changed his shirt, his opponent was still missing. He arrived a minute later, also sporting a new shirt, and played resumed. More than two hours later, when Madsen won the fourth set, 6-4, to secure the match, 3 sets to 1, the two couples were long gone, watching doubles on court 7, unable to even name the players they'd been so impressed with on court 18 that morning.

The few fans scattered around the court gave the two players a standing ovation. A kid asked Madsen to sign his giant tennis ball, and he did it with a smile that would have been no bigger if he'd just won the semi-final and was playing two days later for the title. Winning a match without throwing a single point, without even wondering what the gamblers expected him to do, was the most liberating thing he had done for months.

There was no one there to share in the victory, no media interested in speaking with him. He didn't care. He packed up as many official tournament towels as he could jam into his Wilson tennis bag and headed to the players' lounge where he would get a free massage for the sixth straight day. Despite the four-hour match, he nearly skipped to his destination. *I won a match at the French Open.*

Chapter 47

Just as Monday was the tournament highlight for Tobias Madsen -- whose next match against a seeded player lasted 90 minutes, netted him all of 4 games, and was never in doubt -- Monday turned out to be the highlight of the week for Gil.

Tuesday morning the couples split up and again used their grounds passes to wander. After lunch, Gil kissed Sam goodbye and headed to a rental locker just outside the grounds. There he retrieved his tennis bag and flagged down a cab to deliver him to Club de Lutece, 30 minutes away.

He was welcomed like the Prodigal Son returning to his father, and he wondered what lies Di Pietro had told the good people in charge.

"We have your courts all set up," said an eager assistant named Henri, practising his English. "And your group is already out there, preparing." Smiling, he added, "You have a great challenge ahead of you, monsieur."

"Ha, I think you're right Henri. Merci beaucoup."

"Gil! Over here!" a voice rang out as Gil approached the courts. He'd already surmised they were the right courts, since all the other courts were empty.

"Come on over," Howard Forrester continued, projecting his voice like he was atop the Eiffel Tower, trying to get the attention of someone on the ground. Since Gil was only two courts away and closing the distance by the second, he had no trouble hearing the old man.

"Good afternoon Howard. Everyone. How's the trip so far? What a great day we have."

"We certainly do Gil. Let's get started. Not a moment to

waste."

Sizing up the prospects for the next two hours-plus, Gil called an audible. Excusing himself, he doubled back to the clubhouse and found Henri. "You play, right? I mean, you give lessons?"

"Oh, oui monsieur, why?"

"There's €50 in it if you come and help me keep this group busy for two hours, maybe a bit longer. Whadya say?"

"Oui, oui Monsieur Gil," he said, almost jumping over the desk he was standing at while calling members to remind them of the doubles league the following evening. "That would be magnifique."

When they got back, most of the Memphis group was hitting with each other, warming up. Howard Forrester was pacing at one end of the courts, checking his watch the way his grandchildren checked their phones.

"Are we ready, Gil?" he asked, his tone about 20 per cent crankier than 10 minutes earlier.

Gil formed two groups, and strictly for his own pleasure put Howard Forrester in young Henri's group. He didn't for one moment think the man would go along with it, but he got a kick out of watching him inch over to Gil's group and nudge someone toward the other group.

Gil waited for him to complete the maneuver, then said, "We'll start like this and switch courts halfway through. Alright, let's have some fun. Or, what's the French word Henri, amusement?"

"Oui monsieur."

They ran through half a dozen drills, starting with cross-court groundstrokes from both sides, then volleys, a few overheads and then some situational doubles. It looked like a regular Saturday morning at The Racquet Club of Memphis.

When the time came for the groups to switch courts and do a different set of drills, Howard Forrester suddenly felt the need to sit down and stretch out his aging Achilles. Play had resumed by the time he completed that task and had a drink of water. He had positioned himself closest to Gil's court, and just to be polite, didn't bother crossing through that court to join the rest of his group on Henri's court. Instead, he just joined the players who were lined up single-file to hit a series of feeds from Gil, pick up a few stray balls, and head to the back of the line.

"It takes us old folks a while to pick up those balls and get back into line," he yelled in Gil's direction. "Better to have an extra person over here."

Gil looked at Henri, unsure whether the kid understood what was happening, and just nodded at Howard Forrester as he reached the front of the line. "Here you go Howard, an overhead…"

He popped up a ball about 100 feet in the air, far enough back that Forrester had to retreat a few steps to line it up. Raising his racket in his right hand and pointing his left skyward, as taught, he swung ferociously and missed the ball entirely. He did, however, make solid contact with his left shin, causing him to scream an English word Henri had not yet learned.

"Eye on the ball," Gil yelled out encouragingly as Forrester hobbled back to the bench where he'd last been seen stretching his Achilles. This time, he soaked a towel in water and applied it gingerly to his throbbing shin, which was already turning a shade of greyish blue, contrasted nicely by the green Har-Tru courts.

The two hours were coming to an end and a few players were starting to pack up, their desire to play in Paris satiated. That's when Howard Forrester suddenly sprung back to life, limping toward the group. "Who wants to play some doubles against Gil and me?"

"Oh, that sounds fun," said Dorothy Campbell, who went

by Dot. "You and me Dot," said Pernell Jackson. "We'll serve first Howie. You've got a ringer."

Henri escorted the other four players back to the clubhouse where they could change and get a drink. Gil stayed and played 45 minutes of slow-motion tennis, where lobs begat lobs and rallies went on for forever. With the score 3-2 for Team Forrester/Pence, Henri reappeared courtside, wondering if he could be of any further assistance. Gil pounced on the opportunity like it was a short ball in a long rally. He mumbled something that sounded like French so only Henri could hear it, and before the boy could react, Gil turned around and announced their court time was up.

"Pity we won't get to finish the set," he said. "Great playing everyone. Henri will take you to the clubhouse."

As they waited for the players to pack up, Gil slipped the boy another €20, along with a wink and a pat on the back. "Merci, Henri. Merci."

Chapter 48

No matter how proficient he was at it, Nik always felt a little queasy after whipping one of his athletes back into line. He'd never been in therapy, but he assumed he had some sociopathic traits. How else to explain the ease with which he could ruin the career, and potentially life, of someone like Tobias Madsen, who had done nothing wrong and didn't deserve to suffer as he was.

On the other hand, did sociopaths feel this kind of, well, not exactly guilt, but unease?

He mulled those questions over for the first half hour of his Eurostar train trip home. It took just over two hours from Paris to London, a feat that still amazed him, even if he felt slightly claustrophobic going through the Chunnel. By the time he had emerged on the British side, his unease had been replaced by giddy anticipation. He hadn't seen Lola in a week, and she was the only thing on his schedule that night.

"Whatcha say we skip Square and eat in," he texted with the requisite number of suggestive emojis. "I'll get Thai takeaway and come to your apartment around 6:00."

It had been nearly a month since he'd revealed his dark side to her, and far from driving her away, it had brought them closer together. They still danced around some topics, but the freedom to tell her 90 per cent of what he was doing, instead of 30 or 40 per cent like before, made both of them happy.

Reaching into his soft leather briefcase, he fingered a red velvet bag. It contained the sheer chemise he had purchased that morning at Cadolle, with the help of a beautiful and patient assistant. She knew exactly how he should spend his €200, and he took her advice enthusiastically. She had spent about 15 minutes wrapping it in layers of silken tissue paper, dusting it with scented confetti and gently enveloping it in velvet. Nik assumed newborn babies were not swaddled to such a degree.

As he touched the bag, he closed his eyes and imagined Lola wearing the chemise, however briefly, that evening. He drifted off with that image in his mind, his hand still touching velvet. He woke as the train slowed, on the outskirts of London. Wi-Fi was spotty on the train, and his phone hadn't buzzed once while he slept.

"5 mins to the station," he texted Lola. Unable to resist, he added, "I have a surprise for you."

From St Pancras International station, it was a 20-minute car ride to his apartment. He laid his briefcase down gently then jumped in the shower.

From his closet he pulled his favorite jeans and an Everton hoodie she had given him for Christmas. His phone was dead, so he had to plug it in to summon a car. The 10 minutes of charging while he waited did little good. He shrugged, grabbed his briefcase and stuffed the phone in his breast pocket. *I'll plug it in at her place.*

His driver suggested a new place for Thai. Feeling adventurous, Nik agreed. Judging by the smells of the joint while he waited for his order, the driver knew what he was talking about. He would reflect the recommendation in his rating.

He arrived at Lola's just after 6:00. Carrying his briefcase delicately so as not to crush the contents, he juggled the food in the other hand and used his elbow to push the lift button. Normally he would have texted that he'd arrived, but his phone was nothing but a paper weight at that moment.

Without a warning, she hadn't unlocked her door, so he

rang the bell, again with a rather dextrous elbow. He rang again when nothing happened. "Jesus," he muttered as he carefully put the food down and found the right key on the chain in his coat pocket. The door was spring-loaded, like a hotel, so he had to back in, keeping it open with his foot while reaching back to pick up the food. It wasn't exactly Prince Charming arriving on a white stallion, but he was in, and increasingly giddy about what the evening had in store.

"Hello! Guess who?" he said as he headed for the kitchen. "Can you smell this food? I nearly started on the way over."

When he got no response, he wondered if she was in the spare bedroom on her elliptical, wearing her Beats headphones and oblivious to the world. With the food placed safely on the counter, he headed down the hall. He peeked in but saw only a lonely elliptical, the headphones draped over the handles.

He listened carefully for the shower but didn't hear that either. Returning to the front hall, he checked to see if her keys and purse were in the usual spot. They were. It wasn't a huge apartment. She could have popped out to see a friend in the building or even for a quick swim in the top floor pool, but why leave her keys?

Confused but unconcerned, Nik went back down the hallway, past the spare bedroom toward the master. It hadn't occurred to Nik she would be sleeping, so he was surprised to see her under the covers.

"Hey, you, wake up. I missed you."

When she didn't respond, he crawled onto his side of the bed and repeated his greeting. Only then, lying beside her, did he notice how pale her skin was. She wasn't snoring at all, which was unusual. When he touched her cheek, he screamed. It was cold and clammy. He'd never felt skin like that. He pulled his phone from his pocket to call 999, but it wouldn't come to life.

He searched frantically for hers, then stopped just as abruptly and went back to her side. Taking a deep breath, he pulled her arm from under the covers and felt for a pulse. Nothing. He tried her neck. *Maybe. She might be alive.*

He ran back to the front hall where he'd seen her purse. Her phone must be there. He found it and fumbled to unlock it.

When he finally made the call, he forgot her address.

"Calm down sir, if you can. You're calling from a mobile phone. We need to know the address."

"Yes, yes, OK. Yes. Ah, I think she's still alive. We've got to hurry." In her purse, he found a Cable TV bill. He recited her address to the woman on the line like he was repeating codes used to disarm a missile.

"OK, well done sir. They're on the way."

It seemed to Nik that he could hear sirens by the time he had run back to the bedroom and searched again for Lola's elusive pulse. *Oh shit, the door. The lobby. How will they get up here?*

He called 999 again. It was a different person, but her computer told her about his call. "They'll be there very soon."

"I know, I know. I just need to know if I should leave her and go down to the lobby. They have to get in, right? Or can they get in? I don't know what to do."

"It will be faster if you go down and let them in. Or have someone do that. But sir, please be careful you don't lock yourself out of the apartment. People do that sometimes. Take a deep breath. OK. Take another. Good. OK. What's your plan?"

His plan was to keep her on the line, as he dashed down five flights of stairs holding Lola's phone to his ear, jumping the final three steps to each landing. The sirens were blaring when he got to the lobby. Two paramedics charged toward the door. He let them in and pressed the lift button with enough force to hurt his thumb. *Should have used my elbow.*

The paramedics did not run and yet somehow kept up to

Nik, who felt like he was running as hard as he ever had. With two free hands, he easily unlocked her door and led them down the hall to her bedroom. Then he excused himself, went into the guest bathroom and threw up. His head was pounding and he started to cry.

"Sir, sir?" One of the paramedics was knocking on the bathroom door. "Sir, are you OK? We need to ask you some questions."

Nik pulled himself up and glanced in the mirror. The difference from less than two hours earlier when he got primped at home and set off for the evening was dramatic.

"Yes, sorry. What? How is she?"

"She's unconscious, but alive. We found this on the floor," he said, handing an empty pill bottle to Nik. "We assume that's her name, that these are hers?"

Nik knew Lola took the occasional sleeping pill when he was working late and she couldn't get to sleep. "Ya, those are hers, but she would only take half of one usually. Is that what happened?"

"We're not sure right now, but her symptoms suggest she took quite a few. The date of the refill is just last week, and it was 40 pills."

"But she's alive, you said that, right?"

"Yes sir. Sorry, what's your name?"

"Nik. Ah Nikolai Popescu. I'm her boyfriend. Sorry, is that important?"

"I just want to use your name Nik, that's all."

"Which hospital? I'll meet you there."

"St. Thomas'. Go to emerg."

Three minutes later, they were gone, sirens blaring. His driver tried to keep up but lost them almost immediately, as traffic filled in like flood water after parting for the ambulance. When Nik arrived at the hospital he burst into the emergency room showing every emotion he was feeling.

After a brief back-and-forth, he learned Lola was being treated. No, he couldn't see her or be in the room. Yes, he could avail himself of a hard, plastic chair while he waited. Coffee was indeed available, one floor up.

He sat and slumped, only then realizing what he had brought into the hospital with him – Lola's purse, his briefcase, and an umbrella. He couldn't remember taking any of those things from the apartment, holding them in the car he'd summoned or gathering them up when he arrived. He piled his belongings on the chair beside him. The briefcase was open at one end, and he could see a flash of red velvet. He started crying again.

Chapter 49

As the plane began its descent, Sergei's ears popped, waking him suddenly. For a moment, he thought the woman leaning in to speak with him was from the Red Cross, but then he remembered he was on a Swiss Airlines flight.

"We're landing in Zurich very soon," she said in perfect English. "Please put your seat up, sir, and thank you for flying with us."

He did as he was told and nodded off again. When he woke the second time, passengers all around him were standing awkwardly, emptying the overhead bins and waiting for the front door to open and the bye-byes to commence. Unlike other flights he could remember, they were delivered in French, German or English.

Still groggy, he sat back and took his time gathering his belongings. It had been years since he'd travelled alone, without Svetlana for support and backup.

The airport ran with all the efficiency he expected and within 30 minutes he was in line for his rental car, an Audi S5 he had requested when booking. It was a 90-minute drive to Schaan, Liechtenstein, which had a population of 6,000 and remarkably was the largest municipality in a country of 37,000 people.

It was a glorious drive, through the Swiss countryside and into Liechtenstein. The border between the countries was marked by a sign and nothing more, like passing between Georgia and Florida, minus the tacky billboards advertising discount towels and firearms.

He arrived in Schaan at noon and had lunch outdoors

at Restaurant Specki. The schnitzel and beer were a cliché, but he couldn't resist and enjoyed every last bite. He left his phone off and pulled a single sheet of paper from his inside jacket pocket. He'd studied it a dozen times already that day, but gave it one more look before paying for his meal and leaving by foot for his real destination, LGT Bank – The Liechtenstein Global Trust as it was known when founded in 1920.

Almost from the moment it was created, as a private bank operated by Liechtenstein royalty, LGT was a tax haven favored by the wealthy around the world. In 2008, a German investigation, together with international outrage about tax avoidance and fraud, had forced the country to close some loopholes and share some information with the European Union. That prompted a few charlatans to shift money to other, less established havens. But LGT was still a very good place to open an anonymous account if you planned, for example, to bribe an athlete to throw a tennis or football match.

For more than a year, Sergei had steadfastly ignored the funds deposited by the gamblers, knowing full well if he touched them he was one step closer to being complicit in their corruption. He'd never taken a penny and never thrown so much as a point, as his burned-down house and beat-up wife demonstrated. But there was a princely sum sitting in an LGT account with his name on it, and he'd finally decided it was time to move it somewhere else, to an account the gamblers could not monitor – at least not so easily.

The LGT was unlike any bank he'd ever been in. It seemed more like a nightclub, with what appeared to be priceless artwork on every wall and a hostess who was determined to meet his every need.

He dictated the account number he'd memorized and produced his Russian passport as proof of who he was. He rarely thought of himself as Russian, but in the world of passports and immigration law, he was as Russian today as ever, despite six years of living in the U.S.

"Yes, we have your account here," the woman said, warmly. She pushed a slip of paper across the desk. "Here is the balance."

Sergei tried to play it cool, but gulped slightly at the number: €470,372.84.

"What would you like to do with the funds?" she asked.

"I'd like a certified check, please."

"Those are the only kind we issue," she smiled. "For what amount? All of it?"

"Yes please, all of it. Oh, and can you tell me the last time there was a deposit?"

"Certainly sir. I see it was three months ago. You'll get a report on all the activity when you receive the check," she said. "It will be ready momentarily."

He waited nervously, half expecting someone from the Tennis Integrity Unit to come storming in and suspend him from the tour. But when he looked around, his fear abated. No one in the bank appeared to be stressed about anything. The town itself felt more like a Disney creation than a real place. People tooled around on bicycles, nodded hello to their neighbors and were in no hurry to get anywhere.

"Here you are sir," the hostess said, returning from a private back room. "Your check. Is there anything else we can help you with?"

"No, thank you very much. You've been very helpful."

"It's our pleasure. Remember we are here whenever you require banking services," she smiled.

"Yes, of course," he said, turning to leave. "Oh, one more thing. Your town is absolutely beautiful. I had no idea. Had never heard of it."

"We are a bit of a secret, but we get a fair number of

tourists, mostly from other parts of Europe. And of course, we have customers like you who come from all over the world."

"Is there anything you suggest I see before leaving? I have the rest of the day."

"People go to Gutenberg Castle," she said. "It's at least 700 years old, and it's free. But my favorite is the Kunstmuseum. It's not far, in Vaduz. A beautiful building. Do you like modern art?"

"I think so. Probably more than an old castle. I'll check it out. Thanks again."

The drive was less than 20 minutes, and the anticipation masked for the moment a feel of foreboding about what he was doing. Withdrawing the money was an irreversible step.

After the French, Gil flew back to Michigan to spend two solid weeks training with Coach, gearing up for the summer and fall seasons. Rather than join him, Sam convinced Svetlana to extend her stay in Paris and have a girls week. Svetlana had never done anything like that. She had been with Sergei since she was 18, first as infatuated girlfriend, then as supportive wife. Friendships were rare and never substantial. Sam was the closest thing she had to a true friend since she arrived in the foreign land of Mobile, Alabama, barely an adult, completely out of her element.

"Well, yes, I'd love that. But let me talk to Sergei."

"Of course," Sam said with a wink. "But tell him you deserve it."

Sergei was taken aback by the idea, but not necessarily opposed. He had been toying with the idea of playing in the Poprad-Tatry tournament in Slovakia, but hadn't broached the subject yet with Svetlana. He could see how happy she was spending time with Sam. *Why not?*

"You spend the week with Sam, and I'll go play in Slovakia.

It will be good for both of us."

Although they had agreed, both felt odd the next morning when Sergei headed to the airport.

There was a direct flight from Paris to Bratislava, and from there he could drive to the booming city of Poprad. But rather than book that flight, he headed for the Swiss Airlines ticket counter and booked a seat to Zurich, a slight detour on his way to Poprad, where he would be the No. 4 seed among the 32 players battling for their share of €64,000.

The Kunstmuseum was everything his banking hostess had promised, and he lingered there for much of the afternoon. Maybe it was the art; maybe it was the knowledge of what he'd chosen to do. Either way, he was in no hurry to drive back to Zurich and resume his journey to Poprad.

It wasn't until the next day, while driving a humdrum Toyota Camry from Bratislava to Poprad, that he pulled over and turned his phone on for the first time since leaving Paris. He scrolled down to the unnamed number at the very bottom of his caller list, inhaled sharply, and began typing.

"This is Sergei Ivanov, as I'm sure you know. You have damaged my life enough. I can't run anymore. I will do what you ask. But you must stop threatening us. And you must never, ever go near my wife again. Never mention this to her and never involve her. If you do, I will walk away."

He punched send before he had time to reconsider. The beep of the phone signalled the message was gone and that his life had changed forever.

Chapter 50

A doctor found Nik near the waiting room, halfway through his fourth cup of coffee, pacing furiously up and down the hallway.

"Mr. Popescu? Did I say that right?"

"Close enough," Nik said, trying but failing to smile. "How's Lola? What's going on?"

"We have just pumped her stomach. That's not a pleasant experience, but it will stop some of the drugs from getting into her system. We don't know the timeframe, so a lot of the medicine may have already moved into her bloodstream."

"Is she awake? When will we know if she's OK?"

"She's back asleep, but that's OK. We are monitoring her. We will run some tests, but her pulse is steady, and that's a good sign."

"Will she recover fully? Could she have, I dunno, brain damage? I mean, how serious could it be?"

"The chances of anything permanent are quite low. We will want her to speak with a psychiatrist before she goes home. That's standard when someone overdoses."

"Ah, OK. So, she could come home tomorrow?"

"We'll know more when she wakes up, but my guess is she'll be here beyond that. We'll be moving her from emerg to the ICU soon. She'll spend the night there. I know you want to be here, but my advice is to go home, get some sleep and call in the morning. You can't see her until she's out of the ICU and in a regular room."

Nik took the advice reluctantly and summoned his third driver of the night. He hopped in the back and slumped from exhaustion. The man turned his head around, waiting for instructions. "Ah, sorry, it's been a weird night."

"No problem mate. Where to?"

Without really thinking, Nik gave him Lola's address. It felt like the right place to be, and that was good enough for the moment.

The neighbors who had gathered in the hallway and lobby of Lola's building during the paramedic action were long gone when he returned. In the car, he'd noticed how late it was, well after midnight. There was a note on Lola's door from a woman two doors down whom Nik had met a few times. It offered support and prayers.

I'll talk to her in the morning when I know more.

He let himself in. Only seven hours earlier, he'd done the same thing, juggling the food, giddy about the prospects of spending the evening with her. He pulled a bottle of Red Ember from her fridge and sprawled on the sofa. His mind raced through every moment, replaying scenes on a loop. He grabbed a second beer and walked back toward Lola's bedroom. It was a mess, with sheets and pillows strewn about, along with the remnants of packaging the paramedics had ripped open to get at tubes and needles and whatever else they'd used while he was in the bathroom crying.

He sat on the floor, leaning on her bed. None of it made sense. She'd never hurt herself before, never been depressed, at least to his knowledge. They hadn't talked while he was in Paris, but three days earlier she had been excited about their plans for the evening. Why would she take all those pills?

He dozed off, his neck pushed awkwardly against the bed, ensuring he wouldn't sleep for long. Before his neck woke him, his phone buzzed and did the job.

"Heard it went well in Paris…" read the text from Humph.

Half asleep, Nik was puzzled. Unless there was a full-scale crisis, the partners didn't text each other for updates. And they certainly didn't do so at 1:00 a.m.

The next text, arriving 30 seconds later, jolted him completely awake.

"How's everything going? Safe trip?"

Nik remembered the moment he'd realized his Uncle Fritz was not the kind and generous man he'd assumed while growing up. He remembered the instant he saw him for what he was – an insignificant man obsessed with money.

He watched Fritz lie to a customer to avoid returning a few lei, the equivalent of 50 pence. It shattered all his illusions and tainted not just the future but also the past. He looked at everything through a new prism of skepticism. His mother said the scales had fallen from his eyes, when he told her about the experience several years later. Whatever it was called, he had precisely the same feeling the moment he read Humph's second text.

They don't trust me. They really did hack into my phone, not to follow Madsen but to check up on me. They ran a background check on Lola, not to protect me but to protect them.

He was so tired he could hardly think straight, and yet the thoughts just kept coming, in a torrent he couldn't stop. Moments and comments that meant nothing at the time suddenly seemed sinister. He had kept to himself to such a degree Lola had been ready to leave him, and yet the partners knew so much about him. Their casual comments, as he now saw, reflected a level of knowledge well beyond anything he'd given freely.

By 5:15, six beers in, he had identified a web of deceit all around him. He set his phone for 8:00 so he could call the hospital first thing and reluctantly gave in to sleep. The web slipped seamlessly into his dreams, where he had trouble separating the real from the imagined.

His phone buzzed at 8:00, as requested. Sleeping on the

floor beside the bed, he had spent nearly three hours with his right arm pinned under his body. It was dead asleep and unresponsive as he tried to reach for the phone. So he tried reaching with his left, but was unable to prop himself up with his right. The alternative was to lie on his back and use his feet to push himself in reverse toward the beeping phone.

He silenced it on the third attempt, and then felt the surprisingly painful tingles as blood started flowing again in his right arm.

Ironically, Lola's night had gone better than his. She woke on her own around 7:00, and by the time Nik got through to someone who knew something, she had been moved from the ICU to a room four floors above. He was welcome to see her that morning, and there was a chance she would be discharged before dinnertime.

He straightened the place up a bit and punched his phone to request a driver. On his way out, he stopped at the apartment two doors down.

The woman didn't recognize him and spoke only through the two-inch gap allowed by the security chain.

"I'm Lola's boyfriend. You left a note last night."

"Oh, yes, yes. Sorry," she said, fumbling with the lock and eventually swinging the door wide open. "How is she? What happened?"

"Not exactly sure," he fibbed, Fritz-style. "Seems like an allergic reaction. They weren't taking any chances with the ambulance last night, but it looked a lot worse than it was."

"Uh huh, I see," she replied, warily. "But she's not home yet?"

"It was late. They kept her overnight just to be certain. You know. Anyhow, I'm heading there now, so I'll tell her you asked about her. Thank you so much."

"Yes, tell her we're all worried. She's a lovely girl you know. Lovely. Maybe you should shave before you go, young man."

He rubbed his chin reflexively and smiled. "I didn't get much sleep last night. Thanks again."

It took almost as long to find Lola's new room and get permission to breach the doorway as it had taken the night before to get her admitted to the hospital. Nik downed another two cups of hospital coffee during the process, but kept his cool, outwardly at least.

If a nurse hadn't led him directly to the right room, he wouldn't have believed it was Lola lying in the bed. Her face was swollen almost beyond recognition, and there were half a dozen tubes and wires poking out of her, connected to equipment that formed a kind of picket fence protecting her bed.

"Hi sweetie," she whispered as he stood above her, fighting back tears.

He leaned down and kissed her forehead, then found a chair and pulled it next to her. Neither spoke for several minutes, as they held hands and he rested his head awkwardly on her chest.

A nurse interrupted the moment when she arrived to update Lola's chart by poking and prodding her. It turned out she was doing much better than it appeared. Her voice was weak because of a raw throat, which happens when doctors jam in a tube and pump out the contents of your stomach. Her face was swollen on only one side, where a bruise marked the spot.

"You're doing brilliantly," the chipper nurse declared. "The psychiatrist will be down in an hour or so. And the doctor will be by soon too."

While they waited for her next two visitors, Lola sketched out what had happened to her the day before, as best she could remember or deduce.

She had gone out for lunch that day with her girlfriend, Amber. She had a salad and an Appletini, and felt good when she left the restaurant, sometime around 2:30, she figured. Not long after she got home, her head started to hurt. It was so bad, she took two Advil and got into bed.

"That's all I remember. My head was killing me. Sorry, pun. Maybe it was bad enough to affect my memory, but I swear I didn't take any sleeping pills. I sure as hell didn't take the whole bottle. No way."

"Do you remember what Amber ate or drank?"

"Ah, I think she had a sandwich and wine, maybe. Not sure. But she's fine. I texted her this morning before you got here. Told her what happened."

"But those sleeping pills were yours, right? I mean, you have a prescription."

"Ya, you know that. I take 'em once in a while. One at most. I honestly don't remember getting the bottle last night. And I promise you, I was not sad or depressed in any way. I did not try to hurt myself. Certainly didn't try to kill myself. No way."

"I know. I believe you. Let's hope this shrink figures it out too."

"Ya, can he keep me here if he doesn't like my answers?"

"Probably. I don't know. We can start by asking him. I mean, if you want me to stay in the room while you talk to him."

"Definitely. Don't leave me," she said, squeezing his hand hard enough to hurt.

To Nik's eye, the shrink looked to be about 105. *Every patient could be his last.*

"Good morning Miss Farmsworth," he said in a raspy voice, looking not at Lola but at her chart, which he held very close to his face while he fiddled with his reading glasses. "Had a bit of a rough night, did we?"

"Feeling much better now," Lola said, looking at Nik and rolling her eyes.

"Yes, well some of these prescriptions can be very dangerous. I don't think these young chemists take the time to explain that to people. It's just: Pop in to the grocer's, buy your fruits and veg, and pick up your meds. Well, as you now understand young lady, they're very powerful."

"Yes sir, you're right," she answered, playing along.

"You don't seem upset or down at all. How have you been feeling?"

"Very good sir, ah doctor. I was excited last night because Nik was coming over."

"This is Nik? Hello, young man."

The pleasantries went on another few minutes until the aging psychiatrist scrawled his name on a piece of paper and bid them good day.

"That was weird," she said.

"Ya, let's get you home, OK?"

He was bursting to tell her everything he'd figured out the night before. The problem was he couldn't prove it, and if he was right, she was still in danger. It would have to wait until they were home and he could lay it all out for her. She had to know.

Chapter 51

Sergei wasn't sure if it was good news or bad news when he didn't hear back immediately from the gamblers. Arriving in Poprad by late afternoon, he checked in at the tournament and found the meagre accommodations that came with his entry. Travelling solo, he didn't much care about the motel. Anything fancy would have been wasted on him, as he constantly checked his phone for a message.

He ate in his room, a take-out pork Ramen he was surprised to find within walking distance of the motel. He also picked up half a dozen local beers and downed two with dinner.

At last his phone buzzed, close to midnight in Slovakia, with a cryptic message from a new, untraceable number. It was the result of several hours of intense meetings at Garfunkel, about which he knew nothing.

"With respect Eva, you're too close to this to be rational." The warning came from Humphrey Cox, who made sure he was all the way across her office when he said it.

"Relax Humph, I'm not going to bite," she said. "I know what you're saying. I've been trying to turn this guy for a year, and he's been a pain in the ass."

"Right, that's the point. Why now? What's changed?"

"Constant pressure? Who knows? Maybe it's been the wife who kept him on the straight and narrow. Maybe he's tired of listening to her. Maybe she's pregnant and he's more concerned than ever for her health. Beats me. The point is, he's finally coming around."

"Well, maybe he is and maybe he's not. He emptied the account. He could be getting ready to run."

"Then why text us? Why not just take it and go?"

"Don't know. I'm just saying we should be cautious. That's all. We don't need this guy so badly that it's worth a big risk."

"OK, I'll agree with you there. Let's start small with him and see what happens. We still have all the leverage. More now that he's taken the money. Let's push him and see what happens. Leave the wife out of it, like he asked, and see what he's willing to do."

Sergei put the phone on a table to read the text. He couldn't steady his hand to hold it. "Glad to hear you've had a change of heart," it read. "Please do the following at the Poprad tournament and we will start to replenish the account you emptied this week."

He assumed they would know he took the money, but the mention of it still shook him. The demand was relatively simple: lose the second set of his first match in the tournament.

It was a demand Garfunkel had used before with newly recruited tennis players and served more than one purpose. In the 2-of-3 set format, the player could still win the match despite losing the second set. So he wasn't being asked to knock himself out of the tournament. Also, the request was not so detailed as to require specific actions in specific games, which was more difficult to remember and execute under pressure.

Eva and Humph would also learn something about Sergei's mindset by seeing how he approached the demand. If he lost two straight sets by lopsided scores, it would suggest his spirit was broken and he didn't care about appearances. That wasn't much use to Garfunkel, which relied on unexpected match outcomes to win underdog bets. However, if Sergei fought hard and won the first set, it suggested he was pushing back against them and hoping to win, despite them. If he got to the third set and played hard, he could be very useful to them.

Had Sergei known how he was being evaluated, he would not have changed anything. *I'm damn well not going to lose this match because of them.*

He read the text three times, then responded as instructed with the letter 'y' to indicate he understood and would do it.

It was after midnight, and he was exhausted after two days of travel. But he couldn't sleep. He thought of Svetlana, in Paris, with no idea what he had just agreed to do. He thought of Coach Wilkins and Sally, in Mobile, his biggest supporters. What would they think, if they knew? His worry exhausted him further, until eventually he slipped into three hours of fitful sleep.

Normally, he would have spent some time the night before a match looking up his opponent on YouTube. Even the most obscure players usually could be found, although the footage might look like it was shot with something Thomas Edison worked up in his spare time.

Tired and worried, he didn't even bother to look at his opponent's name. He just made note of the time of his match, and planned to head over two hours early to find a warm-up partner. Before he left, he texted Svetlana, asking about her week and giving generic information about his travel adventures. She responded immediately with a string of heart-related emojis and little else. He hearted her back and headed to the tournament.

The kid he found to hit with spoke English and was reasonably talented. Hitting the ball helped Sergei focus on something other than the gamblers. Near the end of his warmup, there was a commotion at the other end of the practice court complex. It looked like a media scrum had broken out on court 4. In the middle of the gaggle of reporters, tournament officials and wannabe warm-up partners was a skinny kid who towered above everyone else.

"Who's that?" he asked his hitting partner across the net when they stopped to pick up balls.

"You don't know?" the kid said, prompting a withering look from Sergei. "Right, you're not from around here. That's Zupan Mlakar."

"Who?"

"Zupan Mlakar. He's from Kosice, here in Slovakia. He's kind of a big deal."

"I can see that. Is he any good?"

"He's the best around here, for sure. Local players find it hard to play someone so tall. He's 7 feet, at least."

"Is he in the tournament?"

"Ya," the kid said, looking skeptically at Sergei, as if waiting for the punch line of a joke. "You're playing him. Today. I figured you'd know that."

"Ha, normally ya, I'd know. It's a long story. Never mind about that. Tell me everything you know about him. Have you ever played him?"

"Three years ago, we played in a school tournament. But he was a foot shorter then and not doing tennis full-time. It's all he does now. At first everyone said he should choose basketball, but he's terrible. He can't even dribble a ball."

"But he can play tennis? That's weird."

"I guess. It's what you'd expect – big serve, three steps and he's at the net, hitting volleys. He can't move much, but he doesn't really have to."

"OK then, let's work on a few passing shots, eh? You stay at the net. See how many I can get by you."

"Alright, but he's got at least an extra foot of wingspan, just sayin', you know?"

"Just volley them back to me. If you can," Sergei added with a smile. Despite everything going on around him, he still loved being on court, hitting balls with someone who could keep up with him. And this kid was keeping up just fine.

They hit for another 15 minutes. Sergei was dripping with sweat from firing forehand and backhand passing shots at and around the kid. Between rallies, he watched Mlakar warm up three courts away.

Their match started 30 minutes late, following a titanic battle between two nobodies that went to a tiebreaker in the third set. The kid offered to sit with Sergei while he waited. He took him up on the offer. It was an entourage of one vs. a dozen or so hanging around Mlakar.

At the net with the umpire, calling the coin toss and choosing ends, Sergei realized just how tall – and skinny – the guy was. *He could snap in two if I hit one right at him.*

In a strange country, playing someone he'd never heard of, Sergei's instincts were to ease into the match. Extend some rallies and see what came back from the other side. But he knew he had to lose the second set, and that didn't give him any leeway to go easy in the first set. So instead he started with all the fury he could muster. He hit second serves nearly as hard as firsts and went for corners every time. He served and volleyed every chance he got and hit more drop shots in the first set than he had in many entire tournaments.

Mlakar did not respond well. He broke his first racket after the fifth game, when he lost his serve to go down 4-1. He broke his second when he lost his serve yet again to drop the first set 6-1.

Sitting in their chairs, waiting for the second set to begin, both players had a problem. The kid's problem was obvious to anyone watching: He was getting his ass kicked by some Russian dude he'd never heard of. Sergei's problem was known only by those watching the match in the Garfunkel headquarters -- Eva, Humph and a handful of betting whizzes. Their job was to cash in on the long-awaited arrival of Sergei Ivanov to the Garfunkel stable of crooked athletes.

Normally, they would spring to action the moment the first set ended.

With Sergei in complete control, the live odds of Mlakar winning the next set would climb sky high, somewhere around +600. Which meant betting on the 7-footer to win the set would deliver winnings of 6x whatever sum they bet. They had bets ready to go at sites around the world, covering their tracks and avoiding suspicion at least in the moment. But the first set had been so convincing, Eva and Humph had their doubts.

They wondered if Sergei had changed his mind and would steamroll through the second set as well. They wondered if he had lied all along to set them up so they'd lose money. Even if none of that were true, they worried especially that the tall kid whose name they couldn't pronounce might just give up and tank the second set. He'd already broken two rackets and received a warning from the umpire. He looked like he was about to cry, not stage an epic rally to win the second set and even the match.

"Let's do half of the usual," Humph suggested to the room. No one had to explain why; they were all in agreement.

"OK, yes, good idea Humph. Do it," Eva said to the techs in the room. "This is supposed to be a test anyway. If he passes, they'll be other times to cash in."

Sergei had never once lost a game on purpose. The closest he'd come was to gear down a notch or two when he felt tight and was afraid of injury. But even then, he was trying to win. Losing without making it obvious was difficult, he quickly realized.

He was serving to begin the set and double faulted twice right out of the gate. He then hit two other balls so wide the ball boys were in danger. Down 1-0 in less than a minute, he planned to lose the second game as well, and then play out the set somewhat normally to lose 6-4. But Mlakar was not cooperating.

He had spent much of the changeover after the first set trying to hold back tears. When he wasn't crying, he was swearing at himself and everyone around him. This was his first big tournament in his own country, and he felt like he was back on the stupid basketball court, where everyone expected greatness and he could hardly put one foot in front of the other.

Winning the first game of the second set should have given him confidence, but his opponent had played so badly, it did no such thing. He bounced the ball, ready to serve. He bounced it some more. And more. He heard snickers in the crowd. He knew how stupid he looked, but he couldn't bring himself to toss the ball. Somehow, the mechanics of the serve had disappeared from his brain, and the only thing he knew how to do was bounce the damn ball.

If Sergei was confused, the Garfunkel brain trust was apoplectic. "What the fuck is he doing?" Eva screamed. "Who is this guy?"

There are no timeouts in tennis, but Sergei called one anyway. Not officially. But as the kid continued bouncing the ball, looking bewildered and scared, Sergei held up his hand and pointed to the crowd. "Can you ask those people to stay still and turn off the flash on their cameras?" he asked the umpire.

It was a ridiculous request. There were no more than 500 people in the entire stadium, and no one anywhere was moving. Plus, it was a bright sunny day, and not even the most uneducated photographer was using a flash to take pictures.

The umpire, however, was grateful for the excuse to intervene. The 7-foot kid with the funny name seemed to be having a breakdown right before his eyes, and he welcomed the chance to help him, as much as he could within the rules.

"Please take your seats. We'll wait while you do," he said into the microphone. Then he looked at the section of crowd where Sergei had pointed, as though it were home to a gaggle of flagrant etiquette abusers. The people in that section looked around for the culprits among them. There was no one. No one was moving. The umpire kept pointing and waiting.

Sergei walked toward the net, breaking the trance the kid was in so he finally stopped bouncing the ball. "Weird, huh?" he said directly to the kid, punctuated with a friendly wink. "Just play," he said quietly to him. "You'll be fine."

Few noticed the exchange, diverted by their neck-craning efforts to see what was causing the problem in the crowd. Finally, the umpire was satisfied with the crowd behavior and signalled the players to continue. The kid bounced the ball three times, tossed the ball a mile in the air and hit a serve at 128 mph right up the middle, out of Sergei's reach. He flailed and missed, smiling all the while.

Whew, OK. Let's lose this set.

He did, 6-4 as planned, and then reignited his game to win the third set 6-3. "What the hell happened out here?" Mlakar asked him as they shook hands at the net. Looking up, Sergei again smiled. "I'll tell you someday kid. But not today."

Chapter 52

Tobias Madsen looked like a sixth grade student in detention, sulking quietly and waiting for time to pass so he could leave. He hadn't played since the French, in part because he was trying to extend the high he felt from winning a match in his first Grand Slam. But also because he knew when he resumed play on the Challenger Tour, the gamblers would reappear and take control of his life once again.

Reluctantly, he'd accepted a flight to London, where the team that got him kidnapped in Paris wanted to meet and discuss their new idea. *Can hardly wait.*

With little else to do, he was partially thankful for the free trip, which he figured he could extend long enough to see some Wimbledon matches starting the next week. But he wasn't giving off a thankful vibe that morning, sitting in Morton Reid's kitchen, drinking coffee, waiting for the others to arrive.

Because the Paris plan had been such an abject failure, whatever Reid, Catalano and Clancy came up with this time was almost guaranteed to be better. Or so he hoped, allowing himself a glimmer of optimism he was careful not to reveal.

Within half an hour, the troika had assembled, along with a few of the faces Madsen recognized from Paris. They seemed not the least bit embarrassed by their performance there, greeting him as though they were all one-time colleagues reunited for a secret project.

"Alright, let's start by acknowledging what a bloody mess Paris was, shall we?" Reid said to the room. "Tobias, again, you have our commitment to do better this time."

"Thank you," he murmured, obliged to say something.

"Let's also acknowledge our adversary is well-informed and well-trained. They were two steps ahead of us the whole time, and we can't let that happen again."

Nods around the room indicated agreement.

"That's why we've asked you here today," Clancy jumped in. "Now that we've got a better idea of what we're up against, we've come up with a whole new approach."

No one made a move for the door or the bathroom, each curious to see the new plan before deciding whether to participate. At the head of that line was Madsen, who expected a plan worthy of Houdini.

The first bit of good news was that the new plan would not use him as bait. "We don't like to use that word, but let's face it, that's what we were doing in Paris," Clancy said. "Didn't work; won't try it again."

"Thank you," Madsen murmured again.

"The only thing we have that might give us an edge is the communication Mort's been receiving, on and off, for the last year. Someone seems to know something about the gamblers and is sharing information, for what reason we don't know."

It was the first time Madsen had heard that detail, and it caused him to sit up noticeably straighter on his kitchen stool.

"Whoever is sending the info is very cagey," Reid said. "It's been specific, without giving any hint about the organization itself – where it is, what it's called, or certainly who's involved."

"So how does that help us?" asked a voice from across the room belonging to one of Clancy's helpers.

"We're betting... Ha, sorry, no pun intended," Reid said, amusing himself if no one else. "We're betting this organization fixing matches is also involved in legitimate, legal gambling. It makes sense operationally to do both, and some of the references in the leaks we've received made reference to legit odds of different sports."

"And if that's true," Clancy again jumped in, "it gives us a glimmer of hope we could identify it by manipulating things the same way they do."

"Obviously, not the same way exactly," Reid said, nervously. "We're not going to lean on people or throw matches."

"But we're going to mess around with the tournament enough to smoke them out," Clancy parried. "We're going to do that. We've got to take some bold action or we'll never get anywhere."

"What tournament are you talking about?" Madsen asked, at last curious enough to participate in the meeting.

"Didn't we mention that?" Clancy said with a grin. "Wimbledon."

"You're gonna fixes matches at Wimbledon? Christ, how?" Madsen said.

"No, no, no, we're not actually fixing matches," Reid said. "Let's be clear about that. We simply can't do that."

"Too bad," Clancy said. "OK, yes, I realize we are restricted in what we can actually do, but we can still smoke them out. I mean, if we're right the gamblers are associated with a legal bookmaking firm, there are only so many of those big enough to do something like this. Of course, if it's not connected to a firm we can identify, we're nowhere again. So, ya, the odds still aren't good. But at least we have a plan."

"Hooray for the plan," Madsen said, as derisively as he could, surprising himself with his vitriol.

"Hang in Tobias," Catalano said, slapping him on the knee. "Give us a chance."

The plan, as laid out over the next 20 minutes, was to bet heavily on a variety of underdogs in the first two rounds of Wimbledon, bankrolling the inevitable losses with most of the Integrity Unit's budget for that year. The theory was that a firm operating entirely above board would be able to handle the increased volume without much difficulty.

But a firm that ran a legal operation as little more than a front for its larger, more profitable match-fixing operation might have to choose between the two if there were enough pressure on its legal side.

"It's not exactly Sophie's choice," Clancy said. "But if most of your eggs are in the match-fixing side, you jettison the legal side if things get too crazy."

"What do you mean by crazy?"

"Thousands of bets flooding in on unexpected underdogs. The same on their live betting sites. So many bets that even if they're not losing money, it takes significant resources to manage them and figure out what the hell is going on," Clancy answered.

"The key is we don't have to win these longshot bets," Reid said. "We can't count on that. But we can increase the volume in certain areas enough to cause havoc. Or at least, we think so. We've been talking with the ITF, and they're keen to make this happen. We've pitched it as, perhaps, more of a sure thing than it really is, but we've been poking around at this for years. Now's our chance to make something happen."

"They've got a lot more resources than we do. They've connected us with some serious computer whizzes. They can make this happen with algorithms, just flooding the zone with endless longshot bets."

"OK," Madsen said, slowly. "And then what? Why does any of that matter?"

"Because if we're right, the dirty firm – or firms, could be one more than one – might stop taking public bets while it handles the crisis," Clancy said, lifting his coffee mug in an awkward toast. "We monitor firms all over the world. When we see one pull back, even for a few hours, we swoop in."

"And what does swoop in mean?"

"Depends where it is, but ideally we work with local law

enforcement and raid the fucking building," Reid said, suddenly animated. "Put these assholes in jail."

"I'm all for that," Madsen said, smiling for the first time. "You'll forgive me, though, if I don't really expect it to work."

Chapter 53

Nik got Lola into her apartment and propped up on the sofa, without running into any nosy neighbors. "I'm dying for a beer. You didn't drink it all did you?" she asked, noticing the empties on the counter.

"I would have but I fell asleep," he laughed. He opened a Red Ember for each of them and sat on the floor, at her feet.

"Can I tell you something? Are you feeling well enough? 'Cause it can wait if you'd rather just rest for a while."

"Tell me whatever you want."

"OK, here goes. I think someone tried to kill you. I know that sounds crazy, but I think that's what happened."

"That is crazy, but it makes more sense than suicide, which I have no memory of trying. Do you know something?"

"Well, um, I think...I don't know, but I think, maybe, it was someone from my office, or someone they sent. I don't know this for sure, but I seriously think they've turned on me, on us."

It wasn't every day Lola heard there was a killer after her, and she didn't know how to respond. Plus, she still didn't feel 100 per cent. So, instead of saying anything, she fell back onto the couch and began to laugh. Everything about the last 36 hours was absurd, and she just let it all out.

Nik took her beer, placed it on a table and then held her hand. She continued to laugh, resting occasionally to catch her breath before starting all over again.

When she finally stopped, clutching her sore stomach, he scrambled her some eggs and paired them with two slices of toast. She was more hungry than she realized, and finished everything but the crusts, which he buttered again and consumed.

"So, getting back to the part where someone tried to kill me?" she said as he cleaned up the kitchen and washed her plate.

"Right, I remember saying that."

"Please elaborate, because this is a first for me."

"Me too."

"Really? I mean, I've been wondering about how far you go to keep athletes in line. Don't people get hurt? Or even killed?"

"Listen to me, OK?" he said, once again kneeling beside the sofa. "I've never done anything remotely like this. And, as far as I know, no one at Garfunkel ever has. Although, I have to admit, I'm less sure about everyone else now than I was a week ago. But I swear baby, I've never had anyone seriously hurt and absolutely not killed."

"Seriously hurt? That leaves some room for knocking about, right?"

"Sure, I told you, we're breaking a bunch of laws and sometimes we have to scare someone to motivate him. But think about it, what good is a tennis player with a broken leg? How can he help us then?"

"About as good as a dead girlfriend?"

Her joke landed with a thud, reminding them of their apparent new reality. Fueled by more beer, and eventually more eggs, they continued talking, trying to assess things rationally. That was difficult, given how tired they both were and how being the target of a killer was a new experience for them.

He woke before her the next morning and popped out for sausage rolls. He was sick of making eggs, and he assumed she was sick of eating them. When he got back, they shared coffee in bed.

"I think I know what we have to do," he said, finally, when the sausage rolls and small talk were both depleted. "But first, I have to ask you something? And you have to answer me honestly, OK?"

"Of course. Always."

"Lola Farmsworth, will you marry me?"

Chapter 54

When they had decided, two weeks earlier, to meet in Marburg, Germany, on July 1, nobody had bothered to figure out exactly *how* they would all get there.

Gil was coming from Ann Arbor, where he'd spent two weeks missing Sam and dulling the pain by smashing balls, fed to him by her father. Coach had to be available in the summer to help his new recruits get established for the fall. He'd also grown weary of travelling and was much more comfortable in his routine at home.

Their agreement allowed for Coach to spend a lot of time at home, with Gil coming to him as often as possible. It wasn't a tactic others on the Challenger Tour were using, but so far it had worked. When he got to the main tour, Gil would have to either convert Coach to full-time or find someone else. But that was a problem he only hoped to have the following year, one he would never face if he didn't buckle down and train hard during the times he did have Coach's time and attention.

He was flying from Detroit, direct to Brussels, a four-hour drive from Marburg. On paper, it was the most gruelling of the itineraries, but in reality it wasn't even close.

After a week spent eating, drinking and shopping in Paris, Sam and Svetlana set out for Marburg a day before Gil. They drove the six hours in a Mercedes convertible, Thelma and Louise-style. If they had been good friends when the week started, they were closer to sisters when it ended. Svetlana, in particular, had never had so much fun and said so every 30 minutes for the entire trip.

Having spent money on flights the previous week to Zurich and Bratislava, Sergei too decided to drive. Sadly, he was still in possession of his Toyota Camry, which behaved like a sick mule on the 11-hour drive. European-built cars of all sizes and descriptions whizzed by him relentlessly while his Camry, abused by two years-worth of rental drivers, wheezed along in the right-hand lane.

When he had to traverse even a moderate incline, never mind the foothills of the odd mountain range, the gas pedal seemed to lose any connection with the engine as he jammed it into the floorboard.

He arrived last, late Saturday night – stiff, cranky and immune from the charms of Marburg and its 72,000 citizens.

The charms of Svetlana were another matter, however. He soon forgot about his lousy travel day when he found her, waiting for him in bed in the aptly named Welcome Hotel Marburg.

"Tell me all about Paris," he said, snuggling next to her after the briefest of showers.

"Did you really drive 11 hours to talk?" she teased, stroking his chest and nibbling on his ear.

"Now that you mention it, Paris is kind of overrated. I can wait to hear about it."

"Yes, and I can wait to hear about Poprad, which I understand is the Paris of Slovakia."

Both couples were noticeably chipper when they met for breakfast the next morning. It took most of an hour for each member of the quartet to report on their previous two weeks. Aware of the public setting of the restaurant, Sergei skipped over his trip to Liechtenstein and focused on his play in Poprad, emphasizing his road to the finals and not the second set of his first match, thrown away to appease the gamblers.

The women skipped over some details of their time in

Paris too, although they knew full well next month's credit card statements would reveal all. Gil's two weeks had been so monotonous there was no need to skip over details or shade the truth.

The tournament started the following day, so the guys planned to hit that afternoon. Not with each other. They found their burgeoning friendship easier to nurture if they hit separately during practice sessions. Playing in events with small fields, it was inevitable they would meet in a match at some point, possibly that week, so they tried to keep their tennis work separate from their personal lives.

The women had no such compunction and had their afternoon fully planned out. It was to begin with the players' meeting where they looked forward to catching up with a few wives and girlfriends they only saw sporadically at common tournaments.

The couples met again for dinner, giddy with anticipation. None of them would sleep well that night. There was always a level of excitement the night before any tournament started, but that wasn't the cause of their insomnia in Marburg. The reason they couldn't sleep was because the next day they were going to fight back against the gamblers, enacting a plan they'd spent two months drawing up.

The risks were great, with no guarantee they would change anything. But they were past caring. It was something Sergei and Svetlana didn't think would ever happen. Lying next to his wife, Sergei remembered the look of terror on her face when the attacker pushed his knife against her throat. He saw their house burning to the ground and relived Svetlana's tortured reaction as he admitted his terrible secret. Finally, they were going to punch the bully in the nose. And it felt wonderful.

Chapter 55

"Congratulations Nik & Lola," read the banner affixed to his office door, like celebratory police tape. He'd let the office know Lola said yes and officially took two days off to celebrate. They spent the celebration time not as many engaged couples might but instead planning how and when Nik would walk away from Garfunkel.

It wasn't the kind of job people left with two weeks' notice and a going-away party. Workers on the legal side might well do that; several had. But no partners had left since the company began. Nik believed at least some of those partners had tried to have Lola killed, so he didn't expect they would wish him well on his way out the door.

They'd rented a room, using cash and fake names, at the Greyhound Hotel in Sutton, far from both Lola's apartment and the Garfunkel office. The Greyhound wasn't the kind of place that normally rented rooms absent a credit card, but Nik made a convincing case they were hiding Lola from an abusive ex who would track them down unless they paid cash.

It didn't hurt their cause that the roll of cash he offered to cover five nights was enough to pay for a fortnight. The clerk checked them in without any fuss. With Lola comfortable and safe, Nik arrived at the office as the excited fiancé, happy to discuss wedding plans with anyone who asked.

He slipped under the banner and into his office, leaving it in place as proof of his happiness. Within half an hour, Humphrey Cox ducked under the banner and strolled in. "Bloody well done mate," he exclaimed, giving Nik a handshake and two-pat hug. "I'd no idea you two were that serious. Good on ya."

"Thanks Humph, it felt like the right time, ya know?"

"I bloody well do not," he chuckled. "But I'm happy for you both. Happening soon?"

"Probably not. We've basically been living together for a while now. I think she'll give up her place. We'll figure out the wedding at some point."

"Well, don't leave it too long. She won't like that."

As Humph rambled on, spewing relationship clichés, Nik tried to meet his eyes and look into his soul. Not surprisingly, that didn't reveal a lot. Was it possible one of his best friends, certainly his best friend at work, had tried to have Lola killed? Did he know any of what had happened the previous week? He was going to find out.

When Humph had exhausted his bromides and left, Nik sat at his desk and surveyed the room. The microphones were not visible, but he could make a reasonable guess about their locations. Wherever they were, they'd certainly pick up his voice while he sat at his desk. And so he began to perform as he hadn't since playing Mordcha, the innkeeper, in a high school production of Fiddler on the Roof. He'd hoped being in the musical would give him an edge attracting the attention of Elena Rusu, but she turned out to be more of a Tevye groupie.

Calling Lola's empty flat, he had a long conversation with her voice mail app, asking repeatedly if she'd had any recurring symptoms of what she evidently had told him was a nasty case of food poisoning a few days earlier.

Calling the hotel he'd just stayed at in Paris, he booked a more luxurious suite for the upcoming weekend, mentioning he would be travelling with his brand-new fiancée. "Yes, champagne would be lovely. Merci, beaucoup."

He then booked a train for two, eschewing the easy online

process for the phone, repeating travel dates until the booking agent wondered if he was drunk or stupid, or both.

Next was the call to House of Garrard, a jeweller established in 1735, the same year the British Parliament made it a crime to accuse someone of witchcraft. Modern thinking had changed many attitudes, but it was still the expectation of most that Nik would spend handsomely on an engagement ring. Lola did not share that view. Although Nik could afford to buy her a ring for every finger, she extracted a promise that he wouldn't waste the money on even one. Nik kept that detail to himself as he discussed the cut, clarity and color of various options available to him.

Wandering the halls, he accepted congratulations from many more people before slipping out for lunch. He felt like an MI6 agent as he drove haphazardly to Sutton, constantly checking his mirrors to be sure he wasn't being followed. His cell phone was off, and when he arrived at the Greyhound, he opened the boot of the rental Jaguar and grabbed the burner phone he had purchased that morning.

It sprang to life, anchored by one of half a dozen SIM cards he bought with the phone.

"Hi, it's me. Everything OK?"

"Ah, yes. Can we talk?"

"Not yet. I'll be up in 15 minutes."

He picked up coffee and croissants in the hotel restaurant and headed to the 4th floor, where Lola greeted him by reporting an uneventful morning.

"Perfect, that's why we're here," he whispered into her ear as he kissed her cheek. He then unwrapped a second phone, inserted a SIM card and handed it to her. "Alright, from now on, this is the only way we communicate, OK? Texting, calling, everything. Unless I email you from work. In that case, respond like everything is on track for Paris this weekend."

"Very good. But let me ask you one question: What's your name?"

"It's Bond. James Bond."

"Oh, Mr. Bond, do you have to hurry back to the office?"

"As a matter of fact, I do not. Why?"

"Well, I noticed this suite has a very large shower, with two heads and some well-placed grip bars..."

It was impossible for the Greyhound to run out of hot water in the middle of the day, with so few people in their rooms, but they gave it their best shot. And the next day, when making up the room the maid noticed the bar of soap she had placed in the bathroom the day before had been reduced to the size of guitar pick.

Leaving Lola under the covers of the King-size bed, Nik brought his burner phone to life and signed in to a bank account in Singapore. It had been a while since he'd signed in and it took several passwords and a few minutes. But once he was in, he was happy with what he saw. Tapping more keys, he launched a series of new transactions, some of which would not be complete for 24 hours. He would check again tomorrow, using a different SIM card and logging in again from scratch.

"Any requests for dinner?" he asked as he tied his shoes and prepared to leave. "Are you on the menu?" she smiled.

He didn't stop to answer, fearing he would stay too long. Instead he simply winked as he left the room, ensuring the door locked behind him. He looked up and down the hall and took the stairs to the lobby.

"Where the hell have you been?" Humph yelled at him, as he headed toward his office, where someone had removed the "Congratulations" banner from the morning.

"Lunch. What's the problem?"

"I called and texted. Didn't you take your phone?"

"Forgot it. What's going on? What's the panic?"

The panic was Wimbledon, and it had most of the building in an uproar.

With everything else he was doing, Nik had forgotten it was Day One at Wimbledon. Matches began in early afternoon, and almost immediately weird things were happening on the Garfunkel tennis board.

There were huge bets on players who had just qualified the week before, who had never attracted betting action of any kind. That wasn't really a problem. In fact, big bets on probable losers would net Garfunkel a profit. It was the live betting area that was in a real uproar.

Simply put, Garfunkel had never experienced so much live betting during a tennis tournament, and that included finals and semi-finals that were watched by hundreds of millions of potential bettors around the world. The TV ratings for the midday, opening round of an outer court match at Wimbledon were too small to measure. And yet, there were millions of bets coming in from thousands of locations, wagering game by game, sometimes point by point.

"Our whole system is bogging down," Humph said grimly, looking at the various screens in his office. "It's a volume thing. Where the hell are all these bets coming from?"

As more and more live bets arrived, the system started to choke. The software was written to account for volume, but this was unprecedented. During the Super Bowl, for example, the system accepted millions of live bets on things like which team would get the next first down, whether a team would kick a field goal and whether the next pass would be caught. But there was a limited number of items on which to bet during a single football game.

Wimbledon money was coming in on every possible bet on every possible match, and then adjusting and betting more with lightning speed before the each bet was settled.

The system was designed to quarantine those bets, setting them aside and dealing with them later so things didn't get backed up. But there were too many bets for the quarantine protocol, and no matter how many Garfunkel programmers typed furiously on their keyboards, they couldn't slow the cascading effect.

"We need to find out what the hell is going on," Humph said, bolting from his office and heading to the bullpen where most of the furious typing was taking place.

He got there one minute after Eva Vasquez, who was huddled with a chief programmer in front of a computer in one corner of the vast room.

"Eva, what the hell?" Humph said, rushing over.

"We're implementing Ethan Hunt," she said quietly. "We can't let this infect everything."

Ethan Hunt was named after the Mission Impossible character who managed, with superhuman strength and cunning, to always save the day. Garfunkel had never implemented it, but Humph had to agree this was the situation for which it was designed. Every few months, like an elementary school holding a fire drill, the partners went over the system to ensure it was functioning properly.

Other oddsmakers had systems in place to stop crashes and protect bets. The Garfunkel system had to go beyond that, managing both the legal, public apparatus and, more importantly, the match-fixing side that was more complex and profitable.

It was the most complex program the company had ever created, and it had only ever been tested in simulations.

At 3:34 p.m. on the first day of Wimbledon, Eva Vasquez gave the order to run it for real.

Immediately, the Garfunkel website responded, suspending betting options for anything related to Wimbledon and freezing action that was underway. The ingenuity of Ethan

Hunt was that it could target only the betting event behaving erratically. Shutting down everything would be easier but would ruin Garfunkel's reputation among gamblers. The program had to surgically remove the Wimbledon problem without affecting millions of dollars of other legal gambling, and without having any impact on the other, private part of the business.

The programmers had compared the operation to shutting down a single reactor at a nuclear power plant, an analogy that explained nothing but scared the hell out of the partners. "So, we're not going to do it every day?" Humph had joked at the meeting. "Got it."

Less than a minute after the Garfunkel website suspended Wimbledon betting, Nigel Clancy let out a whoop that scared several people sitting near him. "We've got one," he yelled. "We've got one."

Clancy, Catalano, Reid and Tobias Madsen were sitting in their own bullpen of 20 computer programmers. From one location, they were flooding gambling websites around the world with Wimbledon bets. The effect was immediate, as several sites slowed down perceptibly. But none reacted the way Garfunkel had, with a red banner across the top of its site announcing all Wimbledon bets were being suspended.

"Get the information on this site, Garfunkel," Clancy bellowed to no one in particular. Within minutes, someone had produced a file folder labelled Garfunkel. They had a file for every gambling site they knew about, many of them based in Britain. It had taken two weeks to assemble all the information, some of it very spotty about firms that seemed to barely exist in the offline world.

"Madsen, get over here. Take a look at this file," Clancy yelled. "This is the first hit. See if you recognize anything or anyone."

Madsen found an empty seat between two very focused computer geeks and started flipping pages. There were newspaper clippings, bank statements, bios of various people and a lot of information that seemed superfluous at best. But he dug in anyway. What else was he going to do?

At Garfunkel, the partners had locked themselves in the Dungeon to evaluate the rapidly changing situation. Ethan Hunt seemed to be working. The two distinct gambling platforms were disengaging from Wimbledon, leaving the rest of the boards up and running.

"Holy shit, it's working," Vasquez said. "We might get through this after all."

During all the times the partners had met in the Dungeon, they'd never heard a knock on the thick metal door that separated them from every aspect of the outside world. But they all heard it – the distant ping of someone tapping on the door from outside.

"What is it?" Vasquez barked into the intercom.

"We've got another problem," a shaky voice responded from the other side. "You need to see this right away."

In the 50 seconds it took the partners to open the giant door and listen to the nervous messenger, the Garfunkel organization lost €2-million, although no one realized it until later. That was on top of what the messenger estimated was another €60-million or €70-million lost so far that day in the same way.

"We're not losing money on Wimbledon. We've shut it down. It's contained," Humph said, dismissively.

"It's not Wimbledon sir," the messenger said quietly. "It's something else entirely. Has anyone ever heard of the Marburg Open?"

Chapter 56

The answer, as their blank faces suggested, was no – none of the partners had ever heard of the Marburg Open. To be fair, there were people in Marburg who hadn't heard of the Marburg Open, but none of them ran a gambling website that accepted bets on the tournament.

Possibly the worst time to run a professional tennis tournament is during Wimbledon, when serious tennis fans everywhere are focused entirely on the grass courts of England. But the Marburg Open persisted, running annually during the first week of Wimbledon.

It was played on clay, one of about 1,000 things that distinguished it from Wimbledon.

This year, for the first time ever, the tournament was attracting an enormous amount of betting. On a normal day, when the whole firm wasn't relying on Ethan Hunt to keep its website and backroom systems up and running, the warnings about heavy betting in Germany would have been noticed.

So too would another anomaly that jumped out to the partners when they opened their computers in the Dungeon and started looking at the Marburg bets: Every single bet was paying off. There had been thousands of bets placed on first-round Marburg matches, and the gamblers had won 100 per cent of them.

"There's a bug in the system. That's not possible," Vasquez said in disbelief. "We have to freeze it."

"That won't work," reported the tech who had been rushed into the Dungeon for the first time ever and was looking around in amazement. "Two reasons: First, you can't run Ethan Hunt a second time while it's walling off the Wimbledon stuff. Second and more important: The money is gone. Every one of these bets took the money out of the account right away."

That was unusual. Most bettors left their winnings in their Garfunkel account to pay for future gambling, withdrawing only if they had a stretch of good luck and built up a reserve.

"Wait," Vasquez sputtered. "Are you saying we've lost €70-million in bets and all the money has vanished?"

"There's nothing to put a hold on," the tech said somberly. "The accounts were set up to withdraw automatically. We've tried tracking some of the money, but it bounces around a dozen accounts worldwide and then we lose the trail."

"Holy shit," one of the partners chimed in, finally realizing what he was hearing. "Do we even have €70-million to cover this?"

"Well, that's another problem," the tech said, tired of bearing bad news and sensing it might be his last day on the job. "It's been a policy of Garfunkel from day one that we covered our losses. You wanted to establish the brand as a legit place to wager. It worked. That's our, er, your reputation."

"Get to the problem," Vasquez said, forehead in her palms, looking down at the table.

"Well, the system is set up to pay out the bets no matter what. Even if that means drawing down the credit line. It was supposed to be a seamless transfer, so bettors always got paid."

"And...?" Humph said, when no one else would.

"And, there was only about €40-million in cash on hand when we opened for business today. Last I looked before I came down here, we had drawn down about €34-million on our line of credit to cover the bets so far today."

"We're going into debt to cover this shit?" Vasquez screamed. "Why haven't we stopped it? What the hell are you doing?"

"The only way to stop it is to shut everything down," the tech said, calculating how quickly he could reach the door if needed. "We didn't even notice it until 20 minutes ago, and we can't make that decision ourselves."

"OK, give us a few minutes in private to talk," Vasquez told the tech. "But don't go anywhere. We will call you back in five minutes."

He left the room and kept walking to his desk to gather his things and out to his car before anyone noticed. Nothing good was going to happen, and he wanted to be as far away from it as possible.

"Someone tell me how we're losing every single bet," Vasquez started. "Someone must have hacked in. There's no other way."

"There might be another way," Nik said, speaking for the first time since the meeting started. He had felt obliged to join the partners and play along, as he would in normal circumstances. "I just looked up this stupid tournament to see who's playing. Our old friend Sergei Ivanov is entered. Did anyone know that?"

"What are you saying, that one guy and his annoying wife have figured out a way to steal us blind?" Vasquez asked. "Come on Nik, get real."

"I don't know what's going on, but it's a pretty amazing coincidence, wouldn't you say?"

"OK, so he's there. Fuck, whatever. What are we going to do about it?"

"We're down €82-million now. That's €42-million we've borrowed," Humph said, scrolling frantically up and down his screen. "This has to stop right now before we lose everything."

The vote was unanimous, although it was really a formality. Garfunkel was Eva Vasquez, and she would decide how they proceeded. Her anger was not softened when she called for the tech to return and discovered he had left the premises.

Chapter 57

For the few hundred fans in attendance, it was the Marburg Open they had always known – high-level matches featuring promising youngsters on the way up and once-promising veterans on the way down: the regular tournament experience they looked forward to enjoying every year.

It was anything but regular, however.

For weeks, the two couples had been reaching out to players, opening up about the terror Sergei and Svetlana were living through, and asking for their help. Most were stunned and pledged their support immediately. Some didn't know the Ivanovs well but trusted Gil and Sam, which was enough for them to get on board.

A few were uneasy and refused to go along with the plan. But in a gesture of goodwill, they pulled out of the tournament. As a result, all 32 men entered at Marburg showed up Monday morning ready to help. Their travelling companions were on board as well. Some had given their coaches the week off, to avoid awkward conversations and conflicts of interest.

Simply put, the plan was to beat Garfunkel at its own game. Every player in the tournament would throw points, in a pre-determined pattern. The games would appear normal, but were more like professional wrestling – a choreographed exhibition in which not just the outcome was known but also the means of getting there.

Even if everything went as planned, which was asking a lot, they were not absolutely sure they had targeted the right firm. The Marburg group had the same problem as Madsen,

Catalano and their crew in London. They had to identify Garfunkel as the organization behind all their troubles.

Poprad had provided enough clues to convince them it was worth enacting their Marburg plan. They tracked bets from dozens of sites while Sergei was following the Garfunkel instructions, confusing the hell out of young Zupan Mlakar. What caught their attention was the *lack* of betting on the Garfunkel site. Every other major site was losing money on live bets while Sergei alternated his play between great and awful, following his script. Whoever was cashing in on his performance was not betting with Garfunkel. That suggested, but certainly didn't guarantee, Garfunkel was the culprit.

Sam and Svetlana were set up in a conference room at the tournament. With them were half a dozen wives, girlfriends and one boyfriend, each with at least two laptops and crystal-clear Wi-Fi connections. Every computer was logged into Garfunkel, following a specific match. Thanks to some agile computing work by a friend of Sergei's who preferred to remain anonymous, the log-ins appeared to be coming from all over the world.

The handful of volunteers who ran the tournament every year were far too busy to realize what was happening.

As each match began, the bettors flooded the live-betting options, following the script each player had. At changeovers, players reviewed what they were to do during the next two games. There were bets on double faults, broken serves and even washroom breaks. There was an over/under bet on how many times one notoriously slow player would call for a trainer, and there were bets on which matches would go to tiebreakers.

If there was a bet to be made on a given match, they made it. Initially, they placed small bets, partly to avoid detection. But also because their seed money was limited. That morning,

Sergei had deposited the Liechtenstein Global Trust certified check for €470,372.84 into a business account at Volksbank, which had a branch 10 minutes from the tournament site.

"We've set up a fund to process player revenue and expenses," he explained over the phone a week earlier when he opened the account. "There will be a lot of activity during the tournament and then we'll close the account. Is that going to cause any problems?"

The answer was a definite no. So long as Volksbank was able to charge its usual processing fees, it did not care how long the account was active or how busy things got the next week. The more transactions the better.

Because they won every bet, relying on the players to remember and execute their scripts, the original €470,372.84 multiplied very quickly. With the help of the same computer friend, they were able to route their winnings through multiple channels before landing back, 10 minutes down the road at the local Volksbank.

As a reward for taking huge risks to cooperate, Gil and Sergei had offered each player a payment equal to what the champion would receive. They planned to run the operation for one day and then let the tournament play out with no further interference. So the losers on day one would get as much as they could have by winning all their matches. Everyone else would get that plus their legitimate winnings from playing out the week.

"How long will it take them to notice and shut it down?" Sergei asked his computer friend. The answer was a shrug of the shoulders. "Could be 10 minutes or 10 hours. They must have defences, but maybe not against what you're doing. I'm sure it's never been tried."

With each set of each match, Sam, Svetlana and their gambling partners upped the ante, wagering as much as €1-million on a specific point or game, confident they couldn't lose. Each time the win registered in their account, the funds disappeared from Garfunkel, and they did it again. And again.

By 5:00 Marburg time, 4:00 London time, they had amassed over €92-million. Matches were nearly done for the day, which was the only thing that slowed down their winning streak.

"Would be nice to hit €100-million, wouldn't it?" Sam whispered to Svetlana as they relaxed for the first time all day.

"I can't believe this is real money, that it's really happening," Svetlana said.

The level of disbelief in Marburg did not even register compared to the level of disbelief in the Garfunkel Dungeon. At 3:50, the bank had called, alarmed by the ballooning withdrawals from the firm's line of credit.

When Vasquez downplayed it by mentioning "technical issues," the bank capped the line to protect itself and its loyal customer. "Until you have it figured out, it's not prudent to extend further credit," the vice-president-of-something-or-other told Vasquez.

Out of options and sinking in debt, Garfunkel closed all its betting operations at 4:15 London time, one minute after its losses from the Marburg Open tipped over €100-million. The message on its website and mobile app platform said the site was closing for scheduled maintenance and would reopen the following day. No one in the Dungeon thought that would happen. Some thought it might take a week. Maybe two. Others knew the truth: Garfunkel was dead.

Chapter 58

It took Tobias Madsen nearly an hour to get through all the material in the Garfunkel folder. There wasn't really that much, but his enthusiasm waned after 10 minutes when it started to feel like a waste of time. There was so much going on around him, with people on computers making bets around the world, and he was flipping through a paper folder.

He took a break and got some coffee, lingering near the screen being run by an attractive brunette who pushed her glasses up onto her head while she attacked her keyboard. When she noticed him, he smiled and offered her a coffee.

"Sure, ya. But make it tea with milk, thanks."

"I'm Tobias," he said as he set the cup down beside her.

"Jenny," she answered with a smile. "Later, OK? I've gotta concentrate."

"Sure, of course. Later."

The encounter energized Madsen enough to carry on with the folder. Near the back, he saw a newspaper article with a grainy photo that hadn't aged well. But it didn't matter. He knew the face.

"It's him. This is him!" he yelled, getting up and running toward Clancy, holding the article above his head like his country's Olympic flag.

"The name, what's the name?"

That required someone to have a very close look at the cutline below the photo, where half a dozen names were listed in a confusing jumble that didn't seem to relate very well to the photo.

"This must be it. Nikolai P-something," Clancy said, the

clipping six inches from his face, which was scrunched up like an apple doll. "Is there someone here under 30 who can still see?" he yelled.

"Yes sir, it says Nikolai Popescu," said the volunteer millennial who had come to Clancy's rescue and examined the photo. She wrote it in large letters on the front of the file folder.

"Alright, let's get on this. We've got a positive ID of our Paris guy, working at this place, ah, Garfunkel something or other. It's time to move."

With that, nearly everyone in the room ran off in different directions. Morton Reid was one step behind Clancy, heading for the door. Liz Catalano was running to join them when she saw Madsen, sitting quietly by himself. "Tobias, great work. We did it. We're gonna catch him. You should just relax tonight. I'll let you know what happens. Have you got a ride back to the hotel?"

"Sure, sure, don't worry," he said, smiling broadly. "Go get them."

There had been a time when Madsen dreamed of being part of the big round-up of bad guys. He liked the idea of being there when someone handcuffed his tormentor and shoved him into the back of a car. Or chased him down an alley and tackled him on the cobblestone. But those dreams had died in Paris. The reality of the confrontation had sobered him, and he was happy to leave the next step to the professionals.

As the room cleared, he leaned back with his feet on the desk in front of him. He closed his eyes, raised his arms above his head and yelled, "Yes." That was when he noticed the tea-loving brunette sitting across the room at her computer.

"What's this all about?" she asked, walking toward him. "I'm a forensic accountant, brought in by the tennis people. I never really got the whole story. Are you one of the tennis people? Why are you still here?"

"Oh, I'm definitely one of the tennis people," he said, standing up and extending his hand. "I'm Tobias Madsen, middling tennis professional, no longer under the thumb of gambling thugs. It's wonderful to meet you."

"Ah, Jenny McElroy, nice to meet you as well. Care to grab a drink and tell me what the hell this is all about?"

"Love to Jenny. Love to."

Chapter 59

With the Dungeon door ajar, the remaining partners could hear the sirens in the distance. They scrambled to their offices. Some began shredding paper, a pointless task given the electronic trail they'd left behind over the last decade.

Others bolted from the building, only to be turned back by police who had blocked outgoing roadways and were methodically tightening their circle. Humph stood at his desk, stabbing at his keyboard, erasing files as quickly as he could. On the other side of his closed door, people were running up and down the hall in full panic, like they were on an actual sinking ship, rather than a metaphorical one.

An email notification popped up on his screen, catching his eye because it was dated six years earlier. Try as he might, he couldn't ignore it.

He clicked, and a series of .zip files began unfurling across his screen, like a deck of Solitaire playing cards. File after file -- spreadsheets, emails, memos, contracts, all backdated to cover the previous decade and beyond. As quickly as they popped up, they disappeared again, saving themselves in a series of new file folders the computer was creating.

Tired and confused, he didn't understand what he was seeing as he stood there, in a trance. The buzz of his mobile phone jolted him back to the present.

"Humph?"

"Ya, Eva? Is that you? Where are you?"

"Humph, I'm sorry. Truly. You deserved better."

"What are you talking about?"

They were his last words. From behind him, stepping out

from the washroom attached to his office, Eva Vasquez raised a Maxim 9 pistol with built-in silencer and shot him twice in the chest.

With his body, police would find a hard drive full of information identifying Humphrey Cox as the brains behind Garfunkel, the architect of an illegal gambling scheme that reached around the world, coerced hundreds of athletes to cheat, and challenged the legitimacy of dozens of sports leagues and associations.

For weeks, athletes would come forward to add their names to the growing list of those who were threatened, attacked or injured by Garfunkel strongmen. Many, however, would choose never to go public, instead returning to the life they had known, absent the threats and pressure.

Without looking back at her erstwhile partner, Vasquez quietly slipped out of his office, into the cacophony of the building. If anyone stopped her to ask what they should do, she told them to meet in the boardroom. She would be there momentarily to explain all.

She kept moving, repeating the mantra calmly as she went. Eventually, she reached the basement. Instead of turning right to the now-abandoned Dungeon, she headed left, toward a dead end hallway. When she reached the end, she lifted a floor board in the extreme corner, revealing a lighted number pad. She keyed in a six-digit code and stood back as a wall panel beside her slid open, revealing a stairway that led to a tunnel. She stepped in and closed the panel door behind her. The floor was solid dirt and easy to run on. As she began to run, motion detectors turned on lights in cascading, 50-yard lengths, leading her more than two miles, beyond the Garfunkel compound, beyond the police dragnet.

She slowed as she reached the end, gasping for air. It had been years since she'd run so far, and her lungs burned. Entering the same six-digit code into an identical keypad behind a plastic panel, she watched as one side of the tunnel began to slide open, revealing a garage, with its own double door to the woods beyond.

As the door slowly opened, Vasquez could only gasp in disbelief. The garage was empty. Where there was supposed to be a Range Rover, fueled and ready to go, was just empty space. As she got closer, she saw an envelope with her name typed neatly on the front. Suddenly shivering and light-headed, she ripped it open.

Eva,

You bet against the wrong team. I thought you understood odds.

Thanks for the wheels, and go to hell.

Nik

She threw the note away, then thought better of it and stashed it in her pocket. Next, she secured the sliding door, locking it from the garage-side to ensure no one could follow her out. There was still plenty of daylight, and she knew the woods very well.

She flinched as the door creaked, letting her out into the warm evening. It took a moment to get her bearings, and then she set off, walking briskly. After five minutes, she came across a small pond and dumped the gun. She was starting to breath normally again when she heard the sirens...and the dogs. So many dogs...getting closer. As she ran, branches slapped her face, and arms, cutting into her skin. No matter how quickly she ran, they kept getting closer.

Chapter 60

It wasn't until they saw the Garfunkel site suspend all betting that the operation felt entirely real to Sam and her cohorts. To that point, it felt as though they were playing an online game, with a growing pot of credits in their account.

"We shut them down," Svetlana said, jubilantly. "Look at that."

Sam gave her a silent high-five and continued closing up the makeshift computing center. As the totals escalated during the day, they had rethought their original dispersal plan. "We can't have 32 players lined up at the Volksbank withdrawing €30,000 in cash," Sam reasoned.

Instead, they had sent Sergei on a delicate mission late in the afternoon. Armed with a large duffel bag, he'd arrived at the Volksbank ready to make one very large cash withdrawal. He'd also transferred the balance of the funds back to his old friends in Lichtenstein, where he knew they would be safe and untraceable in a new account.

At the appointed hour of 7:00 p.m., he strolled into the Hinkelstein pub to an ear-splitting roar from the patrons. A small payment that afternoon had ensured they had the place to themselves, and now all the players and their partners were eating and drinking, reliving a day like none they'd ever experienced.

"I could have beaten you if they'd let me play," said Carl Schubert, the lowest ranked player in the tournament. He was speaking to teenage phenom Henry Zuk, the odds-on favorite to go on and win the tournament legitimately. He was taking full advantage of the relaxed German drinking age rules.

"Sure, sure Carl. Whatever you say."

Gil stood on a chair near the bar and whistled to get everyone's attention.

"Before we get started, I have to say, you guys were fucking amazing today," he proclaimed, prompting more than a minute of hoots and hollers throughout the room.

"We broke some rules today, but we did it to make a difference. I have no idea what's going to happen to these Garfuckers, but I do know one thing: We took €100-million from them today."

The reaction to that declaration was less joyous and more disbelieving. Many of the players had not heard the final tally, the scale of which was well beyond what they imagined.

"Wait? How much?" someone yelled. "What are you going to do with so much money?"

"That's going to attract a hell of a lot of attention," someone else yelled.

"Yes, absolutely. This is the plan," Gil continued. "Remember, the goal here is to put these guys out of business, hopefully in jail, for what they've done to Sergei and Svetlana. And so many others we don't even know."

A mild round of applause indicated grudging acceptance of the sentiment.

"So, we want to give most of this money to the Integrity Unit. Anonymously of course. They're the ones who can fight this. Not us. But before we do that, we also thought we should bump up your shares too. We were thinking €100,000 each. How's that sound?"

"Excuse me, Gil?" Henry Zuk raised his hand, amid the cheers, like he was still in high school. "Excuse me, but if I take this money, if any of us take this money, couldn't we be caught, thrown out of tennis?"

"Absolutely, which is why we're not just splitting the

€100-million 32 ways. We make this donation to the Integrity Unit and quietly suggest they don't look into Marburg. They're gonna have so much to do. They're gonna catch actual gamblers. They don't need to worry about Marburg, do they?"

"Also, it's not traceable," said Sergei, who stood on a chair next to Gil, holding the duffel bag aloft. "We're talking cash folks. Be smart with it. Don't spend it all at once or deposit it all together. There's no trail that leads to any of you. None."

There were a few more questions, but they gave way quickly to more revelry as players lined up to receive their €100,000. It was more than most of them had ever won, combined, playing tennis. It was more than some of them would ever win.

With the official business complete, the party really took off. Amid the chaos, Gil and Sam signalled to Sergei and Svetlana, and the two couples slipped out quietly, back to the Welcome Hotel.

There wasn't much more to say, as they sat in the quiet of the wood-panelled bar and toasted their success with a bottle of Longmorn Speyside single malt scotch.

"To us," was all Gil could think to say.

He thought he saw a tear in Sergei's eye.

Chapter 61

Nik drove the black Range Rover along the dirt road, out of the woods and straight to the Greyhound, where Lola was ready and waiting. Using supplies she'd picked up that morning at a chemist's, Lola became a redhead, while Nik went bald.

As the sun went down and streetlights came to life, they loaded four suitcases into the vehicle and headed southeast to Folkestone, where a short trip on the Eurotunnel car train would deliver them to Calais that evening.

From her purse, Lola retrieved new passports and other paperwork to support their new identities: a Romanian couple returning from vacation. It helped that Vasquez had kept the Range Rover off the grid, so the new registration papers didn't conflict with previous records.

They boarded the train without incident and drove into France 45 minutes later. It would take nearly 24 hours to reach Bucharest, and they were in no hurry. When they crossed into Belgium, they began looking for a hotel. In Ghent, they checked into a secluded little inn, paying for two nights just in case. Only then did they dare switch on their new mobile phones and see what was making news back home.

Reports were largely unconfirmed, but the BBC had a few strands of the story. Police had found a body, reportedly a Garfunkel partner named Humphrey Cox, who was shot to death inside the building.

"Shot? Poor Humph," Lola said.

"Ya, poor Humph, who tried to have you killed," Nik

reminded her. "Poor guy."

In addition to dozens of people picked up at roadblocks, police had also arrested a woman in the woods far from the Garfunkel compound. Her identity had yet to be confirmed.

"They used dogs to track her down," Lola said in amazement, reading ahead.

"Maybe we should get a dog," Nik smiled, pulling her close for a very long hug.

"I was thinking more along the lines of a baby," she said softly, pushing back to look into his eyes. "We're going to build a real life in Bucharest, right? You promised."

"And I meant it. But could we start with a dog? Just for a while?"

"I suppose. But making a baby could be a lot of fun," she purred, pulling him back onto the sea of throw pillows covering the bed.

Enticing as her offer was, Nik's mind was elsewhere, remembering his first days at Garfunkel, and the exhilaration he had felt working numbers and beating the system. Of course, it wasn't so simple, which was why he soon realized it couldn't go on forever. Everyone needed an exit strategy.

"So many lives changed today," he said, wistfully.

"All those athletes, dozens of them, suddenly free," she said. "Sorry, but that's good news for me. They never did anything wrong, did they?"

"You're right, you're right. They're probably celebrating too."

"Maybe poor Tobias Madsen will finally be happy," she said.

"Who? What did you say?"

"You heard me," she said. "Tobias Madsen."

"But. How?"

And suddenly, Nik felt it happening for a third time in his life – an instant awareness of what he'd been missing, the scales falling from his eyes.

Uncle Fritz, Vasquez and Humph, now Lola.

"You knew?"

She answered with a smile Nik had never seen before, mischievous and triumphant with a hint of mystery.

"The leak. To the tennis idiots. Seriously? You?"

Doubling down on her smile, she rolled him over, giggling and smothering him in pillows, free at last from the secrets she held.

-THE END-

Afterword

Thanks for reading *Tangled Strings*.
Please leave a review and rating where you bought the book, to help spread the word to others.
You can find my first novel, *Pulling Strings*, at christopherclarkwriter.com